Greek Island Friendships

Ian Wilfred

Greek Island Friendships
Copyright © 2024 by Ian Wilfred

This is a work of fiction. Names, characters, places and incidents are used fictitiously and any resemblance to persons living or dead, business establishments, events, locations or areas, is entirely coincidental.

No part of this work may be used or reproduced in any manner without written permission of the author, except for brief quotations and segments used for promotion or in reviews.

ISBN: 9798322888758

Cover Design: Avalon Graphics
Editing: Laura McCallen
Proofreading: Maureen Vincent-Northam
Formatting: Rebecca Emin
All rights reserved

Greek Island Friendships is dedicated to the lovely and hugely supportive members of the Ian Wilfred Readers group on Facebook.

Thank you so much to every one of you for giving my words a chance:

Zayla, Elaine B, Betty, Liz, Julie, Jane, Claire W, Rosy, Kim, Ann, Rachael, Claire J, Gill, Elaine M, Sally, Hayley, Janice, Sue H1, Sue R, Marie, Shona, Sonja, Tracey, Dawn, Katerina, Pam, Debbie D, Rosie, Jayne, Christine, Grace, Bernadette, Jane Mc, Karen H, Jane M, Daisy, Andrea, Lynn, Sue D, Ruth, Liz M, Wendy, Jeanette, Elaine F, Katie, Debbie B, Elaine S, Chris, Paula, Aisling, Pauline, Gillian, Linda C, Deryth, Sue H2, Beth, Evie, Rosemary, Susanna, Sue B, Debbie V, Bethan D.

Acknowledgements

There are a few people I'd like to thank for getting *Greek Island Friendships* out into the world.

The fabulous Rebecca Emin for organising everything for me and who also produced both kindle and paperback books. Laura McCallen for all the time and effort she spent editing the book, Maureen Vincent-Northam for proofreading, and the very talented Cathy Helms at Avalon Graphics for producing the terrific cover.

Finally for my late mum who is always with me in everything I do.

Chapter 1

It had been two weeks since Lena had received a letter from her dad's lawyer and today was the day she would go and meet him to discuss what her late father, Stelios, had left her in his will. She was nervous and still feeling numb with the pain of his loss. She also felt guilty that she hadn't mentioned the meeting to her mum, Mariana, who, even though Lena was twenty-five, would have insisted on coming with her. But that would inevitably have ended with an argument in front of the lawyer, and given her mum hadn't been part of her father's life for over twenty years, she ultimately had no need or right to be there.

It felt very strange walking through the centre of Athens. Having lived here all her life she knew it as clearly as she knew the back of her hand, but today it felt different. It seemed a long time since she had done this walk because it had been – four months, to be precise. The last time was when she had lost her job at the bank. The strange thing was that she hadn't given that day or the job a second thought since then, but that was likely because so much had happened in the interim. Looking at the time on her phone she saw she had an hour and a half before her meeting, just enough time to get a coffee and think through what she wanted to ask the lawyer. She wondered if she should make notes to prepare but she didn't have much to go on given that all the letter had said was that she had inherited a property and some money from her father's estate. But where was the property? Given her father's far-flung business interests it could be here in Athens just as much as it could be somewhere else in Greece.

As she sat drinking a coffee she thought back to her dad's funeral. There had been so many people there but apart from her mum, her dad's sister, Fotini, and her dad's godson, Pavlos, she hadn't really known anyone. It was as though her dad had lived several separate lives. Ok, she knew she had an older half-sister, Callisto – their dad had talked a lot about her during those last few months of his life and Lena knew she was now running his property business – but so much about him was still a mystery even now he was gone. She was grateful for what information she did have, and that he had talked more about himself in those final weeks she had spent with him than he had in all of her life; his time working in London when he was young and how he went on to become the successful businessman, but also the things he had messed up in his life – mostly relationships: Callisto's mum, Lena's mum... Those weeks the two of them had spent together had meant a lot to Lena, and she knew he had been trying to make up for all the years he hadn't seen her. But then, that wasn't entirely his fault. No, the bulk of the blame should definitely be laid at her mum's door. Mariana was the reason that Lena and her dad's relationship had only really been formed as adults, and they had never been able to share a typical father and child connection during the early years of her life. But Lena understood that her mum had her reasons, and she didn't blame either of her parents for what had happened in the past. She was content to focus on the now and had appreciated the time she had with her father.

Thinking of her dad's sister, her aunt Fotini, Lena wondered how she was doing. She knew she should have contacted her or gone to the island of Vekianos and visited before now, but then that would likely have caused trouble with her mum as the two women hadn't spoken for years. Lena knew

Fotini wouldn't be in a good place. She had been very close to her brother and had cared for him in the last few months of his life. Perhaps she could ask the lawyer how her aunt was doing? It was entirely possible he might be having meetings with her as well. A thought suddenly crossed her mind: would Fotini be there today? Would this meeting be like ones you see in films where everyone sat around a big table as the will was read out? If that was the case, it meant her half-sister Callisto would definitely be there as well. Lena could feel herself starting to panic. Why hadn't she thought of this possibility before now?

Pulling herself together she paid for the coffee and headed to the lawyer's office. She hoped there would be a bathroom where she could check herself in the mirror. Looking at the time she saw she was ok and would still be early. As she crossed the road towards the lawyer's office she saw it was a very impressive building. Walking up the steps and into the reception she tried to calm her racing heart as she nervously waited her turn behind the two people in front of her.

'Good morning,' she said once the receptionist was free, 'I have an appointment with Mr J Bouras.'

The receptionist looked at her a little oddly and Lena started to panic – surely she hadn't got the wrong lawyer's office? – but then the girl smiled at her.

'Sorry, I didn't quite hear you and was a little confused. Can I take your name, please?'

'It's Lena Drakos.'

The girl looked at her computer screen and then started to tap something on the keyboard.

'Thank you, Miss Drakos, if you would like to take the lift to the third floor, the office you need is to the left.'

'Thank you, do you have a bathroom I could use

first please?'

'Yes, they're just next to the lifts,' she said, pointing Lena in the right direction.

Lena thanked her again and headed to the lift. This was it. She needed to pull herself together. Her dad would never have meant for this to be a horrible experience. A quick look in the mirror told her she didn't look great; the bags beneath her eyes were dark and heavy and she had visibly lost weight since her dad's death. Oh well, it was too late to do anything about it now. Besides, today wasn't about how she looked, it was about closure.

Coming out of the lift and turning left as instructed, she knocked on the door of the office with the sign reading 'J Bouras' and walked in. A young woman was sat behind a desk and welcomed her with a smile.

'Hi, good morning, you must be Lena Drakos. If you would like to go through, Joanna is ready for you.'

'Joanna?'

'Yes, Joanna Bouras.'

Lena felt stupid. She had thought it was a man she was seeing. But she didn't have time to digest this surprise before she was in the other office and shaking the woman's hand.

'Hi, Lena, please come in and take a seat. I'm Joanna. Now, can I get you a drink? Coffee, juice?'

'Could I just have some water, please?'

The woman nodded and went over to a unit in the corner and took out a bottle of water from a fridge. She poured it into a glass and placed it on the table in front of Lena.

'Now, Lena, there's no need to worry about any of this. It's all straightforward and we can take it slow. If you want to ask any questions at any point, please just stop me. I'm here to help you.'

'Sorry, I thought ... I thought I was seeing a man

and it's slightly thrown me. But in a good way,' she rushed to add. 'Sorry, I didn't mean to be rude.'

'Don't worry; you're not the first person to be shocked I'm a woman.' Joanna laughed. 'So, first of all, your father wasn't just a client, he was also a friend, so this is a little different for me than usual as I know more about the situation than I would with other clients. Thankfully, it's all very black and white with no grey areas. Stelios ... made sure of that.'

Lena noticed how Joanna's voice had hitched on her dad's name, as though there was a slight crackle of sadness to it.

'Where should I start? As the letter said, you have been left a property. It's an apartment on the island of Vekianos, which I believe you know from visiting your dad there? I do have a photo of the outside, if you'd like to see it. It's just next door to your dad's family villa, so I expect you saw it being built when you were there last. Here's the photo. You can see there are seven apartments: a penthouse that goes all the way across the top floor, which is above two floors with three apartments on each. Yours is on the second floor.' She pointed to it in the photo. 'Now, I can imagine this is a big shock so I'll stop and let you take it all in for a moment before we move on. Do you have any questions you might want to ask?'

Lena didn't know what to say – or ask, come to that – but she appreciated Joanna taking her time. She sat there in silence for a moment or two, just staring at the photo, until Joanna spoke.

'Do you think you would be open to leaving Athens and moving to the little island? I know it's very small, but it's gorgeous.'

'Have you been there, Joanna?' Lena asked.

'Yes, I've spent some time at your dad's family villa sorting out paperwork with your father. It really is a beautiful, tranquil little island. Yes, a very special place for so many reasons.'

Again, Lena noticed something in Joanna's voice and there was a dreamy smile on her face, as though she was thinking back to her visit – visits? – to Vekianos.

'Can I ask you about my Aunt Fotini? Is she still in the villa?'

'Yes, for now. I gather she's going to do it up and rent it out to holiday makers as she has also been left an apartment in the same block as you; the one directly underneath you, on the ground floor.'

'That's nice that she'll be close. I'm looking forward to spending time with her. And the other apartments...?'

'Oh! I didn't even show you the photos of the swimming pool and the garden yet. Here, take a look. Now, are you sure you wouldn't like a coffee?'

'No, I'm ok, thank you, the water is fine. Everything looks lovely. It's a big pool, isn't it. But then, I suppose with seven apartments it has to be. The top floor apartment is huge...'

'Yes, shall we move on to talk about the money? In addition to the apartment, you have been left fifty thousand euros. It sounds a lot but it won't necessarily be enough to live on for very long, so I think you would probably have to consider getting a job if you decide to move there full time. But then, if you only use it for weekends and carry on working here in the city it's a nice sum. Flying to Corfu first and then getting a boat over to Vekianos is a day's travelling though, so perhaps it wouldn't make the best weekend retreat.'

Lena had a strange feeling that she was being given advice. No, it was more than that. It sounded just like what her father would have said. Was this something he had instructed Joanna to do? Had she been tasked with convincing Lena to uproot her life and move away from Athens for good?

'I'm actually not working at the moment. I lost my job ... for lots of reasons. When my dad died I couldn't concentrate, and I was making mistakes – big mistakes – and, well ... I ended up leaving before I was asked to leave.'

'I understand. It's so difficult, when you lose someone you love, to carry on as you had been without all the grief taking over... Yes, very difficult.' Joanna paused as a wistful expression crossed her face. 'Would you excuse me please,' she said abruptly. 'I just need to go to the bathroom.'

Lena nodded as the other woman rushed from the room. She could see this conversation was very difficult for Joanna, but that wasn't entirely surprising. Like she had said, this wasn't a normal case for her – she had known Stelios, and he had been a friend as well as a client.

Lena started to think about the apartment. It really would be so lovely to live there and she was sure she could find a job but ... her mum. What would she say? And would she want to move there with her? That couldn't happen. For one, she didn't get along with Fotini, and for another, the island would be far too small and quiet for her.

'I'm sorry about that,' Joanna said as she stepped back into the office, her professional mask back in place. 'Where were we? Oh yes, the money. We'll get it transferred into a bank account of your choice. Now, any concerns you have about the apartment should all go through this practice. And really the only thing left is for me to give you the keys. Unless you have any questions you would like to ask me?'

'Well, yes, I did have a question actually. You said there are seven apartments? I have one and Fotini another, but what about the other five? Are they occupied by people my dad knew or was ...

related to?' she asked delicately.

Joanna sat up in her chair and composed herself, suddenly looking a bit uncomfortable.

'I think you've had an awful lot to take in today without concerning yourself with your new neighbours. Perhaps the best thing to do is to go over to Vekianos and stay in the apartment for a while. Take in the island, talk to your aunt, and decide what is best for you. Now, I have just a few bits of paperwork for you to sign.'

An hour later, Lena was sat in a park thinking through what had just happened. She loved the island of Vekianos – the harbour with all the restaurants and shops, but more than that the little town of Keriaphos where the family villa that held so many happy memories was located – but one thought kept coming back to her: the apartment block. Who else connected to her father would be there? One person she could count on having one of the units, of course, would be her half-sister, Callisto, and given that Lena's aunt had told her at Stelios' funeral that Callisto was now running their father's property company, she would most likely be up on the third floor in the big penthouse. But that still left four other apartments.

'Dad, what have you done? What's behind this apartment block plan you made and who else have I got to meet?'

Chapter 2

Callisto was still fuming. It had been two weeks since she had received the letter from Joanna Bouras and then had the short, sharp conversation on the telephone. She still couldn't believe her dad's lawyer was a woman she had never heard of and not the lawyer for her dad's property company. Did he think she was still a child and couldn't be trusted with the information? Because she certainly wasn't. She had turned forty just a few weeks ago.

She wondered what he had been up to in the last six months of his life. He should have told her; one, she was his daughter, and two, he had left her in charge of running his company, which meant she needed to know about *all* of his projects – especially those that directly affected her both personally and professionally. Annoyingly, when she had gone to stay with him on Vekianos the building work had been going on right under her nose next door, and when she had asked him about it, he'd said he didn't know anything about it. But then, she did know her dad had kept a lot of secrets. He had every part of his life separated out into different boxes and never allowed any of them to mix. Oh yes, he had his secrets, and no doubt there were more to come. This new apartment block was likely only the start.

Callisto didn't like surprises. She dealt in the facts and that was why she had become so successful. She ran things with her head, not her heart; she was nothing at all like her father.

She had been over to the island of Vekianos to investigate the apartment block and after a lot of persuading – and two hundred euros – she had convinced one of the project managers to show her around, but other than the layout she knew nothing further about the apartment block apart from the fact that her dad had apparently left her one of the apartments. Hopefully today all would be made clear as she had a meeting with this Joanna woman.

'I'm here to see Joanna Bouras,' she said authoritatively to the receptionist.

'And your name please?'

'Callisto Drakos.'

'Let me just see,' the woman said, consulting her computer screen. 'Oh yes, here you are. Please take the lift to the third floor and then turn left. The office you need will be in front of you.'

As she got in the lift she thought about the fact that this was a real reversal; it was normally people coming to *her* office, not the other way around. But even so, she would still be in control. She had come prepared and ready with a list of questions and she wouldn't be leaving until she had answers to all of them.

She walked right into the office without knocking, determined to establish the upper hand right from the start. The secretary greeted her warmly and told her she could go straight through as Joanna was waiting.

Callisto was thrown off for a second, having mistakenly believed the girl in front of her was Joanna, but she quickly composed herself and stepped through to the lawyer's office where a very smart looking woman in her late fifties stood to greet her. Callisto was surprised to find that the lawyer looked familiar.

'Hello, Miss Drakos, it's nice to meet you again. Please come and take a seat. Can we get you a coffee?'

Callisto was caught off guard and racked her brain, trying to place Joanna. She had definitely met this woman before, but where? If she had done any business with her in the past she would have remembered, so they had to have been introduced in a social situation. Was it when she was with her father? It seemed likely, given Joanna was his lawyer. Callisto was beginning to feel she was losing control of the situation, but taking a deep breath she composed herself. She could turn this situation around. She always did.

'No, I'm ok, thank you. Also, I'm on a tight schedule, so could you please get to the reason I'm here today?'

'Oh,' Joanna said, clearly taken aback by Callisto's directness. 'I'm sorry you've had to come if it's inconvenient, but I'm just following the instructions your father left. I won't waste any time. As you are aware from the correspondence and our little chat on the telephone, your father has left you an apartment in his will and so there are just a few legal bits of paperwork to go over.'

'The paperwork can be looked after by my lawyers, that's what I pay them for. Moving on, please tell me how and why you are dealing with my late father's interests. I also need more information on the residents of the other apartments. I presume one will be my half-sister, Lena, but I would like a list of everyone's names and contact numbers so that I have them all together.'

'It's not that straightforward, I'm afraid, Miss Drakos. Firstly, your father, Stelios...' She broke off and took a moment to compose herself.

What was that about? Callisto wondered.

'Sorry, as I was saying, your father instructed this practice to deal with the apartments and so that is what we will do. Secondly, all I am permitted to tell you is that you have been left the apartment, which I have a set of keys for...' She trailed off again as she rooted in her desk drawer and pulled out the keyring, handing it over to Callisto. 'As for the other six apartments, I can't give you any information on who they belong to.'

'What rubbish. Don't you realise I'm now running my father's company? I need to know who will be living in the six apartments underneath me.'

'Underneath...? I'm sorry, I don't understand. I can show you a photo of the block, if you like, but I'm not permitted to reveal any information on the other inhabitants.'

'I don't need to look at anything as I've already been and viewed them. Looking at your expression I can tell you aren't going to give me any further information, so if that is everything, I think we're done. But I will say one thing before I go, this isn't the end of the matter. My lawyers will be looking into the reason for all this secrecy and more importantly, your involvement in all of this.'

'Miss Drakos, may I suggest you just read the paperwork? I'm sure that will explain everything. Now, I require your signature for the key. Please sign here,' she said, pointing to the bottom of one of the forms in front of her on the desk.

Callisto was fuming. Not with this Joanna woman who was obviously only carrying out instructions, no, her anger was directed at her father for doing all this behind her back. No doubt he would have had a huge laugh while doing it. He would have loved seeing how worked up about it all she was.

Five hours later Callisto was back in her house on the outskirts of Athens. Two large gin and tonics had been drunk and the blank pieces of paper she had started with were now full of names of people who could have possibly inherited the other apartments, though the only two she was really one hundred percent sure of were her half-sister, Lena – someone she didn't know all that well but whom she knew she could handle – and her dad's sister, her Aunt Fotini. That wouldn't be the easiest of situations to deal with given their history, but she would cross that bridge when she came to it. Of the other four apartments she suspected that one would possibly be a girlfriend, another perhaps someone who had worked for her dad for many years, and for the final two ... it could be anyone really. Her dad had so many different friends and associates, and Callisto didn't even know half of them.

'Oh, Father, you think you're so clever, don't you?' she asked the room. 'You just *had* to show me that you're still the boss, hm? What you're forgetting is that you aren't here anymore. I am. And that means your little game of throwing all these people together in a complex is under *my* control now, and I am more than capable of getting rid of anyone I don't like. You just look down and watch me.'

Chapter 3

Trisha closed her front door behind her then kicked off her shoes and went straight to the fridge to get a bottle of white wine. In her head she was no clearer with her situation than she had been four hours ago before visiting her lawyer, as he couldn't tell her anything in addition to the letter she'd received from Stelios' lawyer in Athens. The long walk across London had been a complete waste of time, apart from the exercise, which would have done her the world of good on a normal day but only added to the stress today. Walking to and from work every day was something she had missed since she'd retired, but once the weather got better she was determined to make an effort to get out on a daily basis, maybe visiting all the gorgeous parks here in London. Of course she could also take those walks on the Greek island of Vekianos, considering she now owned an apartment there. She still couldn't wrap her head around it, and she didn't have the time to do so now as she needed to change and start to prepare dinner. Her best friend Rachel was coming over and hopefully, what with Rachel being a very practical person, she could advise Trisha what to do about the letter.

'Oh, Stelios,' she said to herself, 'what have you gone and done?'

'That was gorgeous as usual, Trisha. I really wish I could cook like you; I'm always flabbergasted by what you come up with. Where do you get all your ideas from?'

'That's easy: forty plus years in the catering industry! Now, pudding, Rachel?'

'Can we leave it a while and let the main course settle? While we're waiting for that to happen you can tell me what's on your mind. I can tell you aren't yourself today and as all you've wanted to do since I arrived is ask me questions and talk about my boring life, I suspect you're hiding something.'

'You know me too well. Shall we go into the lounge and I'll start at the beginning? Fair warning, it goes back many, *many* years. I'll just fetch us another bottle first as this isn't going to be a five-minute thing.'

'You've got me worried now.'

'Well, Rachel,' Trisha began once they were settled a few minutes later, both with wine in hand, 'the story starts when I moved to London decades ago. It was a few days after my twentieth birthday... Gosh, that sounds so long ago, doesn't it? But here I am now, halfway between my sixties and seventies.'

'Enough about your age, Trisha! You know as well as I do that you don't look a day over forty-five. Now, get to the part of the story that's worrying you.'

'It was my first day at my new job. I was nervous but excited to be working in one of the best hotels in London. Moving from a little Derbyshire mining town to London was huge in itself, but then to be working at this hotel as a waitress in one of the most iconic restaurants in the city... It was a dream come true. Of course, the job itself was less than glamorous and I spent the first couple of years never even going near a table, let alone a customer, but instead shuttling between the kitchen and the wait staff that actually served the food in the dining room.'

'Yes, but look where that job led to forty years later.'

'Retirement?' Trisha joked. 'No, I know what you mean.'

'You were the most revered person in that restaurant,' Rachel said supportively. 'How many managers did you see come and go over the years? The richest UK businesspeople knew you by name and international billionaires – not to mention *royalty* – had so much respect for you.'

'Thank you, that's so kind of you to say. I think the reason they were so nice to me was because I was very discreet. I saw and heard so many things over the years and not once did I ever repeat anything,' she said proudly. 'But back to my story and to Stelios,' she continued.

'That name rings a bell. You've talked about him before ... didn't you work with him and share a flat when you were young? And, if I'm remembering correctly, weren't you a couple at one point?'

'Yes, we actually both started at the hotel on the same day. He was a year and a bit older than me and had come from a very small Greek island called Vekianos, and being the newest members of the team, it bonded us. We were both learning everything together; he helped me with the practical side of things as I learned the ropes, and as his English wasn't so good, I helped him with that. We were lucky that our one day off each week was on the same day as it meant we discovered London together. After six months we both had to move out of the staff accommodation, and because we got along so well it just made sense to find somewhere together. It quickly felt impossible though as everything we looked at was too small or too big, and might require us to share with at least half a dozen people we didn't know.'

'But were you not a couple by then?'

'No, not at that point, but deep down we both knew something special was going to happen between us. Now, cutting a long story very short, we had one week left to find somewhere so we split up, heading off in different directions so we could view twice as many properties in the limited time we had. It got to the afternoon and I arrived at this big house – it was like a mansion and had ten bedrooms – and I wasn't initially keen but at this point Stelios and I were desperate so I decided to look inside. Unusually, I was meeting the owner and not a property agent, and he was very pleasant and showed me around. No one was living there so it felt massive and after about an hour we sat in one of the two lounges and I realised we had crossed our wires. He had the impression I was looking to rent out the whole house and not just two rooms for Stelios and myself. I was really taken aback and didn't know what to say but then it hit me – we could let out the other eight rooms to people we would actually want to share a house with. This was years before mobile phones existed so I couldn't contact Stelios to see what he thought of my idea, but something in my head told me he would tell me to go ahead with it.'

'Trisha, that was so brave! Didn't you have to give him some money up front, and I would think a *lot* of money?'

'I felt brave at the time but as I made my way back to meet Stelios I was feeling more like I'd done something very stupid. And as for the money, I gave the owner all my savings as a deposit. It was complete madness,' she said, before hopping up to grab more wine.

As she went out to the kitchen, all those feelings for Stelios that she had had as a young woman came flooding back; the way he'd looked at her in those first few months, and then, of course, the excitement when the passion took them both over. Renting out the house seemed like it had happened just yesterday, the memory so clear in her mind. But that wasn't all that surprising as it had been the start of their lives changing forever. If it hadn't been for that house, both their lives would have been so different. For a start, she would never have been able to own her own home here in London.

'Here we go,' she said, sinking back down next to Rachel on the couch.

'Thanks. Now come on, what happened next with the house?'

'Sorry, of course. Stelios was over the moon that I had found somewhere for us to live, and he wasn't like me, all panicky and scared, he was excited. I was worried about finding eight other people to share with us, and he was shocked that I hadn't thought of the answer already: hotel staff. We advertised at our hotel and a few others that were close by, and within two days we were able to pick and choose who we wanted from a variety of candidates. Stelios suggested we divided the rent between eight and not ten, so that we could live rent free, which was ideal.'

'This is all fascinating, Trish, but I'm a little confused. What does this have to do with what you're worried about now? Surely it can't be anything to do with that house? And where does Stelios come back into the story? I want to get to the crux of your problem. I'm impatient!'

They both laughed.

'Ok, at this point we were officially a couple, but more than that we were so much in love.'

'Oh, Trisha, I see the tears in your eyes. Are you ok?'

'I was just remembering lots of very happy times. Or, at least, they *were* happy ... now they make me sad.' She took a minute to compose herself before diving back into her story. 'So, after our success with that first house, Stelios and I started to rent additional houses to sublet. It was the start of his property empire and him becoming a big businessman back in Greece, and it allowed me to save money to buy this home. The rest, as they say, is history...'

'But it's not history anymore, is it? There's something bothering you now.'

'Stelios died a few months ago and in his will he left me an apartment ... in Greece. It's a huge shock, surprise, and every other feeling. I assume he left it to me as a reminder of how it all started with that house and as a thank you for how much I helped him with all the others. He always said if it wasn't for me he would still be working in hotels and would never have become the success that he did.'

'How exciting! An apartment in the sunshine... The timing couldn't be better now that you've retired, but I'm still confused. What's the problem?'

'I don't really know, Rachel. I'm sad that Stelios has died, and I wish I had seen him in recent years, even if it was just to catch up and talk about the old days. We hadn't spoken in so long and I just ... I don't feel I'm entitled to a bequest like this.'

'But why not? It's clear that you played an important role in his life so why shouldn't you be rewarded with a holiday home?'

'But it wouldn't be a holiday home. I couldn't afford to keep two homes going so if I accept it, I would have to make a decision. Do I continue my life here in England or do I move to the Greek island of Vekianos? Something tells me that if I chose Greece it wouldn't be that straightforward.'

The two women were silent for a moment, considering what Trisha leaving London might mean for their relationship.

'Can I ask you something?' Rachel finally ventured. 'You said you were in love with Stelios but you obviously didn't end up together. What went wrong?'

'The answer to that is simple: I was stupid. We had been together as a couple for just over two years and we were having a wonderful time. One day

Stelios suggested we go to visit his family on the island of Vekianos, and of course I was happy to agree. It was a holiday in the sunshine, what's not to love about that? And it really was a wonderful holiday. I felt so welcomed by his family and friends and we had a great time spending our days on the beach and eating out at night. There was nothing I didn't love about those three weeks in paradise, especially being with Stelios. We were so much in love and I knew he felt the same. In fact, people kept telling me they had never seen him so happy!'

Trisha could feel tears coming and had to stop and take a few deep breaths before continuing.

'Are you ok, Trisha? You don't have to keep going but I suspect it would be good for you to get this out in the open. But please, take it in your own time.'

'Thank you,' Trisha said, reaching out to squeeze her friend's hand. 'What happened next took me by surprise as it had never crossed my mind, not in a million years. Stelios asked me to leave London and go and live with him in Greece. Talk about a shock! I hadn't even guessed that he wanted to move back, let alone wanted me to go with him.'

'And you said no?' Rachel asked tentatively.

'I didn't even think about it, I told him I had a career in London and I couldn't move to Greece. I gave up the man I was in love with for a silly job.'

Chapter 4

Lena could not believe she had arrived at Corfu airport. It was a journey from Athens she had done quite a bit over the last few years, when her dad was back in her life full time, but to get a taxi to the port to take the boat over to Vekianos now that he had passed it was so strange. She had thought that with her dad gone she would never be visiting the island ever again.

Up until she'd met Joanna her head had been messed up over her dad's death, but now she was even more confused. She owned an apartment on the island, which she was very grateful for, but what was she going to do with it? Her mum's advice had been to sell it but Lena knew that was only because her mum never wanted either of them to visit the island again.

Eventually, sat waiting for the boat to take her over to Vekianos, she had calmed down a little bit and started to think of all the times she'd made this journey in the past; the excitement of knowing her dad would be meeting her off the boat and that the two of them would head straight from there to the villa in the little town of Keriaphos where Fotini would be waiting with her big smile and so many treats that she would have cooked and prepared. Lena had spent her time on the island with her dad either on the beach or in the garden or swimming pool. They had been such happy times, and she still struggled to forgive her mum for denying her the chance to have an entire lifetime of memories with him. But like her dad had said when they'd gotten back into contact and spent more time in each other's life, they had to put it all behind them and focus on the future. But now her dad had died it felt as though that future they'd anticipated was gone for good.

The boat to Vekianos took just over an hour and Lena's thoughts were soon consumed with seeing her aunt. She was looking forward to being able to talk about her dad with someone else who had known and loved him. They could chat about the happy times on her 'happy island', as she used to call it.

Once off the boat she walked to get a taxi. She knew it might take forever as there weren't many on the island, but she didn't mind as she was in no rush and it would give her time to get back into her 'island headspace', shedding all thoughts of Athens for the time being.

Finally stood outside the gates of the apartment block, she watched the taxi pull off and went into her bag for the keys. There they were. The key fob had the number 'six' on it and it was joined by three keys, all marked: one for the main gate, one to get into the apartment block, and then finally, one for the apartment itself. Grabbing her two suitcases and bag, and closing the gate behind her, she turned and stood looking at the apartment block. She took a deep breath, relieved to find that everything looked just like the photos Joanna had shown her. To the right of the small modern apartment block in front of her was the swimming pool and the big patio area.

Suddenly she got the strange feeling that she was being watched. Was Callisto looking down at her from the big top apartment? Not up to facing anyone just yet, least of all her difficult half-sister, she quickly ducked her head and walked up the path with her bags. Letting herself in through the main door she headed up the stairs to apartment six, needing to make a further two trips to get all her luggage up. Now was the hard part: opening her apartment door and going in.

Come on, Lena, pull yourself together! Remember that you don't have any memories here; they're all next door in the villa.

Unlocking the door she held it open while she brought her bag and then the cases in. Closing it behind her she turned to get her first proper look at her new apartment. The first thing that hit her was the amount of light coming in from the huge window in front of her. Stepping further inside she saw a bathroom on one side of the hall and a bedroom on the other. Moving forward she stepped into a big, open space with a kitchen in one corner with a dining table and chairs, and in front of the huge patio doors were two sofas.

All of this was now hers? It was overwhelming and she felt a little shaky and very hot. Walking over and opening the doors out onto her patio to let some air in, she took in the view of the sea in the distance. Holding on to the railing her first thought was that she felt she was at home, but how could she when she had never been in this apartment before? Looking at the walls and the furniture she was pleased to note that everything was to her taste, almost as if she had chosen it herself. Then it hit her. The reason it was such a perfect fit for her was because her dad knew her so well.

She was interrupted from her thoughts by a noise, a knocking, and she quickly realised someone was at the door. She just hoped it wasn't Callisto; she wasn't ready for her yet. Lena wasn't the type of person who could ignore a knock though, so she had to open the door.

She was pleased to see her aunt's smiling face when she did so.

'Hello, Lena! It's so lovely to see you. Come on,

let your old aunt give you a hug.'

Once in her aunt's arms Lena couldn't say anything, all she could do was cry, which then started Fotini off. For some strange reason Lena felt safe for the first time in a very long time, and it reinforced that she'd made the right choice coming here. This is what she needed. To be here in the place her dad loved, with her aunt. Eventually they both calmed and sat down on one of the sofas. There were so many questions Lena wanted to ask her aunt, but she had no idea where she should start.

'It's so lovely to have you here, Lena! We have so much to talk about but there's no rush; we'll have lots of time for that if you're planning on staying. So, I need to know, are you using the apartment as a weekend escape or are you making it your permanent home?'

'If you had asked me that an hour ago, I would have said I don't know, but once I stepped inside I knew this is where I'm going to live. So, yes! I'm moving here and this will be my home. Of course I need to find a job, but first I need to settle in, and I'm looking forward to spending time with you and talking about Dad.'

There were more tears from both of them.

'I'm so glad to hear that, and it will be wonderful to have you close with me moving in just downstairs. Now, I have to ask, have you seen or spoken to Callisto since your dad's funeral? She's been here to visit and check out the apartment block but I didn't speak to her as she only came and walked around the apartments for an hour or so and then left again. I presume because she is now running Stelios' company that she'll be up in the penthouse, but she'll likely still be annoyed that she didn't know anything about this place. To be honest, I was the only one who did as I was living at the villa with Stelios and so saw him undertake all the planning meetings.'

'Dad's lawyer told me you were moving in and renting out the villa. Is that right?'

'Yes, darling, the villa is far too big for me and I need to earn a living. It was actually your dad's idea and he put plans together to have the villa modernised. The work will start once I'm moved into my apartment.'

'Are you happy about all that? Won't you miss being in the villa?' Lena asked, concerned that her aunt didn't seem entirely happy with the prospect of moving.

'No, I don't think so, but time will tell. Now, with me, you, and Callisto, that leaves four other apartments. Do you have any idea who will be in them? No one else has arrived yet.'

'That was the question I was going to ask you!' Lena said with a laugh.

'I have to admit that I find the whole thing very funny. It's just the type of thing Stelios would do, throwing all these people into one complex and then letting them fight it out. Well, I don't mean actually fight, but rather argue. Though with your sister in the picture there's no telling what might happen!' Fotini laughed, but her smile appeared a bit forced.

'Oh well, I guess we'll meet our new neighbours whenever they arrive. For now, I'm still living in the villa for a few more weeks – or months, I'm not quite sure how long – and you must come over for dinner tonight. I realise it won't be easy for you to be back at the villa without your father, but I think the sooner you do it, the better. Shall we say seven o'clock?'

'That would be lovely, Fotini, thank you. I thought I would go for a walk now and buy a few essentials so my fridge isn't empty. I'll leave all the unpacking until another day.'

'That sounds like a great plan. I know this is all

very odd for you, Lena, and some days will be more difficult than others, but please do everything at your own pace. Don't rush into anything. Try to enjoy this opportunity your father has left you. I need to be off now but I will see you over at the villa at seven.'

Lena felt a little bit better for having talked with her aunt, and less alone. She wasn't convinced her aunt was going to like living in an apartment rather than the villa though, so she would need to make sure she knew she had Lena's support if she decided against it in the end.

Picking up her keys and bag she headed out of the apartment and down the stairs. Closing the main door behind her she looked over at the pool and the big patio area. This really was a lovely place and she felt very lucky for this opportunity she had been given. Walking through the big gate and down the lane her heart did seem to jump as she passed the villa, but she needed to focus on the now. There would be plenty of time to look back to the times she had spent here with her dad and work through her grief.

Once at the bottom of the lane she turned to the left. Looking at the time on her phone she worked out that she had a few hours before she needed to be back at her aunt's so she decided a glass of wine in the bar overlooking the beach would be a good idea. She could leave any food shopping until tomorrow as long as she stopped on her way back to buy some milk and cereal for the morning.

She could feel the ocean breeze when she turned the corner and there it was: the most welcoming, and her favourite, sight on Vekianos. Seeing the cove laid out in front of her she was reminded of the first time she'd seen it when she was just a little girl and her parents had still been together. The memory brought a lump to her throat and tears filled her eyes as everything she had been trying to put out of her head came flooding back. All those hours on the beach with her dad, just the two of them, the laughter and the silliness they'd shared together. Why did he have to die? Why hadn't they spent more time together? So many whys. As she walked down the little boardwalk to the restaurant something felt different and then it hit her: the side of the restaurant was boarded up. She had never seen the place closed before. Where were the little tables and chairs that usually sat outside? The building looked so sad now. She would have to ask Fotini what had happened. She started to get upset again; everything she loved was changing. Even though it was so nice to be back here, it was so different now. She wasn't in the villa she loved, her dad wasn't here with her, and now the town itself was changing. It was all too much.

She quickly turned around and headed back to the apartment. She had to rethink everything. Maybe the best thing would be for her to go back to Athens, find a new job and go back to her old life. This little town wasn't her future, it was her past, and she couldn't try to relive that life; it would only hurt her to do so. She stopped at the little mini market and picked up some milk, cereal, and a bottle of wine before rushing up the lane to the apartment block. As she got closer she saw that there was a taxi parked outside the main gate and her first thought was that Callisto must have arrived, but she could see the taxi driver taking a suitcase and bags out and passing them to a man, not a woman. She didn't recognise him but he was about her age and very good looking. She held back until the taxi pulled off, hoping to avoid having to introduce herself when she was so emotionally wrought, but whoever the chap was he was having difficulty with the gate even though he obviously had keys. She decided to wait a bit longer but then thought that perhaps it was best to introduce herself and offer him a hand. At least that way she would find out who he was.

'Hi, can I help you?'

'Hello, I'm not sure I have the right key. There are three here in this bunch.'

'Oh yes, one's for this gate, another for the door into the apartment block and then the last to the actual apartment. By the way, I'm Lena. I just moved in today, too.'

'Thanks,' he said, finally getting the right key, 'I'm Jacob. It's nice to meet you.'

She recognised the name Jacob. Something in her head told her that her dad had mentioned him, but she couldn't remember when or why. Lena held the gate open as Jacob picked up all his luggage and as she closed it behind them she turned to find Jacob taking in the pool area and looking up to the apartment block. As he was doing this she found herself staring at him, his lovely dark eyes and floppy hair. It reminded her of hair you'd find on a romcom hero.

'I suppose it's too much to hope that my key will be for the penthouse,' Jacob joked, before quickly adding, 'Sorry, bad joke. It's not yours, is it?'

She noticed him checking her out as he spoke. Clearly he was feeling a connection as well.

'No, that's my sister's ... well, half-sister. Callisto. She's a lot older than me and I don't really know her all that well, but that's a long story and you look like you've travelled quite a distance and will probably be wanting to settle in. My apartment is on the next floor down,' she said, pointing to her balcony. 'Is there a number on the key ring? That will tell you which one you have.'

'Did you say Callisto?'

'Yes, do you know her?'

'No, but I know *of* her. She works with my dad – he's the company accountant – and I don't think they see eye to eye. You said something about a number...?' He trailed off as he shuffled his bags so he could see the keyring. 'Here it is, number four.'

'That's your apartment then.' She smiled kindly.

'Not mine, actually. It was left to my dad, Tassos, in Stelios' will. My dad wasn't just his accountant, he was also Stelios' best friend, and they had been for many years. When my dad was young and starting out on his career Stelios believed in him and gave him a big helping hand up the ladder. It was my dad's idea that I came here as I work from home and he thought it would do me good, but really I think he just wants me out the way. That's another long story.'

'Seems like we all have one, doesn't it? Come on, I'll lead the way. Can I help you with your bags?'

Jacob nodded and Lena picked up a couple of the bags, feeling his eyes on her. She didn't feel at all uncomfortable though, she found she actually quite liked having Jacob look at her in such an appreciative way. Fetching her key out from her bag she used it to open the main door and then held the door open with her foot until Jacob could grab hold of it. As she went to walk away she got her foot caught in one of the bag straps and before she knew it, they had both tripped and Jacob had fallen on top of her.

'I'm so sorry, Lena, what a way to start our relationship! ...And now I've made it worse. I didn't mean we're going to have a relationship-relationship, I just meant we would be living together in the same apartment block, and like, not living together as in living as a couple...' He trailed off and she couldn't help but giggle at the embarrassment creeping across his features. 'Look, I should just stop and get off of you.'

'Yes, that would probably help,' Lena said, another giggle escaping. 'And I knew what you meant.'

As she stood and turned to sort herself out and pick up the bags, she could see how embarrassed Jacob looked. She needed to say something to make him feel better.

'We just need to go up this flight of stairs. I turn left to go to my apartment and you go right. I'm not sure who is in-between us.' As they reached his apartment door Lena said her goodbyes. 'I'll leave you to get settled in. It was nice meeting you, Jacob.'

'You too, Lena. Thanks for the help.'

Back in her apartment she looked at her reflection in the hall mirror and saw she was a little dishevelled. Was it the tripping over or was it that she felt a little giddy about Jacob? She just hoped she hadn't come across all silly and girly because she certainly wanted to get to know him better. Looking at the time she saw she had ten minutes before she needed to be at Fotini's. Thankfully the wine had survived the fall. She tidied up her hair and apart from looking a little flushed she was ok to go.

She had been dreading walking back in through the villa gate, but strangely, now she did so, she felt ok about it. Was that because she had already seen her aunt? Her head was really messed up with so many things going on.

'Hi, Lena, come through and take a seat on the patio. And more importantly, take a deep breath. I'll pour us each a large glass of wine and then you can scream, shout, laugh or cry. I know this can't have been an easy day for you but you've done it, you've made the first step by coming back to Vekianos. Though I wouldn't be surprised if you're feeling a bit out of sorts.'

'Fotini, how did you know?'

'Because, darling, if you didn't you wouldn't be normal! This is a huge change in your life and like I said before, you need to just take your time and accept that you'll have good days and bad ones. You never know, there might be the odd fabulous day along the way as well,' she said, winking. 'Now, here you go, one glass of wine. By the way, I noticed one of the other balcony doors open. Do you know who else has moved in? I wish I knew who all the apartments have been left to. I've been cursing your father for all these secrets. You just know he's having a good laugh about all of this.'

'Yes, it's someone called Jacob. Apparently his father worked for Dad.'

'Oh, Jacob! I've heard a lot about him. His dad, Tassos, was your dad's best friend. They worked very closely and Stelios would never make a business decision without asking his advice. Between us, from what your father said, I've always gotten the impression that Jacob and Tassos don't really get on. I think he lives in England with his mum for part of the year – she moved back to be near her family in London after she and Tassos divorced – and stays with Tassos in Athens for the other half.'

'He seemed nice.'

'That's good then. And that's another apartment to tick off of the list. That just leaves three, but that's where the problems will start.'

'What do you mean?' Lena asked, confused.

'I'm a little worried the odd ex-girlfriend could turn up.'

'Surely not.'

'Only time will tell. One thing is for certain though, your father had a lot of fun putting this little scheme together.'

Chapter 5

Callisto was back in the office after a long weekend partying on the island of Mykonos. She had ignored her phone and the internet, enjoying party after party, so she should be refreshed and raring to go, but what she really needed was a few days to recover. Sadly, that wasn't happening as today she had a dull calendar of meetings. Most of the time she enjoyed the power of being the boss, everyone saying 'yes, Callisto', and having no one to answer to. Well ... almost no one. Tassos, the company accountant, and the one man who didn't seem to care that she held the power, was the exception.

He might have been her dad's best friend but he wasn't hers and it was top of her list to try and get rid of him. Ever since she took over running the company, the two of them had been in a battle of wills and she hated the way it felt as though he was always looking down on her. She knew he didn't approve of many of the initiatives she had started and the changes she had made since her dad had died, but it wasn't like the old days anymore. It was a case of the survival of the fittest. Where her dad had sealed deals with a handshake and trust, she believed in binding paperwork and official process. She had big plans for this company and needed new, young, fresh faces that would do as she said without questioning it. With Tassos, she feared that he could see right through her act, that he knew she didn't have a clue about lots of the things she was doing, and that it didn't matter how hard she worked, he would always know the confidence she projected was all an act. But she was ready for Tassos today, and she was determined to discover whether he knew anything about the apartment block on Vekianos. Obviously he would have known about the actual build, but she suspected he might also know who else was going to be living there. And forewarned was forearmed, in Callisto's experience.

But first she had a meeting with her right-hand man, Santiago. She needed a status report on each of the company's major projects as she had sort of taken her eye off of the ball ever since this apartment business had come to light. Thankfully, she knew Santiago wouldn't have as he was always out to please her. She was aware he also wanted a more personal connection, but Callisto didn't have time for romance right now. She needed him for one thing only: keeping his nose to the ground to ensure all the projects were progressing on schedule.

She sat down at her new desk and took a moment to breathe. Her dad's old office had been given a makeover and it now looked like something from an LA television series – sleek, modern, and expensive – projecting an image that would hopefully convince clients she knew what she was talking about, even if most of the time she felt like a fish out of water. She took a quick glance at the list of projects she needed to check in on, the one she was most interested in being the new luxury villa the team was developing on Vekianos. Callisto planned for it to be her signature development, which would bring her to the attention of the big boys and take her – and the company – into a completely different league. As she reviewed the computer images of the project there was a knock at the door.

'Hi, Santiago, come in and take a seat. We're going to have to be quick today as I have a lot to fit in and I have a meeting with Tassos after this, so I want just bullet points on the three projects I mentioned in my email. So, hit me with the bad news first.'

'There's no bad news, really, apart from the Vekianos project. The team is having an issue with the water and the drains, but that's being looked into and I should have an update for you soon. The good news is that the two villas we're developing on the outskirts of Athens are nearly ready to go on the market, and we're just waiting for the landscaping to be finished, which will be no more than a week or two.'

'That's good and will no doubt make Tassos happy. There's nothing he loves more than money coming in.'

'Yes, hopefully. By the way, I emailed him the figures for the Vekianos build late last week but I haven't heard back from him. One other thing, the planners have sent me an update on the two apartments we're developing here in the centre of Athens. Because your father originally wanted to make it just one apartment, but you've changed it to two smaller ones, it looks like the start of construction will be delayed for a while, while the paperwork approving the change is finalised.'

'So, no very bad news, really,' Callisto said, feeling relieved. 'And once this drain and water thing on Vekianos is sorted out we'll be full steam ahead. Glad to hear there's nothing that can have Tassos moaning. Right, thanks, Santiago. You've done a great job and I appreciate it. I think that's all for now so have a good day and keep me up to date with any issues – well, any big ones. I know you are more than capable of dealing with the little niggles. It's time for me to face Tassos.'

Santiago nodded and headed towards the door before turning back to her.

'Callisto, I was wondering if you would like to have dinner one night ... a business dinner, of course.'

'I'll need to get back to you on that once I've

checked my schedule. Thank you again, for everything.'

As Santiago left the office Callisto knew that dinner wouldn't be happening. She never mixed business with pleasure. Also, he was far too serious for her. It made him perfect for a work colleague, but not as a boyfriend. Still, she had to be careful with him and not upset him as he was a real asset to her and the company.

She was relieved that it was all good news to tell Tassos and that he would have nothing whatsoever to moan about. A quick nip to the bathroom and she would be ready.

Back in her gorgeous new office she was feeling confident, which was unusual for a meeting with Tassos. Normally she was nervous and on edge in case he asked her something she didn't know. Looking back over all the years she had known him, she couldn't understand why they had never gotten along. They were both similar in age – she was forty and he was forty-five – and being from the same generation you would think they'd have the same outlook on life. But in reality they couldn't be more different, and they always seemed to be on opposing sides in any situation.

When the knock came on the door she wondered if she should get up or stay seated and say 'come in'. No, she would be the one to open the door and welcome Tassos. It was the nicer option and would hopefully start them off on the right foot. As she rushed to answer the door she thought that it was meetings like this where she missed her dad the most.

Right, it was time to put on the act of a confident businesswoman. She needed Tassos on her side and she also needed the info on who else might have been left one of the Vekianos apartments.

'Hi, Tassos, please come in. Thank you for coming across the city for the meeting. Take a seat. Can I get you a coffee?' she rushed out.

'No, I'm fine, thank you. A water would be great though, please.'

'There you go,' she said a moment later, handing him the glass. 'So, where should we start? Would you like an update on the three on-going projects before you run through the figures you mentioned you wanted to discuss with me?'

'Yes, that's fine by me, Callisto.'

She was surprised. He was in a good mood and seemed almost as chilled as the glass of water in his hand. She hadn't seen him like this since her dad's death.

'First of all, the two properties on the outskirts of Athens are nearly ready to go on the market – there's just a little bit of landscaping still to do – so that will put a nice chunk of money in the pot. We do have a little problem with the central Athens apartment that I'm hoping to turn into two units rather than the one, but the paperwork on that should hopefully not take too long, and the Vekianos luxury villa is nearly ready for construction to get started. That's the one I'm most excited about. Would you like to see the plans? I was nervous we wouldn't get planning permission for such a large property but with a little persuasion we got the go-ahead. It's going to be expensive to build but what a property it will be, and with the magnificent sea view I know it will sell quickly to high end buyers. So, I think that's covered everything.'

'It all sounds good and I have to say your dad would be very proud and happy that you completed the two villas here in Athens. That was his last project and it's such a shame he isn't here to see it finished. He also would be thrilled with the price we agreed with the buyers as the profit on them is going to refurbish his family home on Vekianos.'

'I didn't know that. Why does Fotini need it refurbished? Surely she'll be fine living in it as it is.'

'It was stipulated in your dad's will that that's how he wanted the profits allocated so it's going ahead regardless of how you feel about it,' he said sharply. 'Now, moving on to the plot of land on Vekianos. The property looks very impressive, magnificent actually, and I cannot tell you how many years Stelios has wanted to build on that site. Every time he submitted new proposals the authorities said yes but the projects inevitably faltered because of the same problem: getting water and drainage to the site. Every quote Stelios got was mega expensive so congratulations on sorting that, Callisto. I just hope it won't bankrupt the company.'

She chose to ignore his sarcastic comment. 'What exactly are the drainage problems? Do you know?'

'Because of where the villa is located it would mean laying multiple kilometres of drains back from the beach, and that would have cost thousands because roads would have to be closed for prolonged periods to facilitate the work. Whenever we looked at it in the past, as much as we tried to juggle figures, it always came back to the same conclusion: the cost was too great and would mean we gained little to no profit on the plot. It was actually the only project he and I fell out over as I advised him not to buy the land but he insisted. I always thought there was something more important to him about that location than just the land, but like I say, it was a subject he wouldn't discuss. Anyway, you have clearly succeeded where he failed, and I think that would make him happy.'

At this point Callisto's earlier confidence had faded and she was feeling very uncomfortable and just wanted the meeting to be over. She had been banking on using the money from the two Athens villas but now that profit had to go to refurbish Fotini's villa, and from what Tassos had said about the Vekianos project, the water drainage problem might derail everything. It was too late not to go ahead though as she had invested too much money in it for it not to happen. The architectural plans alone had cost her a fortune.

'Thank you, Tassos, now over to you and the finances,' she encouraged, hoping they could wrap up quickly so she could have time to process everything he'd said.

'Well, there's good news and bad news. Firstly, the bank will be happy when the sale of the two Athens properties goes though as the company is a little in the red at the moment and that's not really what they – or I – like to see. Of course this has happened a lot over the years, with your father, but he always came through in the nick of time. It seems you've inherited that trait.'

Callisto was a bit taken aback. Was that a genuine compliment, from Tassos of all people?

'Now, as your accountant I have to bring this up, and please don't look at it as moaning because what you do with the company money is your own business, but in my professional capacity it would be very wrong for me not to say.'

'I understand. And that's what I want and need from you. So, what's the problem?'

'In short, more money has been spent in the last six months than has been earned ... a lot more. For example, your wage – which is a lot more than what your father paid himself – the refurbishment of this office, and your new car. There have also been a lot of travel expenses. In short, we need to be careful. For now, I can reassure the bank about the two Athens properties, and of course we'll have a significant payday when the luxury villa on Vekianos is sold, but in the meantime we need to cut back on expenses wherever possible to avoid going into greater debt. And that's me done. Do you have any questions?'

Questions? Callisto was doing everything in her power to appear calm even though inside she just wanted to scream. Everything looked a nightmare! Why hadn't she been on top of all of this? They were in a mess and the Vekianos project had to start – and soon – because it looked like it was the only way out of their current money problems.

'No, Tassos, I don't think I do. Thank you again for your invaluable help. Of course, the car and the office expenses were just one-offs, so there will be far less to pay out during the next six months.'

'Yes, and hopefully more coming in. If that's all, I'll be off. Have a nice day.'

'Oh, actually, there was one other thing I nearly forgot. My dad's secret project, the apartments on the island of Vekianos next to the family villa, what can you tell me about them?'

'Not a lot. I knew he was building them but apart from the financial side of things I don't know anything else about the project.'

'So you don't know who he's left the units to?'

'I know your half-sister Lena was left one and your dad very kindly gave me one, too. Actually, my son Jacob has just moved there temporarily – that's how I know for sure that your sister is there; he's met her. Beyond that, I'm guessing you have one, and of course Fotini as well. That would leave three but I can't help you there as your dad could have left them to any number of people.'

'Thanks,' Callisto said as Tassos left her office, leaving her with lots to think about.

Five hours later, and one large bottle of wine consumed, Callisto still hadn't calmed down from the meeting. She felt sure that Tassos had been so nice to her because he knew she had messed up with the Vekianos project. Hearing how strained the company finances were, she was glad she hadn't told him that she had sold her poky little home and put a deposit on a new, bigger one and that would mean bigger monthly mortgage payments, so there was no way she could reduce the salary she had set for herself. She had messed up and her only hope was that this drainage issue wouldn't be as big as Tassos had made out.

Her phone rang, jolting her out of her thought spiral.

'Santiago, please tell me it's good news and we can start on the Vekianos project.'

'Hi, Callisto, what you told me earlier was right. The drains do have to be dug up and taken back at least half a kilometre. The good news is that the authorities are very happy to do that ... but the bad news is that it's going to cost *a lot*. Apparently that's why the land was a lot cheaper in that area. You only have to say the word and the work can begin, but the authorities do want the money up front for the roads to be dug up, plus there's another property along the route and as that would mean digging on their land, it will be an added expense... Callisto, are you still there?'

'Yes, ok, thank you for getting back to me so quickly on this, Santiago. Leave it with me and we'll talk in the morning. I need to think this through.'

Coming off the phone Callisto realised there was nothing to think about. There were no finances in place for all that extra work, which meant the dig just couldn't happen. Then she suddenly had a thought. Why not use the money that was being put aside to refurbish Fotini's villa? There didn't seem to be any rush to get the renovations done so what would it hurt to put that off for a bit while they dealt with this drainage issue? She just had to convince Fotini and Tassos that she was only postponing the villa refurbishment for a short period.

Perhaps the future wasn't looking as bleak as she had thought...

Chapter 6

Sitting in the taxi and leaving the harbour on her way to her new apartment in the little town of Keriaphos, Trisha was thankful for Rachel's advice. Instead of feeling pressured to make the decision on where to live, she would visit Vekianos and take a look at the apartment that Stelios had left her to see if it might be somewhere she'd like to live full time. This way, she could have a little holiday, enjoy the nice weather, and take deep breaths before making a balanced decision.

It didn't take that long to get to the apartment block from the harbour as the island wasn't that big, and the taxi driver was very pleasant as he happily told her all about living on the island.

'Sorry, I should have asked, have you been to Vekianos before?' he said, interrupting himself.

'Oh yes, many years ago. Actually ... it must be at least forty years or more since I once visited here for a little holiday.'

'I expect a lot has changed in all those years! Now, we're nearly there, I think we just need to turn up this lane... Yes, here we are. Judging by the big, shiny gate this all looks very new. You've booked the perfect place to stay as the little beach, restaurants, and shops are just down the hill and it will only take a few minutes to walk down,' he said, smiling brightly at her in the rear-view mirror.

As they drove up the lane memories flooded back to Trisha. There was Stelios' family villa, still looking exactly the same from the outside. Her heart started to flutter and she felt sad, the memories of that holiday still so clear in her head.

The driver pulled up outside the gate and lifted

her case and bag out the boot of the car. She fiddled in her handbag for her purse and keys, and after paying him she stood back and looked at the gates and the building beyond. This was it. There was no going back now.

She wondered briefly if there might be people in or around the pool. She needed to be prepared for conversations. Would the others mention Stelios? She would certainly not be mentioning that her apartment had been left to her in his will as that would no doubt prompt many questions she wasn't ready to answer. No, that was something she would like to keep a secret for now.

She was just about to try the keys when the gate opened and she quickly stepped back out of the way.

'Hi, sorry to make you jump! I'm not used to people coming in here as it's all a bit empty. Can I help you with your luggage? I'm Jacob,' the younger man said amiably, extending his hand to her.

'Hello,' she said, shaking his hand. 'I'm Patricia, though I answer more to Trisha. And thank you, it would be a big help if you could take that case there. It's very kind of you to offer.'

She picked up her carry-on bag, put her handbag over her shoulder, and followed Jacob through the gate. Closing it behind her she could better see the apartment block in front of her. It was even more impressive than it had appeared in the photos she had seen, and the pool looked so inviting.

'This is gorgeous. I love the pool area.'

'So you've not been here before, Trisha? That's a silly question, isn't it. None of us have. In fact, you're only the third person to arrive. There's me, of course, and Lena, who is one of Stelios' daughters – the nice one. We're still waiting for Callisto – the scary one – to arrive. Sorry, I shouldn't say that as she could be a friend of yours! I think I've talked enough for now so tell me where we're headed with these bags. Which apartment number is on your key?'

Trisha tried to take in everything Jacob was saying but it was all a bit confusing. Stelios had daughters? She needed to get in the apartment and take a moment to take it all in.

'Sorry,' she said, shaking herself out of her fog. 'It says number seven.'

'Now that is *very* interesting, Trisha! Oh here's Lena. Hi, Lena, this is Trisha, a new arrival,' he said, turning towards the young woman who had just exited the apartment building.

'Hello! Nice to meet you, Lena.'

'Likewise. Can I help with your luggage?'

'Oh I'm fine, thank you, Jacob's been very kind taking the heavy case. We were just about to head inside. I'm in apartment number seven.'

She couldn't miss the pointed look Jacob and Lena exchanged. What was going on?

'Ok, well ... enjoy!' Lena said, a smile on her face that Trisha couldn't quite decipher. 'As Jacob is helping I think I'll be off. Welcome to Vekianos, by the way, I'm sure you're in for a lovely and interesting time here and I will no doubt see you around soon.'

With that Lena headed to the main gate and Trisha followed Jacob to the apartment door. He was a lot faster than her and after he held the main door open for her he went up the flight of stairs two at a time, not stopping until they reached a big door on the top floor.

'This is apartment seven, Trisha – the penthouse! It goes right along the whole length of the block and I expect you have the most fabulous views looking for miles. If you have your key ready I'll take your case in.'

'Oh, no, you've done enough already. Please just

leave it by the door; I can manage it from there. Thank you so much, Jacob, you have been an enormous help.'

'If you're sure? I think I'll see if I can catch Lena up. By the way,' he called from the top step, 'if you need anything or have any questions, I'm in the apartment underneath here – number four. It's my dad's but he lives and works in Athens and so I'm staying here for a bit. Bye for now.'

What a nice, helpful young man, Trisha thought to herself. And he was obviously very interested in Lena judging by the way he'd blushed as he said her name. There was nothing quite like young love... Thinking of love, there was no avoiding the fact that Vekianos was the place she was last in love, all those years ago.

But enough of those thoughts. Turning to the door she couldn't help but say, 'What have you done, Stelios? The penthouse? Why me?' Putting her bag down and getting the key with the number seven fob on it she unlocked the door and stepped inside. The first thing that struck her was the light that hit her from the big windows. She put her big bag down and then wheeled the suitcase inside. Closing the door behind her, she walked into the big space, which was full of sunshine. In the main room there were three huge, pale blue sofas and the sight of them had her welling up. Pale blue was her favourite colour, which had to mean Stelios hadn't just given her the apartment, but also that he had chosen the furnishings. It was clear that a lot of thought had gone into this, and she only wished he was still here so she could ask him why he had gone to such an effort on her behalf.

Two hours later she was still crying and still very confused and still didn't know what to do. She had walked around the apartment so many times but still couldn't take it all in. Three bedrooms, two bathrooms, stairs up to the roof terrace and a big open plan area with a gorgeous kitchen. She hadn't gone up on the roof terrace just yet because she didn't want to get spotted and also because she knew the view would look towards Stelios' family villa, which she wasn't ready for. She had sent a quick text to Rachel to let her know she had arrived ok and she would call her later on, once she had settled in. She decided to put all her clothes in the wardrobe in one of the bedrooms and as she wheeled her case along the corridor she thought she heard a knock at the door. She paused and stepped back to listen. Yes, there was definitely someone knocking. She did her best to pull herself together and then opened the door with a smile.

'Hi, Lena, can I help you with something?'

'Hello again! I was just thinking as I was walking back from the shop that you probably haven't got milk or coffee or that sort of thing, so I wondered, would you like to pop down and have a coffee with me? I've also got some very special Greek pastries that are to die for. I'm at number six, just down one flight of stairs. I'll go and put the kettle on and you come down whenever you're ready.'

With that Lena was gone. There had been no opportunity to say yes or no so Trisha would have to go down, but to be honest, a coffee would be very welcome and this could be the first step to finding out why she was here. Why Stelios had left her an apartment, and not just any apartment, but the penthouse. Picking up her phone, keys, and handbag, she closed the door behind her. She was about to have a coffee with Stelios' *daughter*. This was so odd.

She took more deep breaths as she walked down the stairs and along the corridor. Lena's door was wedged open.

'Hi, Lena, it's Trisha,' she called as she let herself in.

'Come in, come in! How do you like your coffee?'

'Black no sugar, please.'

'Ok that's easy. Would you like to go out on the balcony? I'll bring the drinks out.'

She felt more comfortable with the idea of being on someone else's balcony than she thought she would on her own, but she still wasn't ready to look over at the villa. Walking through to the big sliding doors she saw that the apartment was very similar to her own but on a much smaller scale. It made her feel worse. As Lena was Stelios' daughter, shouldn't she be up in the top apartment?

'There we go, one coffee and a couple of pastries right out of the oven less than an hour ago. Not my oven, but the bakery down the hill.'

'Thank you, this is very kind of you. I really appreciate it.'

There was then a silence and Trisha suspected that they both felt a little nervous, not knowing who should say what ... or more to the point, ask what.

'Didn't Jacob catch up with you?'

'Yes, he was hoping we could spend the day together on the beach or go for a walk.'

'And didn't you fancy that? He seems a very nice young man.'

'Oh, yes, that would've been nice, and he is lovely... Perhaps another day. To be honest, I was more interested in you, Trisha. Sorry, that sounds ominous, doesn't it? I didn't mean it to be. I'm just intrigued as to where you fit into my dad's apartment of secrets. At the moment it feels as though my dad is playing a game with us all. In a good way, of course, he wouldn't do anything horrible,' she hastened to add.

'I really wish I could answer that, Lena, but I honestly don't know why I'm here. I'm as much in the dark as you. Of course, I knew your dad, he was a good friend many years ago, but for him to leave me an apartment here in Greece? It's all beyond me and if I'm truly honest, it's a bit scary. I keep wondering what surprise is going to come next.'

'Oh, please don't be scared! How about I tell you what I know? Hopefully that might help. But where should I start? Well, there are seven apartments in the building. I have one – Jacob mentioned he told you I'm Stelios' daughter. I'm the youngest child but more about that later – and then my dad's sister, Fotini, has another – number three, on the ground floor – Jacob's in number four, which is his father's apartment – that's Tassos, he was my dad's accountant and best friend for many years – and you are in number seven. My half-sister, Callisto, has one of the apartments as well, so that leaves just two more mysteries to be solved.'

'That makes things a lot clearer, thank you. Which number is your sister in?'

Trisha could see Lena looked a little nervous before answering. Had she said the wrong thing?

'I'm not sure... You see, both my aunt and I presumed Callisto would be in the penthouse as she now runs my dad's company and, well ... we just took it for granted that she would be up there. But now we know she isn't.'

'Do you think she will be upset? Should I explain to her that the choice had nothing to do with me?'

'I don't know, but I'm guessing she won't be happy. You see, she doesn't get on with my aunt, and from the stories Jacob has told me, she doesn't get on with his dad either, which is difficult since she is now running the company and they have to work closely together. As for me, I've only even met her once and that was at my dad's funeral. He kept everyone in his life completely separate. We were all in little boxes and those boxes never got mixed up.'

'Oh dear. Callisto definitely won't be happy when she arrives by the sounds of it. But do you think perhaps your father did it this way, giving you both the same size apartment, because he didn't want to favour one daughter over another?'

'Yes, that could be it. I hadn't thought of it like that.'

'But it still doesn't explain why I have the penthouse. I haven't been in his life for many years. We were good friends once, but our lives went in different directions, with Stelios coming back to Greece and me staying in London.'

With that Lena's face lit up with a big smile.

'My dad loved London. He told me so many stories about it and he was always so happy talking about his time there as that's where he learned English properly and started his business. He also said it had a special place in his heart because it's where he met the love of his life. Sadly it didn't work out and he had to leave the woman behind. Her name was Patricia.'

Patricia sat in shocked silence. What had Lena just said? For one thing, Stelios hadn't left her behind; it was her who had rejected his offer. And the 'love of Stelios' life'?

As she was processing it all she noticed Lena's face. The penny had evidently dropped and she had put two and two together.

'Of course, it all makes sense now. *You* are *Patricia* – that's why my dad has left you the penthouse! You were the love of his life!'

Chapter 7

Lena was up early and she had already been and had her first dip in the pool. She also had been into the little pool house, which was basically a big storeroom with tables, chairs, and sun loungers. It made her smile to see that her dad had gone to so much trouble getting everything ready. Perhaps now that there were three of them in the block – four, if you counted Fotini – she could start to put the loungers around the pool. As she moved them out into the sunshine everything started to feel real – the fact that she was here, the fact that the apartment was hers – and she was feeling increasingly comfortable with the situation. It was like she had said to Trisha yesterday, she genuinely believed her dad only meant all of this to be a good thing. The last thing he would have wanted was any upset.

Now, as for Trisha, Lena really didn't know what to think. She liked her and she could see why she was here, but she also felt sad for her as she really didn't think Trisha wanted to be. As soon as the coffee was finished yesterday, Trisha had made lots of excuses about unpacking and having to go and get a few supplies, which made sense, but Lena suspected that there was a lot more to it. Trisha was a work in progress, and Lena would give her the space she needed for now.

As she turned away from where she'd just settled the last sun lounger, she could see Jacob heading towards her. He was dressed casually in shorts and a vest, and she couldn't help but notice his arms, specifically the muscles.

'Do you need a hand?'

'Hello, Jacob, I'm fine, thank you. I just thought I would make the pool area feel a little more lived in with the loungers. There are also a few little tables and chairs to put out but I'm not too sure where the best place for them would be. Perhaps in the shade?'

'That sounds like a good idea. Let me help you.'

As they moved to collect the tables and chairs from the storeroom and arrange them outside next to the pool, Jacob looked Lena over. 'Judging by the wet hair you've been for a dip. How was the pool?'

'Good, thanks. You need to try it. You could dive in now.'

'Perhaps later. I have some work to finish today or else I'll be in trouble. I'm a little behind, what with moving here and one thing and another.'

'Another time then. By the way I haven't asked what work you do.'

'I'm a children's book illustrator.'

'How exciting! An author.'

'Oh, no, I don't write the stories. I just do the drawings.'

'*Just* the drawings? I would think that that's the most important part of children's books.'

'Thank you, that's kind of you to say.' Checking his watch, Jacob said, 'I need to get off. I'm just heading down to the shop as I need chocolate to keep me going. Can I get you anything while I'm out?'

'No, I'm fine, thanks. Have a good day and I hope you meet your deadline. I'm sure you will.'

'Thank you.'

As Jacob left Lena plunked herself down on one of the sun loungers. She really liked Jacob and she got the impression he liked her as well. The way he looked at her when he was talking made her feel good and they were already so relaxed in one another's company.

Thinking about the day ahead of her, she

pondered what she should do. Should she go and see Fotini? She wanted to tell her about Trisha arriving and especially about her living in the top floor apartment. Lena knew it would make her aunt happy because it would mean Callisto would be so annoyed and there would be nothing she could do about it. But first she would try the tables and chairs in a few different places to see what might look best. As she was doing this she noticed Jacob come back and he waved as he headed inside. She found she was secretly hoping he would stop and chat, but she knew he was on a deadline. As she waved back she noticed Trisha coming out of the main door, so she headed over to greet her.

'Hi, Trisha, did you get all your unpacking done and are you settled in? That's probably a stupid question, isn't it, given you've only been here one night.' Lena laughed. 'If you're anything like me it will take a bit of time to start to feel comfortable and for all of this to really sink in.'

'You're right, it's all very strange and if I'm honest, still very uncomfortable. I feel that at any moment your sister will arrive and be angry to find I have her apartment.'

'I wouldn't worry too much. It was only Fotini and I that jumped to the conclusion that Callisto would be at the top, and for all we know that thought might never have crossed Callisto's mind. And if she is upset and wants to blame anyone, she can blame our dad. Now enough of all that, what have you planned for your first day here on Vekianos?'

'I need to get some supplies – mainly coffee as I have drunk all that you kindly gave me – and then I thought I'd take a walk around. I don't think I will recognise much but it will give me time to clear my head.'

'Would you mind some company? We could

make a day of it with coffee to start and then lunch later on. It will only take me five minutes to be ready and I'd be very happy to show you around.'

'Thank you, Lena, I'd like that. I'll wait here for you but there's no rush. I have all day!' Trisha laughed.

Lena went up to her apartment to get changed and Trisha walked over and sat at one of the little tables. Instead of looking towards the pool she faced up to the apartment block. She wanted to feel happy about all of this, but she couldn't. Even though she hadn't seen Stelios for many years he was now completely filling her head. Had she wasted her life? Should she have gone in a different direction those forty plus years ago? At the time she was still so young, so it wasn't surprising that her choices then would not necessarily be the same as those she would make now.

'I'm ready! Trisha, are you ok?' Lena's bright smile quickly turned into an expression of concern as she took in Trisha's emotional state.

'Not really,' Trisha admitted, 'but I'm ready for you to show me around.'

'Follow me,' Lena said, rallying. 'I'll be your tour guide for the day and I'm going to bring a smile to your face. That's a promise!'

'Thank you, I'm really hoping you can. Now, lead the way to the coffee.'

As they came out the gate Lena pointed out the family villa, which of course Trisha recognised, but neither made any further comments about it. They walked to the end of the lane and turned left, heading down the hill to the little town and the beach.

'It really has changed. I can't remember any of these properties but they're quite nice and I'm sure the visitors who use them bring in a nice income stream for the community, which is good.'

'They certainly do. They've all been here as long as I've been visiting. Now, there's a little path you can cut down to get to the town but it's a little steep so we'll go the longer way and stick to the road so you don't miss anything.'

'Thank you. So far you've been the perfect tour guide and once you find the coffee I will happily grant you five stars.'

They both laughed and carried on, Lena pointing things out as they passed.

When they got to the road that ran behind the little beach, Trisha said, 'I remember this! It's good to see not everything has changed. I'm pleased the little shops and restaurants are still here as I would have hated it if it had all been modernised. I can remember your dad and I used to come down here to the beach and there was a place that served coffee overlooking the little cove. I hope it's still there.'

'I'm afraid it's closed now. It was my and my dad's favourite place as well and I was so disappointed when I came down here the other day to find it all shut up.'

'Oh well, not to worry, we'll just find somewhere else. There's a restaurant over there with tables outside and it's in this gorgeous street perfect for people watching. What more do we need?'

They headed over and the waiter made them very welcome. Coffees and cake were ordered, and they both smiled.

'This is nice, Lena, thank you for showing me around.'

'It's my pleasure! Are you feeling a little better? You don't seem so tense now we've had a bit of a walk in the sunshine.'

'You're right, I do feel better. It's nice to come out and get some fresh air. You must think I'm silly,' Trisha said, blushing a little.

'No, not at all!' Lena rushed to reassure her. 'I

think you're just in shock and with everything that's happened and it's understandable. Can I ask you, are you ok talking about my dad? Like I said yesterday, I loved hearing his stories of when he lived and worked in London; it just seemed like all you did was go to parties.' She laughed.

'Yes, we certainly did party well,' Trisha said wryly, 'but we worked hard as well. Times were very different then. Lots of things were spur of the moment. We would finish work at midnight but there was always somewhere to go from there. London seemed to never go to sleep.'

'If you don't mind me asking, were you and my dad a couple?'

'Yes, we were a couple for about two and a half years. We had a lot of fun together, both loving the life we had. Life was very cheap for us in those days as we ate for free in the hotel we worked at and we didn't have rent as we managed the house we were living in. That was actually the start of your dad's business ventures and I know he became very successful, which I'm so happy about.'

'Yes, he talked about renting houses out and then subletting them, and told me how once he came back to Greece he invested the money he'd made into holiday accommodation, which then led him into building properties. I asked him how he never seemed to get bored with his working life and he said it was because every day was different and no two projects were ever the same.'

'I'm pleased he was happy with his life, and I just know you would have given him so much joy. And your sister, of course.'

'Yes, my mum and dad split up so there was a period when I didn't see a lot of him, just the odd holiday, which he had to fight with my mum to get as she was very angry and bitter with him – and still is. I realise now though that it's herself she's angry with, as she was the one who messed the relationship up by cheating on him.'

'That's very sad but I'm glad to hear you got to spend some time with your dad here on beautiful Vekianos, which I know he loved so much. When we used to talk about Greece it was always about him growing up in this town. On that note, do you fancy having a little walk and showing me more of this place? And of course we need to go to the beach, which I remember very clearly.'

Trisha paid the bill and they headed along the road until they came to the boardwalk that led down to the beach.

Reaching the beach they perched on the steps of the boarded up coffee shop and as they sat down they both stopped talking. They were in their own separate worlds remembering the times they had each been there with Stelios.

Although for Trisha it had only been for a few weeks many years ago, it was still so clear in her mind as it had been a very special holiday. Stelios had been so proud to bring her to his hometown and for her to meet his mum, dad, and all his friends.

They seemed to be sat on the steps for ages in silence but it was a lovely silence, both embracing their different memories, which were very similar in a lot of ways.

'This place is beautiful and so special,' Trisha said at last, breaking the contented silence. 'It's strange how for decades none of this has ever entered my head but now I'm here the memories are so clear.'

'Can I ask you something? It's probably none of my business but I'm curious to know, why did you and my dad split up?' Lena asked softly.

'You know, if you had asked me that question back in London a few months ago I would have given you a completely different answer than I would now. I would probably have said that it was because we wanted different things out of life, but answering you here, now, I would say that it was because I was stupid and silly and too young to see the big picture. I gave him the wrong answer when he asked me to move here to Greece with him. It's taken me years to realise it but I should have gone with my heart and not my head.'

Chapter 8

Callisto clocked herself in the mirror. She looked worse than she felt and that was saying something. Her life was a mess and though she had spent days trying to sort it out she hadn't gotten anywhere and now she had only one option left, and she had to put her plan into action today. But first, she had to pull herself together and make herself into the businesswoman she was because it was truly make or break time.

Three hours later and with her best power suit on, she was at Joanna's office. She was ready.

As she knocked on the door and walked in she found Joanna waiting for her.

'Good morning, Joanna, thank you so much for seeing me at such short notice. I know how busy you must be.'

'It's not a problem. Please come through to my office. Can I get you a coffee? I was just about to have one myself.'

'Thank you, that would be nice.'

As Joanna went over to a side table to get the coffee Callisto went and sat in the seat she had last time. She placed her briefcase next to her and took a few deep breaths. For years her dad had been telling her to treat people as she expected to be treated but she had rarely done it, which was one of the reasons she was in the mess she was. That changed today.

'So,' Joanna said as she handed over the coffee. 'Have you been over to Vekianos and spent any time in the apartment?'

'No, sadly I've been so busy with all my projects – well, finishing off my dad's, really – and so it's been hectic ... but also very exciting. That's the reason I'm here actually. With all of my work commitments I can't see myself being available to use the apartment more than a couple of weekends a year, and if I did go over, I would prefer to stay in my dad's family villa, with my Aunt Fotini. That would mean the apartment would lay empty most of the time, which is such a shame.'

'That is very sad, Callisto, as your dad meant it to be a little escape for you to get away from your busy work life here in Athens.'

'Yes, if this had happened in ten years' time, when I would have a little more time on my hands, it would have been perfect, but with my dad's shoes being quite big to fill I'm working nearly twenty-four-seven at the job as the last thing I want to do is let him down. I need to keep everything up to his high standards.'

'Yes, I see where you're coming from, but knowing Stelios, he would still have liked you to be able to enjoy yourself and take time off, just like he used to. He worked hard but he equally loved to relax and have time at the beach, or to go for walks around Keriaphos, eat nice food, and spend time with the people he loved.'

Callisto was a little taken aback by the tone of Joanna's voice and even more the emotion in it.

'The thing is, Joanna, and I know my dad would completely understand and realise the reasoning behind it, I would like to sell my apartment rather than it be there empty.'

There was a long silence and Callisto could see Joanna was uncomfortable as she was fiddling with her pen and not making eye contact.

Finally, she said, 'Callisto, did you get a chance to review the paperwork my office sent across?'

Callisto shook her head. 'I had my lawyer look at it instead.'

'Ah,' Joanna said, understanding in her tone. 'Well, I'm afraid that what the paperwork will tell you, is that you aren't allowed to sell the property for ten years.'

Callisto stared at the lawyer, not knowing how to respond.

'When I was putting all of his requests and actions together I pointed out to your father that perhaps the ten year commitment could be a problem, but he was very persistent and completely adamant that the clause be added. I'm so sorry but there's nothing I can do about it. If you wanted to get your lawyers to put up an objection you are entitled to, but I don't know that anything would come of it as your dad really did put a very strong contract together. On another level, a personal one, I think it's worth pointing out that he did this, his last project, out of love for the people he wanted to live there. He didn't make any of the choices he made lightly.'

Sitting on a bench outside Joanna's office a while later, Callisto switched her phone back on and an email immediately popped up from Santiago with a link to the costings for all the drainage and water supply work on the luxury villa project. She groaned. Oh, why had she been so stupid? She had paid for so much initial work on the site, which was now just money down the literal and figurative drain.

Walking back to her office Callisto was upset for so many reasons. She had gained nothing from the meeting with Joanna and she had let her father down. Looking around her office as she stepped inside, she took in all the new furniture and the artwork on the walls. All of it was a waste of money – the money her father had worked so hard for.

Now she had to face her dad's best friend, who

had worked with Stelios setting up the company, and even though she had made steps to try and help the company finances – pulling out of the purchase of her dream home and selling her house in Athens to try and recoup funds so that she could lower her salary – she knew he would still be so angry with her once he discovered how much money had been lost on the drainage issue, and he would be perfectly right to be.

She knew the sooner she got the difficult conversation with Tassos over with, the better, as she could then move on – though to what, when, and where she hadn't got a clue – so it was time to make the call.

'Hi, Tassos, it's Callisto,' she said as soon as he answered. 'I'm sorry to bother you but would it be possible to arrange a meeting today?'

'Yes, that's fine. I can come across the city to your office in a couple of hours.'

'No, it's ok, I'll come to you.'

'Fine. Shall we say around three-thirty then?'

'Thank you.'

That was it. There was no going back.

At three-thirty on the dot she knocked on Tassos' office door. It crossed her mind that she hadn't been to this office for years; no doubt it would be just like her dad's with old furniture and everything falling apart.

'Come in.'

As Callisto opened the door she was flabbergasted. This was not what she had been expecting! Tassos' office was sleek and stylish and it felt a bit like she was walking into a luxury hotel. There was a huge, gorgeous desk, floor-to-ceiling shelving units filled with books and pieces of art, and two sofas and a coffee table in front of the window.

'What a fabulous office,' she said.

'You seem shocked, Callisto. Surely you didn't think I would work in a place like your dad? He was always out on site somewhere or other so he wasn't bothered with how his office looked, but I'm here ten hours a day, five days a week so I need it to be an attractive and functional place to work. If you'd like to take a seat, I'll get us something to drink.'

It wasn't just the office that was a shock to her, it was Tassos' attitude. He was being ... friendly? Well, that wouldn't last long once she told him the Vekianos news and the amount of money that had been wasted. No doubt his attitude would change then.

'There you go. Now, how can I help you?'

'I just needed to fill you in on a few things, mainly the Vekianos project, which doesn't seem to be happening now.'

'Yes, I've had the figures through and I think it's sensible to put it on hold for now, until we're in a better financial situation. You've made the right decision there.'

'Yes, but there are still some bills connected to it that need to be paid, which will hit the budget big time. There's also the flat project here in central Athens. It's going to have to stay as one unit because with the new projections I ordered it appears that the additional cost of undoing the work that's already been done, in order to convert it into two, is now expected to be significant enough that we won't be able to make enough of a profit.'

'That's a shame, but the two villas on the outskirts are nearly ready to go.'

'Yes, but that profit has to be ploughed into dad's family villa on Vekianos, and we know we aren't going to get any return on that investment.'

'I know, but that was never expected to affect the bottom line.'

'But the bills for the architect plans and all the other expenses connected to the Athens apartment and the luxury villa property on the island are huge. They're going to throw us into a lot of debt and I can't see a way out of this mess. I'm sorry, I know it's not just my dad I've let down, it's you as well. I've been so stupid. There is one little light at the end of the big black tunnel though. The sale of my home goes through soon so any profit I make on it can go towards paying for my mistakes.'

There was a silence as Tassos took in everything Callisto had said. She knew the money wouldn't be much to undo the damage she had done, but she hoped it showed him that she was dedicated to making things right.

'You shouldn't be so hard on yourself, Callisto,' he began, more gently than she'd expected. 'Yes, things have gone wrong, but you're also doing a lot right. I'm sure we can get the maximum price for the villas just outside Athens, even if it means holding on to them a little longer. And I know the central Athens apartment will also sell quickly as it's in a very desirable area. And as for the Vekianos plot of land, ok, there has been a lot of expense wasted, but your dad should have never bought it in the first place and you shouldn't feel a responsibility to finish an impossible project for him.'

'But why did he buy it if he knew it was a problem site?'

'I really don't know. It's always been a mystery to me and every time I questioned him about it, all he said was that he had his reasons.'

'Thank you, Tassos, you've been very kind and I know that's not what I deserve. I promise that once the sale of my home goes through I will make sure the profit is transferred into the business account right away.'

'Do you know where you're moving to yet?'

'I'm not sure, but that's the least of my worries. At the moment, I need to concentrate on saving my dad's company.'

'Could I suggest you consider moving to Vekianos? You do actually have a home there ... and you have family. Your aunt and sister are both living there at the moment.'

'Yes, a sister I've only met once, and an aunt who thinks I'm a know-it-all who lives a life I shouldn't.'

As she said goodbye and walked out the office, she got the impression Tassos felt ... sorry for her? The way he had looked at her as she laid her failures bare before him, it gave the impression he actually cared for her. But surely that was impossible. After all, what reason had she ever given Tassos to think well of her?

Chapter 9

It had been a couple of days since Lena and Trisha had toured the island together and today they were going to spend some time at the pool. Jacob was joining them as he'd caught up on his work. Lena planned to use the barbeque and had invited Fotini as well – it was time for the four of them to get to know each other a little better – but first she needed to nip down the hill to the shops for a few treats. As it was still early she thought a walk around to the little beach would be nice, and it would give her a chance to call her mum, something she had kept putting off since arriving. After finding a quiet spot on the rocks she pressed the call button.

'About time you called, Lena,' her mum said sharply when she answered. 'I don't believe all your excuses about being busy. How could you be busy when nothing ever happens on Vekianos? Now, if you were here in Athens, I would understand, but you're not. Now, tell me what's happening. I hope you're not standing for any of Callisto's nonsense or letting Fotini interfere with your life, planning everything. You need to stand up for yourself. Don't let them walk all over you.'

As the tirade continued Lena was reminded of why she had been putting off calling her mum. Because she had wanted to avoid this. Eventually, Mariana stopped for breath, and Lena rushed to reassure her.

'No to everything, Mum, Callisto isn't here yet and Fotini has been very busy so we haven't spent much time together yet. I'm seeing her today though; a few of us are having a little barbeque just to get to know each other a little better.'

'If Callisto isn't there, then who is?'

'There's Jacob, Tassos' son—'

'Oh, I might have guessed Tassos was involved. Your dad would never do anything without his say so.'

'Mum, Tassos was a good friend to Dad—'

'So who else is there?' her mum interrupted.

'No one you would know, only a lovely lady from England.'

'Patricia is there? I might have guessed,' Mariana said disdainfully.

'You know Trisha, Mum?'

'Not *know*, only *know of*. She was the love of your father's life; the woman he should have married.'

'What do you mean? Did he tell you that?'

'Not in so many words but I know that was the case. But I don't want to talk about that. Anyway, I need to go. You may be content just sitting around but I have a busy life to get on with.'

Call over, Lena pulled out her shopping list and walked to the store to get some supplies for the barbeque. It only took half an hour to get all she needed and then she began the hike back up the hill.

'You look like you need a hand, Lena,' Jacob said as she walked through the gate of the apartment block. 'Let me take one of the bags.'

'Thanks, yes, I'm a little overloaded! I forgot just how steep that hill can feel.'

'Glad you made it ok! I'm really looking forward to today. It will be fun getting to know everyone a bit better.'

'It will. I take it you've finished all your work and you can now enjoy some time off?'

'Yes, but just a week, unfortunately. I have another project to start on after that so I'm going to make the most of my vacation time. Perhaps we could have some days out together? I was thinking we could take a trip over to Paxos, or we could have a day on the beach, if you're interested?'

'I'd really like that. Let's make a plan later on. For now, I need to go and put all this in the fridge. Oh, I see Trisha is already by the pool. Hi, Trisha!' Lena called as she headed inside. 'I won't be a minute. I just need to pop up to the apartment.'

Jacob helped her up the stairs with the bags and as he left they shared a lovely smile between them. She really liked Jacob and was looking forward to a week spent getting to know him better.

Once everything was packed away, Lena got changed for her day at the pool. By the time she got back downstairs, Jacob was already there chatting to Trisha.

'All sorted, Lena? I was just telling Trisha you've bought enough food to feed the whole island of Vekianos!' he said with a warm laugh.

'Better too much than too little, I say. That way you don't run out and with leftovers, nothing will be wasted. How are you today, Trisha?'

'I'm fine, thanks, though still shocked I'm here.'

'I feel the same but each day it's getting easier. Here comes Aunt Fotini. Good morning!' Lena called brightly as her aunt came through the gate. 'Come pick a sun lounger. This is Jacob, of course you know his dad, Tassos, very well, and this is Trisha. I'm not sure ... did you two ever meet all those years ago when Trisha visited with my dad?' Lena asked, looking between the two older women.

'Hi, Jacob, and hello, Trisha. We've never met as I was working away on Corfu when Stelios brought Trisha to visit,' Fotini confirmed, looking from Lena then back to Trisha, 'but I do know a lot about you as Stelios often spoke about you.'

'I hope it was all good things!' Trisha said, sounding a bit panicked. 'I feel like I know you a bit as well as Stelios talked a lot about you and your parents.'

Lena and Jacob decided to take a dip in the pool but Fotini settled herself down on the sun lounger next to Trisha.

'I have to admit that I was worried about my niece moving here,' Fotini confided. 'I thought it would likely be a little overwhelming for her to be back here now that her dad is gone, but look at her now. It's as if she's always been here.'

'It does look that way, doesn't it? Do you think that has something to do with Jacob being here?' Trisha asked in a hushed tone. 'They seem to have clicked and I think they could both be very keen on one another.'

'Oh to be young again!' Fotini laughed. 'Not to say I haven't had a good life. No, I'm very happy and I can't complain.'

'It's so easy to fall into reminiscing, isn't it, wondering what you should have done or not done. That seems to be all I've thought of since I arrived! But as my friends keep telling me, I need to move on and look to the future. Live for the moment. Lena tells me you're moving into one of the apartments as well. That will be very different from the villa, I would think.'

'Yes, but I'm looking forward to it. A lovely new home is probably just what I need at my age. The villa is lovely and holds lots of very happy memories – and sad ones, of course –but it's far too big for just me and it needs a lot of work to modernise it. Stelios had been talking about it for several years and once all the work is done it will rent out quite easily and bring in a nice income.'

'And when will the work start?'

'Shortly. Tassos – Jacob's dad – told me that the company is just waiting to finalise the sale of a couple of properties and then the profit from them will fund the refurbishment. In preparation, I've been busy getting rid of things and getting organised. I should probably be starting to plan moving in here, and I have to admit that I'm happier about the prospect now things have changed slightly.'

'You mean with me being up in the top apartment instead of Callisto?'

'Yes, exactly. I think, well, I know, it will be a lot calmer living in the complex without her being around.'

'You don't think she'll move in?'

'Oh no, not if it means having to be in an apartment just like me and Lena. No, I suspect her apartment will stay empty as she is far too busy swanning around the Greek islands, flitting here, there, and everywhere. The last thing she'll want to be doing is coming to the very quiet island of Vekianos. Now, I think I'll join those two in the pool. Will you join me?'

'Not just yet but you go ahead.'

Trisha felt better having talked with Fotini and it was so lovely to see Lena and Jacob getting on so well. This was a happy complex and hopefully that's how it would stay. She didn't yet know if she'd like to live here rather than in England, as it was still very early days, but for now she intended to enjoy the sunshine while she had it.

With so much light-hearted chat between them all, the morning had quickly turned into afternoon and while Lena had fetched the savoury and sweet pastries she had bought earlier, Fotini went back to the villa to fetch some white wine.

Once they were all settled in with their drinks and snacks, Fotini turned to Trisha and asked, 'Do you mind telling us about your time with my brother in London? He used to mention parties but never gave details – probably to avoid painting himself in an unflattering light!' Fotini laughed.

'I don't mind at all,' Trisha said warmly. 'We did have quite a lot of fun with what we called our "upside down life". As hotel staff, we were always working when everyone else was off having fun, and then partying when everyone else was asleep. The clubs we went to were basically jam packed with hotel staff so you didn't feel as if you had to dress up. It was all about unwinding after a hard day's shift. Up to a few months ago I was actually still working in the same hotel, though not partying anymore!'

They all laughed.

'I do miss it, well ... parts of it. The best part about the hospitality industry is seeing people having a good time, enjoying time together with family and friends.'

'Do you have any family, Trisha?' Jacob asked.

'I have a sister, a brother-in-law and a nephew and niece, but sadly I don't see a lot of them.'

'Well, perhaps now you're retired they'll be able to come and visit you here,' Lena suggested.

'Possibly, but I'm not sure if they'd like it. Now enough about me, I think it's time to enjoy the pool. Who's joining me?'

Jacob said he would but Lena and Fotini said they'd watch from the sun loungers.

'What are you thinking?' Lena asked Fotini once they were alone. 'You look like you're in deep thought.'

'I am. I think Trisha has a lot to sort out in her head. Something tells me she has regrets that she needs to acknowledge and work through.'

'Where my dad is concerned?'

'Yes, possibly. I also noticed that when she mentioned her family her voice changed and she looked really sad for a moment. Perhaps now that she's retired it's the first time she's slowed down and started to reflect on her life.'

Lena didn't know what to say and felt a little sad, but she wasn't quite sure why as Trisha's regrets had nothing to do with her. Looking at her phone and seeing the time she thought perhaps it was a good moment to light the barbeque.

'Is everyone hungry?' she called out to the group. 'I thought I might start to get the barbecue ready?'

'I'm always ready for food!' Jacob said enthusiastically. 'I'll give you a hand.'

Fotini and Trish shared a smile at the young man's eagerness and within minutes he and Lena had disappeared together to get everything organised.

'Normally, I would offer to help but I think somehow I would be in the way, don't you?' Fotini asked with a wink.

'I suspect you could be right,' Trisha agreed, and the two women laughed.

For the next hour both Fotini and Trisha lay in the sun, exchanging just the odd couple of words here and there as they watched Lena and Jacob giggling together while preparing the food.

'We make a good team with this cooking, don't you think?' Jacob asked, grinning. 'We'll have to do it together more often.'

'I'd like that very much,' Lena said, returning his grin.

They were soon all seated at one of the outdoor tables and a silence settled over the group as they happily dug into the food.

'I'm absolutely stuffed!' Fotini said at last, leaning back in her chair. 'Thank you so much, Lena.'

'Oh, don't thank me, it was Jacob who was a whiz on the barbeque. All I did was tell him what to cook.'

'Rubbish! I had the easy part. You're the one who did all the planning and organising,' Jacob argued.

'Well then thank you to both of you. You've earned a rest so I will clear things away,' Fotini said.

'No, Aunt, you don't need to,' Lena protested.

'Fotini's right. While she and I clear this all away, you two sit and relax. You could plan what you're going to be doing for the next week!' Trisha encouraged.

As the two young people put their heads together, Trisha and Fotini started to round up the used plates and cutlery.

'Well, Trisha, it looks like we have our first official romance at the apartment block,' Fotini whispered.

'Yes, and here's hoping it's the only one! The last thing I need is a man complicating my life right now. I have enough going on in my head as it is.'

'I'm just the same. The only love I'm not looking for is the kind you find in a book, preferably while I'm sat drinking a glass of wine, thank you very much.'

They both laughed and chatted while they cleared everything up. Once done, Fotini opened another bottle of wine and they made their way over to where Lena and Jacob were on the sun loungers. They were just getting settled when they all heard a car pull up and before long the gate opened.

Stood there was a young man Fotini recognised well. And she wasn't the only one.

'It's Pavlos!' Lena cried. And with that she was out of her chair and running over to greet him.

'Pavlos, it's so lovely to see you! I should have guessed my dad would have left you an apartment. It's so obvious! Everything is even better with you being here, too.'

'Oh dear,' Trisha whispered to Fotini as she took in Jacob's crestfallen expression. He looked as though he had just had all the joy knocked out of him. 'Perhaps that romance we were talking about will never get off the ground.'

'I think you could be right,' Fotini agreed. 'In fact, it looks like another one could be starting!'

Chapter 10

Trisha made her first coffee of the day and headed out onto her roof terrace. The first few steps as she opened the patio doors were hard because she was full of guilt that she had this and all the others in the block only had a balcony, but there was nothing she could do about it, and like Lena kept telling her, it was Stelios' decision, not hers. It was still early and as the sun rose her thoughts went back to yesterday. She had really enjoyed getting to know everyone, especially Fotini. Even the somewhat uncomfortable arrival of Pavlos didn't really spoil the day, although she did feel sorry for Jacob as Lena's attention had been entirely pulled in a different direction for the rest of the afternoon.

Pavlos was apparently Stelios' godson – the son of one of his close friends – and also someone that Lena had seen and spent time with on and off over the years. It was very obvious that they enjoyed one another's company by the way they chatted away happily, but saying that, Lena did try to include Jacob in all the conversations, which was nice. Trisha wasn't sure how Jacob had felt when Lena had invited Pavlos to join them on their days out in the coming week, and suspected that things might get a little complicated, but they were young and she was confident that they would work it out amongst themselves.

She was a little tired after the excitement of the day before so thought perhaps she should have a quiet day by the pool, and when she went down the stairs and over to the sun loungers, she found Pavlos having a swim. She waved and said good morning and he swam over to the side of the pool to greet her.

'Morning, Trisha! Ready for a day in the sun?'

'Definitely. Yesterday was very full on with quite a lot – maybe too much – wine and food and chat. I'm surprisingly exhausted today so I'm going to take it easy. But I have to say it was such a lovely day getting to know everyone. How was your first night? Are you feeling settled in yet?'

'Yeah, I think so, thanks. To be honest it feels almost like a dream and I really don't think it's sunk in that the apartment is mine.'

'I know exactly how you feel. Lena mentioned that you work and live on Corfu. That's not too far from here, is it? I'm told it's a lovely town with lots of history and nice restaurants.'

'Yes, and I'm very happy there, but now owning this apartment has sort of turned my life upside down. As this place is free it just seems to make sense to sell my place on Corfu and live here instead. I don't love my job that much and perhaps I could find one here. My parents have told me not to rush into making any decisions though, and to just take things slow for now.'

'That's exactly what my friend told me, so I'm treating this as a little holiday but also considering whether I might want to settle here full time.'

'But if you moved here wouldn't you miss your family? Oh shoot,' he said, looking at his waterproof watch and moving to the steps of the pool. 'I'm here happily chatting when actually I really need to go and get ready if I don't want to keep Lena and Jacob waiting. Hope you have a nice day,' he called over his shoulder as he collected his things, and then headed inside.

As Trisha got comfortable on the sun lounger she thought about the fact that two people had mentioned her family in less than twenty-four hours. To be honest, it had never crossed her mind to tell her sister, Julie, that she had inherited an apartment. Probably because apart from birthdays and Christmas, they rarely spoke anymore. They'd never had any kind of falling out but since their parents had died they've drifted apart.

She and Julie had never been close, probably because she had gone to London as a very young girl. Trisha had been desperate to leave the little Derbyshire town, thinking she was better than everyone else and deserved more. But now, looking back, she wondered if she should have stayed and accepted the cards she had been dealt. As it was, with her away in London, the care of her parents near the ends of their lives had fallen to Julie, which undoubtedly had contributed to the distance between the sisters.

'...Trisha? Can you hear me, Trisha?'

Trisha snapped herself out of her thoughts and greeted Fotini, apologising for ignoring her.

'You looked like you were miles away! Somewhere nice, I hope? But saying that, I don't think you can find anywhere better than this gorgeous Greek island. By the way, Lena, Jacob, and Pavlos said to have a nice day. They were going out the gate as I came in and they thought you were napping so didn't want to disturb you.'

'Oh dear, I didn't even see them! You're right that I was miles away. How are you doing today?'

'I'm a little tired after yesterday, to be honest.'

'Me, too,' Trisha agreed.

'Is that why you're feeling a bit spacey today?'

'Yes, I seem to have a wide range of things going on in my silly little head. Stupid stuff that has popped up after decades, things that perhaps I should have thought through before. Family things.'

'But if no one was hurt surely you can move on.'

'I'm honestly not sure if anyone was hurt. You see, when I was young I thought I was the bee's knees, better than everyone else in my little town. I thought they were all boring and had no ambition and – I feel terrible saying it, but – I looked down on them.'

'I think you're probably being too hard on yourself. You were just ambitious, and ambition is a good thing! It's what gets the world moving. Look at Stelios; he had tons of ambition and realised from an early age he wanted to make something of his life, so he went after it. That's probably why you both got on so well.'

'Perhaps. But that ambition separated me from my family, it made me feel like I was destined for greatness and made their lives seem small in comparison. I remember just after my sister got married to her husband, Keith, they bought a brand new home. It was a massive achievement for a young couple and they both worked so hard and saved like mad, and my parents were so proud. But when my mum, dad, and I went to visit it was so small and with Julie and Keith talking about how it was the perfect home to bring up a family, it was a light bulb moment. I did not want Julie's life. That would never be enough for me.'

'But, Trisha, you've had a fabulous life! The stories you were telling us yesterday about the people you've met and the respect you've had from some of the biggest and most important people in the world... You said you've even had thank you letters from royalty! Surely it doesn't get any bigger than that.'

'Yes, but at what cost? I'm all alone now and the family life I once scorned suddenly seems like the ideal. I feel terrible for making my sister feel like her life was small, all those years ago.'

Fotini didn't answer at first, as though she didn't want to say the wrong thing.

'Feeling all alone is something I can relate to. I

had opportunities over the years to not be alone but I always had excuses for why it wasn't the right time or wasn't the right person. But I suspect this isn't so much about the past though, as about so much happening in your life in such a short time. You've only just retired, which is a huge thing, and then Stelios pops back up in your life by leaving you the apartment, which would understandably bring up a wealth of emotion. I really think you're being too hard on yourself. You should take your time and enjoy the moment for what it is. As for your sister, perhaps you should call her and tell her you've retired and you've been left an apartment here in Greece. Ask her if she'd like to come and stay so you can spend some time with her.'

'You think it can be as simple as that?'

'I do. Now, I'm determined to cheer you up today so let me take you out for lunch, nothing fancy, just a little good old fashion Greek cooking down at the beach. Why don't we meet outside the gate at one? And there's no need to dress up as it's nothing fancy, just a little place the locals go to.'

'Thank you, Fotini, that's very kind, but you don't need to go to any trouble for me.'

'It's no trouble at all! You'll actually be doing me a favour as it means I'll have a day away from clearing out the villa.' Fotini smiled.

As agreed, Trisha was outside waiting for Fotini at one p.m. and as she stood in the shade she noticed someone walking towards her. She realised it was Jacob and the fact that he was all by himself didn't bode well considering he was meant to be out with Lena and Pavlos.

'Hi, Jacob! I'm just off out for lunch with Fotini.'

'That's nice. I hope you two have a lovely time. I think I'll head in and have a swim to cool down.'

'That sounds lovely. It's gotten quite warm

today, hasn't it?'

'Yes, it's not been the day I had planned. As my granddad in England used to say, "two is a couple, three is a crowd". We've not fallen out or anything, it's just I felt I was playing gooseberry so I made an excuse to come back.'

'I'm sorry your day was spoiled. Oh, here comes Fotini. I'll see you later, Jacob, I hope you enjoy your swim.'

As she crossed the lane to meet Fotini she greeted her warmly.

'You look nice, Trisha, I hope you're hungry!' Fotini smiled.

They made their way down the hill, which now was becoming very familiar, all the while chatting about the different houses they were passing and how things had changed over the years. Thankfully, with the age of the town and it being such a narrow road, the area had still kept its charm and old Greek quaintness.

'We need to sort of go back on ourselves here,' Fotini said, steering them down a side alleyway. 'I can never understand why this path has never been properly maintained given that it's used all the time by the locals. Mind where you walk.'

As they headed along they could start to hear voices chattering away and then a little ramshackle stone building came into view. It was packed inside and out with locals and as they got closer Fotini hugged and kissed many people. It was so lovely to see a community of true friendships. She introduced Trisha to so many people she knew she would never be able to remember all their names, but what a lovely welcome to receive. She got the impression Fotini had told them she had moved into the apartment block as there were huge smiles of recognition whenever Fotini said her name.

'I think that table over there is free and it's in

the shade. Another bonus.'

'The food smells delicious,' Trisha said.

'Yes, sometimes when the wind is in the right direction you can even smell it up at the villa! I'm having the *kleftiko*, which is wonderful, but you're free to choose whatever you like.'

'I'll have the same, thank you.'

Fotini called the order over to a man on the next table, and he passed it on to another table, and gradually it went from one table to the next, all the way to the kitchen where a bell rang.

'Is that how you order?' Trisha laughed.

'Yes, and once the bell rings you know your order is placed. It's so simple, don't you think? They've been doing it that way for generations.'

Within minutes a jug of wine appeared with two sets of cutlery, shortly followed by two huge plates of *kleftiko*, and the two women dug in.

'That was so good,' Trisha said happily once she'd finally put down her fork for good. 'I certainly won't need to eat again today! Thank you for introducing me to this place.'

'I knew you would like it and to be honest, Trisha, it's far easier to come down here and eat than to cook for just myself, and I like the company. There's always someone to chat to and it breaks the day up. And, of course, the most important part of visiting here is the gossip. There is always plenty of that to go around!'

'I expect that conversation over the last few days has primarily been about the new residents of the apartment block?'

'Oh yes. Of course, everyone here knows Stelios designed and had it built but they hadn't heard how he'd left the apartments to people he knew, which has gotten people talking. It's all from a good place though. Stelios was loved in this community and was never happier than being here, eating with the locals, having a laugh and joking around. There was a lot of sadness when he died, and the community has been very kind to me. I have a lot to thank them for as life hasn't been easy all by myself.

'It's like being part of one big family, which I need and appreciate at my age. Now, are you ready to face that hill? It's hard work walking back up but at least we will be working the lunch off.'

'I'm ready but would it be rude of me to say I quite fancy sticking around and taking a little walk around while I'm down here to help me get my bearings?'

'Of course not! The best way of finding out about a place is by wandering around and saying hello to people.'

'Thank you, Fotini, it's been a lovely few hours and I really appreciate you giving me the time.'

They hugged before saying goodbye and Trisha walked back to the main street leading to the beach. It felt so different from where she had just been as it was bustling with visitors heading out on walks or off for a late afternoon on the beach. She walked down the boardwalk at the side of the closed restaurant and though the beach looked busy she didn't mind as she planned to walk over to the rocks at the edge. She wouldn't be climbing them, not at her age, but if she could find one to sit on and look out to sea she would be happy.

Walking down to the edge of the sea, the memories of being here on that holiday with Stelios all those years ago came flooding back. They were happy memories, but that was then, and like Fotini said, she needed to look to the future. She spotted a rock that was just big enough for one person to sit and thought it the perfect place to take in the views and make a call that was long overdue. Taking her phone out of her bag she went to her contacts and hovered her finger over the name 'Julie – Sis'.

Perhaps she should wait and call when she was back in the apartment? But no, she knew if she did that she would then make another excuse. It had to be done now.

Press the button, Trisha.

'Hello, Trisha, this is a nice surprise,' Julie said, having picked up right away. 'Is everything ok? There's nothing wrong, is there?'

'No, everything is fine. I just needed to let you know I'm retired now, and a lot has happened in my life in the past few months. Good things, but that's not what this call is about. I'm calling because I need to say I'm so sorry for everything, I truly am. I haven't been the sister I should have been...'

With that she burst into tears, which led to sobbing. The words just wouldn't come out and she panicked, thinking she should end the call, but before she could, she heard Julie say, 'Trisha, slow down. Why don't you take some deep breaths and call me back in your own time, when you're feeling up to it? I'll be here when you're ready.'

Chapter 11

The big day had finally arrived for Callisto, but it was not the day she had planned. Instead of moving into her luxury apartment in Athens, she was flying to the island of Vekianos. There was just one more big job to do before leaving Athens and she knew it wouldn't be straightforward. No, this meeting with Tassos would be different from her last one as a lot had happened since then, and he would now have all the bills and invoices outlining the exact figures of what she had spent on the now doomed Vekianos project. She had warned him that it was bad, but she suspected it would be even worse than he had assumed. It was a very dark day in her career, but even worse, for her dad's company. There was a knock at her door and she assumed it would be the removals company, come to pick up all her personal belongings. She wasn't taking much with her as she had sold all the furniture to the people buying her home.

As she closed the door three quarters of an hour later, she couldn't help but laugh in an odd, sad way. It had only taken that short amount of time for the men to load her life into the back of a van. Tomorrow, she would unload it at her new apartment on Vekianos, something she had never imagined would ever happen. She took a deep breath, grabbed her bag, and headed out the door to go and see Tassos. She had a feeling that whatever he said it would be bad, but it likely wouldn't make her feel any worse than she already felt.

Tassos' secretary asked her to take a seat in the reception, saying he was running late. It briefly crossed her mind that this might be a sort of punishment – making her sweat it out before they met – but she could admit to herself that it was nothing less than she deserved. Her phone beeped and looking at the screen she saw it was a message from her lawyer to say the deal had gone through and she no longer owned her home. Tassos' door opened and her first thought was that he looked drained and very sad, and she realised that was all her doing.

'Sorry to keep you waiting, Callisto, please come through.'

She followed him into his office and took a seat.

'Thank you for seeing me today, I just needed to fill you in on a few things. First, the sale of my home went through literally five minutes ago, so later on today I'll be able to transfer the money into the business account. I'm not quite sure how much there will be once the legal fees have come out, but it should go a ways towards helping our current financial situation. The other big thing is that I've rented out my office to an advertising company. They've signed a twelve-month contract and their rent will be paid directly into the company account. Project wise, the landscaping on the two villas has been finished and I have a meeting next week to put them on the market, and the Athens apartment work is continuing apace.'

As she was talking he scribbled notes on a piece of paper and she started to find his silence unnerving. Was he happy about the steps she'd taken?

'So that just leaves the Vekianos project,' Tassos said, looking up for the first time since she'd started speaking. 'Can you confirm I have every bill in now, or are there going to be even more shocks?'

'No, I've checked all the spreadsheets and you have everything.'

'Callisto, I don't know what to say apart from ...

why? Why waste so much money on contractor's deposits and on bathroom and kitchen fixtures when the water and drainage situation still hadn't been resolved? Did you really think you would make a profit on the project? It's complete madness. The money from your home being sold will help but everything is looking bleak and will for some time. I think you should go now; I'm not in a good place and I don't want to say something I'll regret later.'

Part of her wished he would just scream and shout at her, but she could see he didn't have the energy for that. As she stood to leave his head was still down, his gaze on the list in front of him on his desk.

'By the way, now that I have no office here in Athens, I'm moving to the apartment on Vekianos. I'll work from there as it should be plenty big enough for me to live and work, what with the three bedrooms.'

'Three bedrooms?' Tassos asked, looking up at her. The look on his face was confusing, as if he was about to say something but stopped himself.

'Right. I'm off. I'll be in touch.'

Out in the fresh air walking to her car, and then driving it for the last time before she sold it back to the car dealer, she couldn't stop thinking about that look on Tassos' face. What had he stopped himself from saying? She pondered on it while she took the car back and then headed to the airport for her flight to Corfu and then the boat to Vekianos. No doubt the first person to greet her would be Fotini, who she realised she would have to mend some bridges with. As for Lena, that wouldn't be so easy as emotion would be involved and they would have to talk about their dad, the only thing they both had in common. At least she would have a bit of an oasis in her apartment at the top of the block. She had a roof terrace to get fresh air and, if she planned it well, she could nip out for groceries when there was no one down in the pool area.

The short flight reminded her of the days when she was a child planning with her dad what they would do on their holiday. Life was so simple then, with lots of laughter, but now it was so different. She had never been to the island without her dad, their past few years together spent in Athens or out on projects while he was training her to run the company. If only she had paid more attention, perhaps she wouldn't be in this mess and moving to a town that was such a departure from the fast-paced Athens world she was used to. Once she landed and got her suitcases she took a short taxi ride to the ferry port for the journey over to Vekianos. The boat ride seemed to take forever and she was starting to feel as though she'd lost control. She knew it would be the same when she got on the island as there would be no possibility of just getting in her car and driving away. No, she would be stuck and she didn't like the sound of that.

As the taxi took her from the harbour to the apartment, slowly driving along the lane, she recognised someone they passed ... but who was it? She thought it might be someone from her dad's funeral and then she realised that it was Pavlos, her dad's godson. It made sense that he would have been given one of the apartments as well. Counting in her head she realised that was five residents accounted for: Lena, Fotini, Tassos, Pavlos, and herself.

After paying the taxi driver she braced herself. She had been here before so she knew the way upstairs, and her main objective was not to look towards the pool area as the last thing she needed was to catch anyone's eye and open herself up to questions. Before going through the main gate she glanced across towards the family villa, the place she had been visiting all of her life. It felt very odd not going through that gate, but then, she would be sooner or later as she needed to go and talk to her aunt. A conversation that would go one of two ways: in her favour, or against her. But that could wait for another day. Pulling the set of keys Joanna had given her out of her bag, Callisto looked at the fob with the number one on it.

Before she knew it she was through the gate and up the path to the main apartment door. Closing it behind her and swapping to the apartment key, she had one foot on the stairs when something caught her eye – apartment one was on the ground floor. Surely that was a mistake? Callisto was convinced that the signs on the wall must be wrong but her head told her to try her key in the door marked one. As it slid into the lock, her heart sank.

Three hours later Callisto still sat on the chair she'd sunk into as soon as she'd stepped inside the apartment. She was numb, upset, angry, and completely baffled as to why she was not at the top of the block and instead stuck in this one bedroom, ground floor flat. She had thought her meeting with Tassos was the worst part of her day, but now she knew arriving here was. Thinking of Tassos, she thought back to the conversation with him and that indecipherable look on his face when she had mentioned working from the top floor apartment. He obviously knew she wouldn't be, but if she wasn't up there, who was? Surely her dad wouldn't have given it to Lena or Fotini ... or even worse, Tassos?

Chapter 12

When the knock came on Trisha's door the last thing she wanted was to chat with anyone after the upset of her failed call to her sister yesterday, but she knew it would be rude to ignore it. As she walked to the door she caught a look at herself in the mirror. Oh dear, she really didn't look good, her eyes all red and puffy from all the tears. Before she could do anything about it there was another knock, so she fixed a smile on her face and opened the door.

'She's here! Callisto is here! Oh, Trisha, I didn't know what to do.'

'Lena, come in. I thought Fotini said she didn't think Callisto would be visiting any time soon.'

'I know but she arrived yesterday, and last night I noticed her walking out the gate and then coming back with bags of shopping. It was very late and dark, so she obviously doesn't want to see or talk to anyone. I'm not sure what I should do. Should I approach her or leave her alone?'

'Come in and take a seat on the terrace. I'll make us a drink and we can make a plan. Coffee ok?'

'Yes, please, a coffee would be lovely.'

As Trisha went off to make the drinks she realised Callisto would soon want to know who was living in the top apartment and it definitely wasn't something she was looking forward to. Hopefully by then she would be looking and feeling better as the last thing she needed to do was erupt in more tears.

'There you go. So what happens now? Who speaks to whom first?'

'I'm not sure. She's definitely going to impact the dynamic around here. The happy little family that we've created is about to change.'

'I hope you don't mind me saying that I don't think everyone in the "happy family", as you call it, is overly happy. I noticed Jacob was a little down yesterday. Would that have something to do with Pavlos arriving and claiming your attention?'

'Pavlos is just an old friend and I'm sure Jacob realises that. The three of us were having a lovely day out together but it was interrupted by a message and then Jacob said he had to leave and go and do some work.'

'Before Jacob got the message, was he ... involved in the conversation?' Trisha asked gently.

'I think so. Pavlos and I did chat a lot about the past, but Jacob seemed fine with it...' She trailed off, biting her lip as she mentally went through the events leading up to Jacob's abrupt departure. 'I've upset him, haven't I?' she asked, looking ashamed.

'I just think he was so excited to be spending time with you and perhaps he felt a little left out. It might not hurt for you to invite him somewhere just the two of you,' Trisha encouraged. 'Although it does sound like you might have your hands full with Callisto.'

'I know. I called Fotini to see if Callisto had spoken to her yet but she said she wasn't even aware she'd arrived.'

'I've not seen the balcony door from apartment one or five open. Which one do you think she's in?'

'I don't think five as that's next door to me and I've heard no noises, so it must be number one. I did think I should go and speak to her first but what would I say?'

'I'm not sure... What's that noise?' Trisha asked, distracted.

The two women looked out over the roof terrace to see a van had pulled up and Callisto was walking down to the gate. Instinctively, they leaned right back so they wouldn't be noticed, and watched as two chaps started unloading the truck and following Callisto up the path. It took them half an hour to carry all the boxes in.

'Well, Lena, I think it's more than just a quick visit. To me, it looks like she's moving in for good.'

'Yes, though I'm not sure she'll have a lot of room left once that van is unloaded.'

'I'm sure she'll make it work. Have you decided what you're going to do about your half-sister's arrival?'

'Not yet. What about you? Any plans for today?'

'I haven't made any but I'm beginning to think at some point today a conversation with Callisto might crop up.'

'I hope you don't mind me asking but is everything ok? You looked upset when I arrived. Is it anything I can help with?'

'That's kind of you, but I'll be ok. I'm just not really myself today as I had a wobbly moment yesterday when I called my sister and told her about retiring and this apartment.'

'Oh dear, wasn't she happy for you?'

'Yes, very happy, but I was feeling emotional about a lot of things and to be honest I shouldn't have called until I'd calmed down some. But I did, and I got upset – far too upset to talk – and the whole thing ended in tears. Eventually I pulled myself together and made my way back up here and after a few hours I called back and Julie was so nice. There was just so much I wanted to say sorry for, but she was having none of it. She said she was happy for me, but I don't know... Everything is very overwhelming at the moment and I just need to get a grip and pull myself together. Is that my phone or yours?' Trisha asked as a ringtone interrupted them.

'It's mine,' Lena said, looking at the screen. 'Sorry, but I have to rush off. Pavlos is waiting for me; we're going out for the day again.'

'That's nice. Just the two of you, or is Jacob going as well?'

'No, apparently he has work to do. But now I'm wondering, do you think he's just saying that as an excuse?'

'I'm not sure. Like I said, it would be nice if you invited just Jacob out for the day at some point. Make it clear to him it's going to be just the two of you and see if he takes you up on the offer. I suspect he's smitten with you, and I think you feel the same, but for now have a nice time with Pavlos.'

'Thank you, Trisha, I will do. Are you sure you don't want me to stay though, just in case Callisto comes knocking at the door?'

'Don't be silly! Go and have fun. I'm sure everything with Callisto will be fine.'

Once Lena had gone, Trisha pondered what she could do for the day. The last thing she needed was to be on tenterhooks waiting for a knock at the door from Callisto, but she also didn't feel she could go and knock on her door either. Perhaps she should get herself and her things together and go down to the pool, that way if they spoke to each other it would be on neutral ground. It also meant Callisto wouldn't immediately know which apartment she was in.

An hour later Trisha was showered and looking and feeling a lot better. She headed down to the pool determined to put herself somewhere that she could see both the main gate and the door to the apartment block. She wanted to be prepared for anyone coming towards her, and by 'anyone', of course she meant the new arrival.

Settled on the sun lounger and reading her book a few minutes later, she looked up and saw Jacob come out the main door and head towards her. She waved and put her book down.

'Hi, Jacob, have you come down for a swim?'

'No, I've decided to go out for a walk to make the most of the gorgeous weather before I start working on things next week. By the way, my dad called me last night to say Callisto would be arriving and he was under the impression she thought she was moving into your apartment. I heard someone moving around under where I am though, so I presume it's her.'

'Yes, I think so, as she's had a load of boxes delivered today.'

'That must be what I heard. Have you seen Lena this morning?' he asked, evidently trying to appear unconcerned but failing.

'Yes, she's gone out for the day,' Trisha said neutrally.

'With Pavlos, no doubt.'

'Yes, I think so, but it's worth mentioning that they're only friends, nothing more. She really likes you, Jacob.'

'Oh, I didn't... That is to say...' Jacob trailed off awkwardly, clearly not knowing how to respond. 'I should really be going,' he finally got out before waving and rushing for the gate.

Trisha couldn't help but smile. It was very clear that Jacob felt the same way Lena did.

As she was swimming a few lengths a while later she noticed the gate open and in came Fotini. She swam to the pool steps and climbed out.

'Good morning! Have you come to have a swim?' Trisha asked.

As Trisha started to dry herself with the towel Fotini moved closer and whispered conspiratorially, 'Have you noticed we have a new arrival?'

'Yes, Lena told me earlier and we saw a load of boxes being delivered. It looks like Callisto is here to stay.'

'Yes, I called Tassos and he told me she's sold

her home in Athens and also rented out her office and she's going to run Stelios' company from here.'

'To be honest, I've been waiting for her to knock on my door to see who I am. That's partly why I've come down here.'

'If it makes you feel any better, you're not the only one she wants to have words with. That's actually why I'm here. She phoned me last night to say that she needs to have a meeting with me about the refurbishment of the villa.'

'Is that a good thing or a bad thing?'

'I'm not sure. Stelios completed all the planning and I know he was very thorough, so I presume it's just about timings, letting me know when it will start and when it will finish.'

'How do you feel about all of that?'

'I'm excited overall. Everything is so old in there and the electrics and plumbing are desperately in need of updating. Plus, it's far too big in there for just me. It was different when Stelios was visiting all the time with friends and his daughters. We needed all the rooms then, but not anymore. And I have to say, now you've all started to move in here, I'm more relaxed about the move and actually looking forward to living in my new apartment.'

'That's good to feel like that.'

'I have to think of the future. I'm not getting any younger and the simpler I can make my life, the better. The apartment is new and modern and will be so much easier to look after. Right, I best get on as I don't want to be late for my niece. I'm a bit surprised she wanted to see me here though, as I thought she would come over to the villa. Anyway, I'm going to try and repair my relationship with her as we'll be living so close now. It would be nice to be friendly, you know?'

'Absolutely.'

Fotini smiled and headed over to the main door.

As she did, Trisha couldn't help but wonder if Fotini was really happy about moving into the apartment block. It had felt a bit as though she was trying to convince herself, rather than Trisha.

Trisha settled herself on the sun lounger and tried to read her book but her head was all over the place. She was glad she'd managed to have the conversation with Julie, although she still felt guilty even though her sister had said she had no reason to, and she was feeling more comfortable here as the little town was so relaxed. And as for the apartment, that was of course perfect and out of this world. She was also really enjoying the company of the younger residents and getting to know Fotini better. Yes, life was starting to feel more settled than it had in quite some time. There was just the one hurdle to get over: Callisto. With that thought she heard the main door close as Fotini stepped outside. Trisha sat up ready for her to join her for a chat, but instead she saw her heading for the gate.

'You know those bridges I was talking about?' Fotini called over her shoulder. 'They've been burnt to the ground and there will definitely be no building or rebuilding of them any time soon!'

Chapter 13

Lena was excited. She was up early and really happy she had taken Trisha's advice and arranged for a day out with Jacob. She had mentioned in the text inviting him that it would just be the two of them, no Pavlos, and Jacob had quickly agreed. They had planned to go on the boat over to Paxos and not come back until late in the evening, a full day of exploring.

She was just getting herself organised when her phone rang.

'Hi, Aunt Fotini, how are you?' she asked as she answered.

'I hope I haven't woken you, but I need to get something off my chest,' Fotini said, sounding grave.

'Oh dear, what's wrong?' Lena asked, getting very worried.

'It's your sister. Yesterday, she asked if I would come and see her to talk about the villa refurbishments. I thought it would just be about the timings and schedule as everything else your dad had already sorted, but oh no, the madam wants to postpone the refurbishment for a couple of years. Not days. Not weeks. Years! I tried to explain how I had been clearing out the villa and I was ready to move in here and she just said that wasn't a problem; I could still move in, but the villa wouldn't get sorted until the year after next.'

'Did you ask her why the need for such a significant delay?'

'Yes, and she said it was because there was a cash flow issue. She hinted that it was something to do with the way Stelios had left things, but I told her

I didn't understand because your dad had said the money for the refurbishment was all allocated and had specifically been earmarked for the project. She reckoned he'd got it wrong but I know my brother and that just wouldn't be the case.'

'So, what happens next? What are you going to do?'

'I've already done something. The minute I got back to the villa I phoned Tassos and although he said he couldn't talk about the specifics of your dad's business finances – and yes, I'm still referring to it as Stelios' company, not hers – the money is definitely allocated for the villa work and the only thing that needs to be decided is when the work can start, which he said was entirely up to me. So I really don't know what game she's playing. I tried to ask him questions about why she was living here and not in Athens and all he said was that it was none of his business and I should ask her.'

'Are you going to?'

'And give her the satisfaction? Absolutely not! No, I'll continue with my clear out and I'll make sure it's Tassos to whom I give the date when the villa will be free to start the works.'

'That's not going to make her happy. By the way, I didn't see Trisha last night as it was late when Pavlos and I got back. Do you know if she's spoken to Callisto?'

'Not yet. After my meeting with Callisto, once I eventually calmed down, I came back to apologise.'

'What, you apologised to Callisto?'

'No, that's never going to happen. No, I apologised to Trisha. I had ignored her when I rushed out of the gate after my disastrous meeting with Callisto, and I wanted to explain why I had been so upset. Actually, we had a nice couple of hours up on her roof terrace drinking wine and chatting. Do you know, I think she's starting to relax a lot more here. I hope she decides to make this her permanent home. I enjoy her company.'

'Yes, so do I.'

'Right, thank you for listening to my tirade. I feel better having got that off my chest. I'd better let you go though. Are you out with Pavlos again today?'

'No, I'm spending the day with Jacob and I'm really looking forward to it.'

'Well, have fun and try to avoid your sister. I'm sure she isn't in a good mood.'

'I will. She's the last person I want to bump into, but saying that, I suppose at some point I'll have to talk to her. Who knows, it might even be a good thing. It would be nice to talk about Dad with the only other person who knew him in the same way I did. Bye for now, Fotini.'

After hanging up, Lena had a quick look through her clothes to see what was suitable for the day ahead. They weren't going to the beach so a nice dress might be ok. She was just about to get into the shower when there was a knock at her door. Oh dear, she had been ages on the phone to Fotini, hadn't she, and now Jacob was here already. She hoped he wouldn't mind waiting a bit.

'Sorry, Jacob...' she began as she opened the door, but she stopped short when she realised it wasn't Jacob on her doorstep. 'Hello, Callisto,' she said warily.

'Hi, I hope I'm not disturbing you, but I think we need to have a chat. Can I come in?'

Before Lena could say anything Callisto had walked past her into the apartment and sat herself down on the sofa.

'I'm sorry, Callisto, but I'm in the midst of getting ready to go out for the day. Could this wait for another time?'

'With Jacob? That's who you thought was at the

door. I'm sure he'll understand that you need to postpone. Just tell him you have family business to sort out with your sister. There will be other days for the two of you to have fun.'

'No, I don't think I'll do that. I can meet you tomorrow or the next day. Today, I'm busy.'

'But this needs talking about today!' Callisto said hotly. 'Give him a call and cancel. Blame it on me. I don't mind if he doesn't like me. His father doesn't so I presume he won't either, no matter what I do. Go on, call him.'

Lena didn't like feeling intimated like this but she knew it might be to her benefit to just get this encounter with Callisto over with, so she called Jacob to cancel. He was very understanding and she felt terrible as she came off the phone. The smug smile on Callisto's face didn't help. Her half-sister might have won this round, but Lena had to trust that there would be other opportunities when she would have the upper hand instead.

'See, that wasn't too difficult, was it? And please don't look so scared. I don't bite. I just feel we need to get to know each other a bit better, and we also need to sort out a few business things, which affect both of us. Shall we have a drink? Black coffee for me, thank you. We can go out on the balcony to chat. Could you bring a pen and paper to make notes?'

Lena did as she was told but she was annoyed that Callisto had taken control of things. This was her apartment, and she didn't appreciate being ordered about, but keeping the peace seemed her best option until she knew more of what this visit was about.

'There you go, Callisto, one coffee, and I have my notepad. So, what would you like me to write down?'

'You make it sound so official! It's not a bit like

that.'

'Isn't it? You're the one who walked in here and demanded that I cancel my day and prepare myself for a business meeting.'

'I have to say, Lena, I saw a little bit of me in that spirited response. It must be in the blood.'

'What? Rudeness and arrogance? Let's just get this over with. Tell me what I should write down.'

'Look, I'm sorry. I didn't mean it to be like this at all. I really do want to get to know you. We should have been in each other's lives from day one, but you know my dad – sorry, *our* dad – liked to keep us all separate.'

'Ok, let's start again,' Lena said. 'I know this isn't easy for either of us. You said there was something about the business we need to discuss?'

'Yes.'

'I've never been involved in any of that though. To be honest, I don't really know what his business was apart from it's to do with properties.'

'Don't worry. I'm happy to explain it all. Now, please don't think I'm criticising Dad, but by building these apartments and leaving monetary bequests in his will, he put the company in financial danger. You see, the profit from each project the company undertakes normally funds the next one, in an ongoing chain. But in the case of this apartment block, he didn't wait for any other developments to finish. Instead he dipped into the company savings. Now, normally this would all even out over time and the coffers would quickly be refilled, but because of some issues we're having with a couple of projects currently in development, the company has been left in the red.'

'I'm sorry, I don't understand what it has to do with me?'

Lena could see for the first time Callisto was looking uncomfortable and it suddenly clicked.

'I'll cut to the chase. Basically, our father gave money away that should have been put back into the company, and to tide the business over I need to ask that you transfer your inheritance back to the company. Of course, it's only temporary, just until a few projects get finished, and then you can have it back.'

What Callisto was saying didn't make sense to Lena. Their dad wouldn't have left the company in a mess as he was very careful about financial matters and would never have wasted company money or made reckless decisions. No, there were definitely things in Callisto's story that didn't make sense, and Lena knew she needed to talk to Fotini and get advice.

'I really hope I've made things clear. I hate to imply our dad was anything less than perfect, but not being well, he didn't have his eye on the full picture by the end.'

'I have to admit I'm a little upset that you would even suggest this.'

'Completely understandable. We both looked at our father as someone who didn't make mistakes.'

'Oh no, Callisto, my upset doesn't have anything to do with our father – it's you. I had hoped that your coming here meant we would spend time together, getting to know each other as sisters, but no, you only want to have something to do with me because you want my money. The money that *my* dad left me.'

'No, you have it wrong, Lena. Of course I want to get to know you better! It's just that the company needs urgent help and until that's sorted I can't relax and think of anything else. Please know that it's not me that wants your money, it's our father's company that needs it.'

'That may be the case, but I'm not doing anything until I've gotten some advice from a friend who knows about these types of financial matters.'

'There's not a lot of time, Lena, and I'm your sister. I wouldn't let anything happen to your money. It's safe with me, you have my word.'

'That might be the case, but I need to do what my father told me to do.'

'I don't understand.'

'Dad knew I could benefit from some help with money, so he sorted out an adviser to help me manage my inheritance.'

'Who?' Callisto asked, looking wary.

'Someone Dad trusted. Tassos.'

With that, Callisto picked up her phone, got up, and walked out without uttering a word.

Chapter 14

Trisha sat on the roof terrace pondering what to do. Would this be the day she would chat to Callisto? She had been on edge waiting for her to appear all day yesterday, so today she was going to go out and just get on with things. The conversation would happen when the time was right.

She decided on a walk down the hill to the shops to grab a few things she needed to pick up, and she also wanted to discover more of the back streets and get a feel for what it might be like to live here as a local. As she stood up, she noticed the person in question go out the gate, get into a taxi, and head off in a hurry. Well, she had an answer for now. There would be no confrontation from Callisto this morning. Perhaps she could stay by the pool...? No, maybe later. For now, she would stick to her original plan and head down into the town.

By the time she eventually arrived it was quite busy, so her first stop would be for a little sit down on the rocks to take in the view and people watch as the world wandered by. She stopped and bought a bottle of water before turning the corner towards the beach. Walking down the boardwalk by the closed café, she noticed the beach was really busy and then it clicked to her – it was Saturday. Fotini had told her it was always busier at weekends, and she was certainly right. Once at the end of the boardwalk, Trisha could see there were no empty rocks to sit on, which was a shame. Taking her flip-flops off she walked on the sand down to the water's edge for a little paddle before heading on to the supermarket and then back to the apartment pool, where it would be much quieter.

Wandering back up across the beach towards the closed restaurant she noticed someone she recognised. It was Pavlos, and he seemed to be coming out of the restaurant with someone. She watched as they shook hands and the other chap locked the door and walked off, then called out a greeting to Pavlos.

'Oh, hello, Trisha! How are you? It's really busy on the beach today, isn't it? I've never seen so many people but it's a nice atmosphere with everyone enjoying themselves.'

'It certainly is. Are you not hanging out with Lena today?'

'No, she's having a day with Jacob. I think he's a little upset that she's been spending time with me but he has no need to be jealous as we're only old friends catching up on things. To be honest, a lot of Lena's chatting is about how much she really likes Jacob,' Pavlos confided. 'I personally think they make a lovely couple and at this time in her life, having lost Stelios, it's good for her to have someone like Jacob around.'

'I agree. I was just about to visit the little supermarket and then head back to the pool as it's far too busy here on the beach for me.'

'I think I'll do the same. Do you mind if I walk back with you?'

'Not at all! Though I might have to take advantage of you and get you to help carry some of my shopping.'

'That's not a problem at all. There's just one thing I need to look at first... I want to work out how many tables will fit on this little decking area here in front of the main doors.'

'Ok, while you do that I'll nip off and get my shopping and wait for you outside the supermarket.'

As she walked off she started to wonder, was

Pavlos looking to open the restaurant back up? How exciting! She made a quick run around the shop and her timing was perfect as Pavlos appeared just as she got outside.

'Thank you, this is a big help. By the way, how are you enjoying the apartment?' she asked as they started up the hill.

'I love it. I'm even thinking of selling my studio apartment over on Corfu so I can move in here full time. And as you have no doubt figured out, I might be working here as well. I'm thinking of combining the money I make on the sale of my apartment and the money Stelios left me and re-opening the restaurant by the beach.'

'That's so exciting! Does it need a lot doing to it inside?'

'Yes, a lot more than I was hoping for, actually, but now I've been in there I have a better idea of what might work best so I can start to ponder on things. But also, seeing it today, when the beach was so busy, it's made me rethink things a bit. If I want to make the restaurant a success, I need to go with my head and not my heart.'

'What do you mean?'

'Well, I initially wanted to make it a classy, fine dining, evening restaurant, but I now realise that's bonkers. It needs to be a daytime beach bar selling snacks, drinks, and ice creams, which perhaps stays open a little into the evening. That's where the money will be. Yes, it's back to the drawing board for me.'

As they reached the apartments, Trisha reached out to take the bags back from Pavlos. 'Thank you again for your help with the shopping. Will you let me reward you with some lunch? I have bread, cheese, ham... What do you fancy?'

'You don't need to go to any trouble.'

'I want to.'

'Ok, then I'll have what you're having, thanks.'

'Great! Why don't you meet me in half an hour down by the pool. I'll bring the food and perhaps also beer or wine. I quite fancy a beer as it's something I haven't had for years. I have some in the fridge I bought.'

'That sounds great, thanks, Trisha.'

They both headed off to their own apartments and Trisha changed into more comfortable pool clothes before preparing the lunch. As she passed the hall mirror she stopped and looked at herself and smiled. She really was starting to enjoy her life here, but then the familiar feeling of guilt hit her. She didn't feel she was entitled to all of this luxury. Stelios had far more important people in his life, so why had he given all of this to her?

As she stepped outside a few minutes later and headed towards the pool with the food she could see Pavlos was sitting there with a notepad and pen.

'Here you go, a beer and a baguette. I've also got some crisps in the bag. I hope I'm not disturbing your work?'

'Not at all,' Pavlos rushed to reassure her as he took the food and expressed his thanks. 'I'm just putting an action plan together. It's all early days so I need to slow down and avoid rushing ahead of myself. It will do me good to switch off and talk about something else.'

'It's good you're excited about it. That means you'll throw yourself one hundred percent into it.'

'I intend to. So, tell me about you, Trisha, have you decided what you're going to do yet? Is it Keriaphos or life back in the UK that's in your future? Or are you still thinking it over? It's certainly a big decision to make.'

'A very big one, especially at my age. The thing is ... everything is new here, and I don't mean just the apartment, but also all the experiences I'm having. Meeting everyone... I really do feel I've gelled with you all, though, of course, I've yet to meet Callisto.'

'She is an odd one. I knew her a lot better when I was younger, but I'm not sure we would get on so well now. But then, I'm not the only one. I imagine it will be difficult for her and Lena to get on, and, of course, I know Fotini hasn't got any time for her. I think it will be very different for you though. We all already knew her, whereas until you came here you weren't aware any of this – or any of us – existed.'

'That's true. And to think we still have one apartment here that's empty. I know it's driving Fotini crazy trying to work out who might move in. I think the problem is that her list of guesses is quite long.'

'As far as I'm concerned, it's a waiting game,' Pavlos said with a shrug. 'The one thing we do know is that it has to be someone who was important to Stelios.'

'I suspect you're right. Can I ask, did you spend a lot of time with Stelios? I understand you're his godson, so I assume that means he was especially close to your parents?'

'Yes, he and my dad started out together. When Stelios came back from England and invested in his first property it was my dad that helped him with the building work. They worked together all the way up to a few years ago when my mum and dad retired to Corfu. So yes, Stelios was in my life quite a lot. I think he and my dad would have liked it if I followed them into the construction business, but it wasn't for me. Although I did work with them when I was a teenager in the holidays and at weekends. That's the way I was brought up – to work and earn money. They drilled it into me, which I appreciate. Oh look, here comes Lena.'

'Have you come down for a swim?' Trisha called

to her.

'No, I thought I might go for a walk.'

Trisha could see there was something wrong – Lena wasn't her normal bubbly self – but before she could ask if she was ok, Pavlos spoke.

'I thought you were out with Jacob today?'

'Yes, I should have been, but Callisto came knocking at my door so I had to cancel.'

So that was the reason she wasn't herself. Something Callisto must have said had obviously upset her. Trisha wished she could help.

'Pavlos and I were just about to have our dessert. Would you like to join us? It's vanilla pie fresh from the bakery, your favourite.'

'Oh that sounds lovely. But only if it's no trouble?'

'Of course it's not! You sit and chat to Pavlos while I nip up to get it. I won't be a minute.'

Trisha took the dirty plates back up with her and was just coming down the stairs with the tray when she heard the main door close. Looking over the railing she saw Jacob and called out to him.

'Hi, Jacob, how are you?'

'I was ok but not anymore now I know why Lena cancelled on me: to spend time with Pavlos! And to think I believed her excuse that she had family business to sort out. She must think I'm stupid.'

Before Trisha could explain that he'd got the wrong end of the stick, he went into his apartment. Back by the pool Pavlos was stood talking on his phone, and as Trisha headed back over he said something to Lena before turning and walking towards her.

'I'm sorry, Trisha, but I need to rush off. Someone has made an offer on my studio apartment on Corfu and I need to call the agent back to see if we can push them a little higher.'

'That's not a problem. See you later and good

luck! I will keep my fingers crossed.' She waved him off and then set down the pies in front of Lena.

'There we are, dessert is served! By the way, I've just passed Jacob on the stairs and—'

'I know what you're going to say, Trisha. He saw me and Pavlos here chatting and he thinks that's why I cancelled my day out with him. I'll have to explain that it was to do with Callisto, as she insisted on having a chat, and if he doesn't believe me he can call his dad who I was on the phone to right after.'

'Oh dear. I'm sure he will come around eventually. I'm guessing by your face you and your sister's meeting didn't go too well,' she prodded gently.

'No, basically she wants me to lend her – no, sorry, not her but my dad's company – my inheritance money, and when I told her I needed to talk to Tassos first she stormed off. I think that's because she knew what Tassos would say.'

'A resounding "no", I presume?'

'Yep. I don't know what it's all about, but Tassos made it clear to me that my inheritance would be better kept where it is. So, first there was Callisto not wanting to renovate the villa for Fotini, and now she's come asking me to fund the company. I think my sister is in a bit of a mess, and the sad thing is she's blaming my dad for everything. When I told Tassos that he seemed a little angry.'

'I know it's just a matter of time before Callisto's next stop will be me, and it's not something I'm looking forward to one little bit.'

Chapter 15

Lena was glad she had talked to Tassos and Trisha yesterday, but the one person she didn't want to tell about Callisto's request was Fotini. She knew her aunt would be fuming, and would no doubt go knocking on Callisto's door demanding to know what she was up to.

The meeting with Callisto had been unpleasant but the worst thing about yesterday was upsetting Jacob. Ok, he was his own worst enemy, jumping to conclusions as he had, but she was just as much to blame because until Pavlos had appeared on the scene she had been giving Jacob all of her attention, and they had made so many plans for the week. Jacob was obviously still angry with her as he hadn't replied when she had texted him last night.

But today was another day and, to be honest, she wasn't in the mood to chat with anyone she knew. It would be a good day to be by herself and in her own thoughts.

She knew that if she went for a walk down the hill and onto the beach someone she knew would stop her for a chat, so she would have to go further afield, maybe catch a boat somewhere. It had even crossed her mind to go back to Athens for a few days, but that would probably just create more problems as her mum would want to know about everything and everybody.

After an hour of drinking coffee and pondering her options, she decided to catch the boat over to Corfu. She threw a few things in her bag and phoned for a taxi to take her over to the harbour and then she was off. For the first time, she hoped she wouldn't bump into anyone on the stairs or on the patio as she headed out. She really wasn't in the mood for a chat. Thankfully, she managed it, and her luck continued at the harbour as there was a boat leaving just ten minutes after she arrived. Perfect timing. She quickly nipped into the little shop for a bottle of water and, as anticipated, someone recognised her – Maria, who used to work in the supermarket back in Keriaphos.

'Hi, Lena, are you living back here on the island now?'

'Yes, for the time being.'

'Oh that's good. I miss your father. We went to school together when we were younger and he was so funny in those days. Is your sister here as well?'

'She is. Sorry, I'm going to have to go, I need to catch the boat to Corfu. Nice to see you!' Lena called over her shoulder as she made a hasty exit.

As she stepped onto the boat she breathed a sigh of relief. She loved to talk about her dad but she really wasn't in the mood for it today.

The boat journey didn't take very long, just over an hour, and before she knew it, she was at the ferry port and wondering what her plan of action should be. She wasn't hungry yet so thought perhaps she'd have a look around the shops as she might see some nice things for the apartment, pieces that would bring a bit of her personality to the space. She also had a think about whether there was anything she needed that she couldn't get on Vekianos. She needed some more towels and she knew just the shop to go in, one that she had been to several times with her dad when she was still a child. The thought brought back memories of where else they would go, and she remembered the little ice cream parlour. Hopefully it would still be there.

An hour later she had picked up a few towels and other bathroom accessories and had made her way to the ice cream parlour. It had not changed a bit, even down to where the ice creams were in the display counter. Her eyes ran along the top row and stopped on the third flavour in – her favourite, cookies and cream. She decided she would have two scoops in a waffle cone.

Ice cream in hand, her day was complete ... or it would be when she found a seat. As she paid and headed out of the parlour her emotions got the better of her when she suddenly realised that this was the first time she had ever been in there without her dad. Making it worse, she was now walking the same path as they always used to, to find a seat. Before she knew it the ice cream was melting all down her hand and the excitement of buying it had gone. Suddenly she smiled to herself. If her dad were here he would tell her that the only way to stop the ice cream from melting was to eat it, and so she did. Once it was gone she was pleased she had had it. It had brought back far more happy memories than sad ones.

After cleaning her hands she decided to head back towards the harbour and then along the sea wall. Everything was so much bigger here in Corfu compared to Vekianos. For a start, the boats moored in the distance were much bigger than the ones she could see from her little island. That thought made her smile: *her* island. Because it was now, she realised, and she was going to make her home there. But what was she going to do for a job? That would have to be her next priority. She decided she'd like to do something very different to the office work she'd done at the bank back in Athens, before her dad passed. Every few minutes she stopped to take in the view and it reinforced her enthusiasm to be living and working by the sea. City life wasn't for her anymore.

She carried on walking and was nearly at the

edge of the harbour when someone spoke to her.

'It's Lena, isn't it?' the woman said warmly. 'Joanna. We met in my office in Athens?'

'Joanna, hi! Sorry, I was miles away. I do remember meeting you, but the meeting itself was all a bit of a blur.'

'Yes, I expect it wasn't an easy day for you. Should I presume that as you're here on Corfu, and as it's only a short boat ride to Vekianos, you must be staying there?'

'I am, yes. The apartment is lovely and things are sort of ok. So what brings you to Corfu, Joanna?'

'I'm just having a mooch around until I catch the boat over to Vekianos.'

'Does that mean you're visiting the new apartment block to see us all?'

'Oh no, I'm not going to Keriaphos, but to a different part of the island. I've kept you chatting long enough though so I'll let you go, but it was nice to see you again, Lena.'

Lena could see Joanna was flustered and couldn't wait to get away. Perhaps this was her opportunity to find out a little more about the last empty apartment?

'I'm not in a hurry. Would you like to go for a coffee? I can fill you in on all the dramas of the apartment block.'

Lena could see Joanna was very hesitant but she wasn't going to take no for an answer.

'There's a little restaurant just around that corner my dad and I used to go to while we were waiting to catch the boat back to Vekianos. They make lovely coffee.'

'Yes, I know the place you mean. I've been there quite a few times. Ok, why not.'

They walked in silence and Lena worried Joanna might have felt forced into agreeing. She was determined to make her feel comfortable.

'Here we are, and look, there's a little table outside with a lovely view.'

Once they'd settled into their seats and the coffee was ordered Lena tried to brighten the atmosphere by filling Joanna in on all the latest from the apartments.

'Is your half-sister, Callisto, living there as well?'

'I think so as she appears to have moved a lot of her things in. She's keeping herself to herself until she has something to say, it seems, but that is what it is.'

'So, Patricia. She's the only one I didn't have any dealings with as her bequest was handled through a lawyer in London. Is she nice?'

'Oh yes, she's lovely and we get on really well. Actually, she gets on brilliantly with everyone, although she still feels bad she has the penthouse, especially since she hadn't had anything to do with my dad for many years. It's strange, really, as I feel I've known her all my life. I think that's because Dad always talked about her and she is exactly like he described.'

'Yes, I remember him talking about her with a lot of affection. I'm glad she's just like he described, that's nice.' Looking at her watch she began to gather her things. 'I have to be off now but it's been lovely chatting to you, Lena, and I'm so glad you've settled into the apartment.'

'But you've not asked about the arrival of the resident of the final apartment,' Lena said, taking her chance.

Joanna gave a little grin, as if she knew Lena was attempting to trick her into naming the person.

'Should I have?' she said, giving nothing away.

'Well, no one's moved in yet and we're all trying to figure out who it might be.'

'I wouldn't worry about it. You never know, they might never move in. Perhaps they have a life somewhere else and don't want to give it up, or they might not feel comfortable being there with all the people connected to your dad. There could be a hundred and one reasons it's still empty. Right, it's been lovely to chat and I'm so happy to hear that everyone is sort of getting on. Your dad really did know what he was doing. Everyone involved was so special to him and all he wanted was to make you all happy. Goodbye, Lena.'

Chapter 16

Another morning and Lena was again up early. She was hoping she would feel better today than she had yesterday but she didn't. Yesterday had been an odd one, full of emotion and lots of thoughts about her dad, which had been good in one way, but upsetting in another, and then bumping into Joanna... That had also been strange. For some reason she got the impression there was something more to Joanna that met the eye and it was something she wanted to ask Fotini about. Had Joanna been more than just a lawyer and a friend to her dad? She hoped her aunt might be able to shed some light on it all.

Lena was also feeling off because Jacob still hadn't replied to her text from the other day. She made herself a coffee and took it out onto the balcony, which was the one place she would miss if she left. She felt calm looking out at the ocean in the distance beyond all the roofs in front of her.

As she was daydreaming, in her own little world, she saw Pavlos walk down to the gate. He turned around and noticed her and waved, which was nice. She waved back as she wondered where he was off to so early in the morning.

Within minutes she noticed someone else heading down the path – Callisto. She was carrying a suitcase but it was only a small case so Lena suspected that her older sister probably wouldn't be gone for long, wherever she was going.

Someone else appeared at the gate soon after – it was like rush hour! – and Lena saw it was Trisha. She had her shopping bag with her so she must be heading down to the supermarket.

When Lena's phone rang shortly thereafter she

went into the apartment to answer it.

'Lena,' her Aunt Fotini said when she answered, 'I was wondering if you fancied going out for lunch today? Being honest, I'm feeling a little down and sorry for myself, and I just know you will be the one to cheer me up.'

'I've been feeling the same way and I would love to have lunch with you. What time would suit you best?'

'Say, twelve-thirty, outside your gate? It will give me time to do a few little things first.'

Lena agreed and hung up the phone, feeling better than she had before the call. As she had the morning ahead of her, she decided to have a swim and a few hours by the pool with her book. She was also hoping Jacob would see her and come and chat. She set an alarm on her phone for half an hour before she had to meet her aunt, and after doing a few laps of the pool she settled on a sun lounger. She hadn't been there long when she saw Trisha come back through the gate and walk towards her.

'Hi, Trisha, how are you?'

'I'm fine thanks, Lena. You?'

'Ok, thanks. I took the boat over to Corfu yesterday, which was very interesting as I bumped into Joanna, the lawyer who dealt with doling out all the apartments. Between you and me, I'm wondering if the final apartment might belong to her.'

'What makes you think that?'

'Well, she was a good friend of my dad's and she's come over to Vekianos but wouldn't tell me why she was here. I'm having lunch with my aunt later so hopefully she can fill me in on anything she knows about Joanna.'

'You'll have to let me know what you discover. For now, I best get a move on or my frozen things will all have melted. Have a lovely lunch and give your aunt my love. Oh!' she exclaimed, turning back almost immediately. 'I meant to ask, how is it going with Jacob?'

'I don't know. He's still avoiding me.'

'Oh dear. Hopefully he will come around soon.'

With that Trisha waved and headed up to her apartment and Lena settled back on the lounger, wondering what she should do about Jacob. She also thought briefly about Callisto's request, which made her think of her inheritance money. It wouldn't last forever so perhaps she should start looking for a job in the local area. Fotini knew everyone here in Keriaphos so if anyone could help her find work, it would be her aunt. She was suddenly even more glad they'd planned to have lunch today.

'You look lovely, Lena. I feel very underdressed.'

'Don't be silly, Aunt Fotini, you look lovely. I'll admit I've dressed up for a reason – and I need your help – but first I need food because I am *starving*. Lead the way.'

They headed down the hill and Fotini led Lena to a little local restaurant in the back street where all the older locals met for lunch.

'I'll have to introduce you to everyone and of course they will be so happy to talk to you as they knew and loved your dad. Will that be ok?'

'That's not a problem at all. Actually, talking of my dad I wanted to ask you about him and Joanna the lawyer. Were they more than friends, do you know?'

'Now *that* is a long, complicated story,' Fotini said with a bark of laughter.

'Really? So you think she could maybe be the owner of the last apartment?'

'I thought so at first but now I don't think so. For one thing, she already has a property on the other side of the island, so she wouldn't need it.'

'But one could argue that you don't need it either as you have the villa,' Lena countered.

'I never thought of it like that. Perhaps you have a point. Let's continue this conversation later though, or else everyone will have an opinion to share,' Fotini joked as they stepped inside the restaurant. It was very busy and as Fotini had warned, everyone wanted to chat to Lena, so it was ages before they even sat down. Eventually they managed it and they both ordered souvlaki and a half carafe of red wine.

'Now, Lena, what did you want my help with?'

'I need to find a job. Nothing high flying, like my sister's, just something basic to earn me a wage. I thought as you know most people here on the island you might be able to help.'

'I don't think your sister is high flying anymore. By all accounts she has made a mess of the company already...' Fotini broke off when she saw the look on Lena's face. 'Did I say something wrong?'

'If I tell you something, will you promise me you won't do anything about it? And by that, I mean: do you promise you won't say anything to Callisto?'

Fotini nodded hesitantly.

'She's asked me for money. She wants me to put my inheritance into my dad's company.'

'More likely she wants the money for herself as she has obviously messed up somewhere along the line. First it was that there would be no refurbishment of the villa and now she's uprooted her life and moved here.'

There was a silence as their food was delivered and Lena could tell her aunt was distracted thinking about the whole Callisto situation. She decided it might be best to change the conversation before things became any more heated.

'Tell me about Joanna,' Lena encouraged.

'I know she was born on Vekianos – her parents

had a house and a little business growing tomatoes over the other side of the island, in a town called Thagistri – and that she went to school with your dad. She then went off to university in Athens, which was a huge thing in those days, and it wasn't until years later – I think once your mum and dad split up – that she and your dad saw each other again.'

'And do you think they were in a relationship?'

'I'm not sure. As you know better than most, he kept much of his life a secret, but I would think if they were he would have told me about it, and I probably would have met her. But you say she's back on the island now? If that's the case, and if the apartment has been left to her, I'm sure we'll find out soon. Now, tell me what's happening with you and Jacob... Why are you laughing?'

'It's all very silly, really. He's in a huff because he has the wrong idea about why I had to cancel our day out and, to be honest, I don't need the hassle or drama. I'm not looking for a boyfriend, just a job and an easy life. I have all the upset I could handle in Athens with my mother, so I don't need it here in Keriaphos as well.'

'I think a job would definitely help, not just the money but also having something to occupy your time. I can think of a few people who would offer you work but I do think you need a special job, by that I mean something you can really throw yourself into and get something out of it in return. I'm not saying a career ... actually, perhaps I am. Give me a few days to mull it over. Another glass of wine?' she offered, picking up the carafe.

There was no more talk of a job or Callisto from that point onwards, but that was mainly because the locals had seen they had finished their meal and so they kept coming up and saying hello, which was nice, and made Lena feel very welcome in the little town.

'Ready to walk up that hill?' Fotini asked a while later.

'Yes, when you are. Did you need any food shopping while we're down here though? I could help carry it for you.'

'No, I'm fine for everything, thank you.'

After saying their goodbyes to everyone in the restaurant, which seemed to take forever, they headed down to the main street, where they ran into Jacob.

'Hello, Lena, Fotini. Just out for a walk.'

'Does that mean you don't need to be anywhere in the next few hours then, Jacob?' Fotini asked.

'Yes, that's right.'

'Good, because neither does Lena, I suggest... No, I don't, I'm *telling* you both to go and sort out your differences. You should be having fun not ignoring each other.'

With that Fotini walked away and they were both left not knowing what to say.

'Jacob, I didn't lie to you,' Lena finally ventured, breaking the uneasy silence. 'Callisto knocked on my door and I explained I was meeting you but she demanded I cancel, and when she left I had to contact your father, and then by the pool—'

'You really don't have to explain, Lena. I've been stupid again. Shall we put it behind us and "go and have some fun", as your aunt said?'

'Why not. Do you know what I fancy doing if you're up for it? Getting the bus down to the harbour in Vekianos and going on one of those little boat trips around the caves in Paxos and Antipaxos, and then grabbing a drink.'

'I've never been to the caves before but so many people talk about them and say how magnificent they are. I've also heard they're very romantic, if you want them to be,' he added suggestively. 'How about it, Lena? Are you up for some romance in your life?'

Lena laughed off the question but she had to admit that part of her had answered with a resounding 'yes' because Jacob was the one asking. They caught the bus to the harbour and chose one of the little boats that could take six to eight people out for a two-hour trip.

'Looking forward to this?' Jacob asked.

'I am. I can't believe that in all the years I've been coming here I've never visited the caves. It's going to be a new experience for both of us.'

The other people on their boat were really friendly tourists, and the minute Lena said she lived on the island there was one question after another. She didn't mind but Jacob's face told a different story. She hoped the excitement of going through the caves would cheer him up.

Two hours later they were standing on the quayside and Jacob did look happier, so the caves had obviously done the trick, and Lena was about to cheer him up even more.

'I really enjoyed that. Do you fancy getting something to eat now, before we head back to Keriaphos?' she asked.

Jacob's smile widened. 'Sounds great!'

Chapter 17

Callisto's head was all over the place and, to be honest, she really didn't know what she was doing getting a taxi to Thagistri, let alone bringing an overnight bag as she had no idea if or where she would be staying. But what she did know was this: she was determined to see the problem piece of land for herself, and to try and find a solution to the drain issue. She also thought that perhaps if she could spend some time in the little town it might click why her father had bought the land in the first place. And understanding his motive might help her understand his vision for the villa. The journey took just less than an hour from Keriaphos and she wondered again why she was planning on spending the night. Yet another waste of money to add to her tally.

'Do you have the address of where you are staying?' the taxi driver asked as they arrived in Thagistri.

'No, I don't... Could you please just drop me somewhere along the main street?'

'Of course.'

They pulled to a stop on a little street with a couple of shops and a restaurant, and Callisto paid the taxi driver and he took her case out the boot of his car. As she stood there she took a look around. Her first impression was that it didn't feel touristy at all, which added to her confusion. Why would her dad have wanted to build a vacation villa in such a quiet and remote spot on the island? She was determined that before she left later today or tomorrow she would know what was behind it all.

Wheeling her case behind her she decided she

needed something to eat as she hadn't had breakfast before she left. Heading the opposite direction from where the taxi came from she noticed a little minimart. Popping her head through the door she was encouraged to find it was very modern and full of stock.

Walking a bit further along the main street she noticed a little restaurant on the other side that stuck out because it looked very chic and modern amongst all the other properties. Crossing over she looked in and found that there were no customers, just one man scrolling on his phone.

'Excuse me, are you open?' she asked.

'Yes, are you looking for coffee or food?'

'Both, actually, but coffee first, please.'

'If you'd like to take a seat I'll bring it over. How do you like your coffee?'

'Just black, please, no sugar.'

As she went to take a seat she noticed a cabinet with big trays of pies and she smiled to herself; she had come to the right place.

'Please tell me that's a spinach pie,' she called over to the owner.

'It is. Does this mean you don't want to see the menu?'

'No, thanks, a large slice of that pie will be perfect, please.'

As she sat down she felt comfortable in her surroundings. This was a really fresh business and it reminded her of the cafés and coffee shops in Athens, not at all something you would expect to find on Vekianos. She thought it was a very brave thing to do, opening something like this in a town that didn't look like it catered to tourists.

'There you go,' the man said as he set the coffee down in front of her. 'Would you like the pie warmed up?'

'Thank you. No, just as it is will be fine.'

The chap brought over the pie and she dived in. It was gorgeous and just what she needed. As she ate she flicked through her phone, not that there was much to look at given that she had no meetings planned and her social life had come to a standstill since arriving here on the island. If this had been a few weeks ago she would have arranged to go somewhere with friends, but sadly, for the time being, her life needed to be focused on rebuilding all that she had broken. And part of that process would be building bridges with her aunt and getting to know her half-sister better.

'Excuse me, could I have another coffee?'

'Of course. How is the pie?'

'Very moreish. I think I'll have to come back and have it again.'

'Well, we're open seven days a week and you would be very welcome. Are you here on holiday?'

'No, I'm staying over in Keriaphos for a while.'

'There's a lovely little cove there that's perfect for a day on the beach, and on the hill there are some fantastic restaurants.'

'Yes, it's nice, though a little quiet for me. I'm used to the buzz in Athens. By the way, do you know of anywhere to stay in the area? I'm only looking for one night as I need to do a little work here this afternoon and tomorrow.'

'You're in luck, as long as you don't mind a very compact studio above a coffee shop that sells the best spinach pie on the island. It's fifty euros for the night but breakfast is included.' The man smiled.

'A place to stay and the chance to enjoy spinach pie for breakfast? Sounds perfect! I'm Callisto, it's nice to meet you.'

'My name's Makis. When you've finished your coffee I'll show you up to the apartment. There's a separate entrance out back.'

With that a group of four people walked in.

'Please would you excuse me? When you're ready I'll show you upstairs, but there's no rush.'

As Makis walked off Callisto was feeling pleased. This would be perfect. She would take her case up to the studio and then head off to view the piece of land. She needed to find where the nearest property was to see what she could do about the drainage, and hopefully she'd discover what the attraction for her dad was with this plot.

An hour later Callisto was standing at the end of the little row of shops and restaurants. She knew the direction she had to go but there was something niggling at her; there was a sign on the road saying the beach was up ahead, but as her gaze followed the road she saw it curved to the right, turning away from the water she could see in the distance to the left. Was there a shorter way to get there by walking? She got out her phone and looked at a map. Yes, she was right, the road looped away from the water before it turned back towards the beach, and there was a path that would take her in more of a straight line, getting her there a lot quicker.

She followed the map to the starting point of the shortcut and soon realised it wasn't a path, but more of a lane, with visible car tracks. She wondered if they led to a property or right down to the beach. As she walked she passed land that had obviously been used for growing tomatoes in the past, as evidenced by the run-down polytunnels that sat ready for the growing season, but was now very overgrown and looked like it hadn't been touched for years. A little further on there was an old building with no roof and one wall that had collapsed, then more land that was overgrown with weeds and a few very old olive trees scattered about. As the path widened she could see the beach and the sea more clearly. She was shocked at how quick she had gotten there, but then she realised it wasn't the bit of beach she had expected to see, the bit she'd visited on her other visits to the site, and she was confused.

After a few minutes of trying to suss out where she was, she decided to turn right and walk along the beach to find the point where it met with the road. It only took a few minutes for things to start to look familiar, and her gaze turned inland again, trying to spot the piece of land her dad had bought. From what she could remember there were four little posts knocked into the ground marking the area out, and it didn't take her long to locate them and head in for a closer look.

There was no doubt that the view from the land was magnificent, there was nothing to beat it, but after walking between the posts half a dozen times – something that no doubt looked very odd to the few people that were on the beach – she was still no closer to figuring out the mystery of why this land had been so important to her father that he would disregard the advice of Tassos and buy it.

Standing at the post nearest to the beach she noticed a bench nearby looking out to sea. Walking the site hadn't sparked any answers so far, so she decided to take a seat and look back at the area from a new viewpoint. But just as she got near to it an older couple got there first. She started to turn away but the gentleman called out to her.

'There's plenty of room for you, Miss. My wife and I don't have a problem sharing.'

Callisto decided there was no harm in being polite for a couple of minutes.

'Thank you, that's very kind,' she said as she sat, trying to leave the older couple as much room as possible.

'Not a problem. It's so lovely to have this bench here, isn't it? We have been saying for years how nice it would be to have somewhere to sit and admire this view, and then a couple of weeks ago ... it just appeared! It's been dedicated to someone who has just died. If I get up you can read the plaque,' he said, starting to shift his weight forward.

'Oh, no, please don't get up on my account,' Callisto implored him. 'And you're right, it's a perfect spot for a bench.'

'Are you here on holiday?' the man asked kindly.

'Yes and no. I'm new to this area but I've just moved from Athens to Keriaphos, which is about half an hour away around the coast.'

'How lovely that you are out exploring the island. Now, I'd best stop talking before my wife tells me to shut up so you can enjoy the gorgeous view.' The man chuckled as his wife gently tapped his arm and Callisto couldn't help but smile. They really were quite sweet together.

Callisto couldn't turn and look at the piece of land as the couple were in the way but she couldn't complain as the view before her was lovely. She was beginning to think that it must have been the reason her dad had bought the land.

The three of them sat in peaceful silence for a few moments but it was interrupted when her phone beeped.

Apologising to the couple as she took it out of her bag she quickly silenced it and then looked at the new message that had come through. It was a text from the company lawyer to say the sales of the two villas on the outskirts of Athens had gone through and the money had gone into the company account. She wanted to shout with excitement, this was such good news! But ... perhaps also bad news, as it meant the finances were in place to start the renovations on Fotini's villa. Tassos would no doubt make sure there was no stopping it going ahead, but there had to be a way of cutting the costs down so she would still have money left to start to rebuild the company.

'Time for us to head back to Thagistri, I think,' the older woman said to her husband. 'We can leave you in peace,' she added, winking at Callisto.

Callisto smiled and as they headed off towards the road she called to them, 'Did you know there's a quicker way back to the town? Instead of walking along the main road, if you just go along the beach in the other direction for a few minutes you'll see a path that will take you straight back in about a quarter of the time.'

'Oh, yes, we know, that's the way we used to go many years ago, but we find it very sad with the house now collapsed and the fields so overgrown and forgotten. There was talk at one point of it being cleared and the house rebuilt but nothing came of it – probably cost too much money – and then there was talk of something being built on this bit of land,' the man said, pointing to the plot Callisto's father had bought, 'but nothing came of that either. Such a shame. Enjoy the rest of your day, dear.'

As Callisto waved them off her phone beeped again with a message from Tassos confirming the funds from the sales had come through. She turned and looked at the plot of land, still none the wiser as to what about it had appealed to her father beyond the view. She decided to walk back to the town and go for something to eat and an early night because tomorrow she was determined to get to the bottom of this mystery. Perhaps she could ask a few questions around the town, see if any of the old locals knew anything.

As she stood up her eyes caught on the plaque and her legs went to jelly, forcing her to sit down before she fell. Her head was buzzing and she started to cry. Who had put this bench here? And why was it here and not in Keriaphos?

As her fingers followed the grooves on the

inscription, the tears came faster and the words blurred.

In memory of Stelios Drakos, a man that was loved by so many.

Chapter 18

It had been a long night. Callisto hadn't slept well, seeing the bench with the plaque every time she closed her eyes. It had upset her, and it wasn't just because she found it strange for it to be where it was on the island, it was also because she didn't know who had placed it there. It *had* to be connected to that plot of land, but she had no idea how.

Then, like a thunderclap, it had hit her. How stupid she had been not thinking of the obvious right from the start; that the person who sold her dad the land could hold the clues to the mystery!

As she showered and packed her case, preparing for the day, she decided she would go down to the café and have some breakfast while she made a plan of action. She had already taken a brief look at the land registry website but it wasn't working so she would have to try again after she ate.

'Good morning, Callisto. Did you sleep well? Was the studio ok for you?' Makis greeted her.

'Everything was perfect, thanks. Can I ask you, have you lived here all of your life? If so, you might be able to help with something I'm working on.'

'I have and I'm happy to help if I can. What's your question?'

'There's a piece of land down by the beach that was sold off a few years ago. I know who owns it now but I'm curious as to who owned it before.'

'I think I know the piece of land you mean. It was owned by a lovely couple who used to employ so many youngsters here in the town picking and boxing tomatoes on the land that bordered that plot. There was no one to take over the business when they got too old to work the land as they only had one child and she lives and works in Athens.'

With that a group of customers came in and started ordering omelettes. Callisto realised it would take a while for their food to be prepared and she would have to wait to find out more from Makis, so she settled in to finish her coffee and then ordered another one.

When a steady stream of more customers soon followed she realised she should probably give up waiting and come back later on, before she left. Hopefully it would be a little quieter then.

Once back up in the studio she tried looking at the registry site, but it was still down. She was one step ahead of where she had been though, as she now knew the piece of land was connected to the crumbling old house nearby. That was a start.

She organised her things, ready to be picked up later, and headed off towards the beach. She opted to go the long way around, instead of down the track, as she thought it might help her understand some of the problems with the water and the drains that had prevented her father from following through with the project. She hoped to see something that would help her put two and two together.

About ten minutes after she started down the road she passed a property. It was lovely, old but big with a swimming pool, and it seemed tidy and well looked after. Carrying on, the road started to wind back on itself, this time going towards the sea, but looking into the distance she couldn't see any more properties up ahead. That was interesting. If the house she had just passed was the only one in the area, that must be where the water pipes and drainage would have to come up to. Given how far it was from her father's land, it was all starting to make sense now why the cost of laying the pipes and connecting them to the local sewage system was so high. But surely her dad must have known that from the start? He was diligent about researching his projects in advance and so would undoubtedly have come across the very obvious obstacle. And yet, he'd gone ahead with the purchase regardless. How odd.

Finally she reached the end of the road and stepped into the beach car park, making her way across it and then up to her father's bench.

Once there she looked at the inscription and said out loud, 'Dad, this bench, this plot of land ... what's it all about? Why did you buy it? Come on, give me a clue and help me out.'

When no answer was forthcoming she pulled a paper map of the area and a red pen out of her bag. She wanted to mark out her father's land and see where it was in relation to the house she had just walked by. Looking at the map and comparing it to the quote paperwork she'd received from the company she'd been looking to hire to lay the drainage system, she realised that the quote called for the tunnels to take the long way around from the town, following the winding road, but why not use the water tunnels along the pedestrian path? After all, there had to be water running to the polytunnels as how else would things have been watered when the land was still in use for growing tomatoes? The cost of running the pipes that way would be significantly less, given how the path ran directly to the plot of land, plus it meant they wouldn't need to dig up any roads or the other property's land. Had she just found a way out of all of their problems?

She took a photo of the map and emailed it to Santiago to see if this alternative solution had been looked into, and if it might be possible. Trying the land registry site again she was pleased to see that it was working, but now she was struggling with another problem – trying to get an internet signal. When it kept cutting off she realised she would have to wait until she was back in the town.

Taking one last walk around the plot of land, she saw someone walking down the track from town, and realised she recognised them.

But why was she here? Was she the clue that Callisto had asked her dad for?

'Hello, Joanna,' she called as the lawyer approached. 'What an unusual place for us to bump into each other.'

'Hi, Callisto, yes, it is, isn't it? But there's a very simple answer. Shall we go over and sit on the bench while I explain?'

Callisto nodded, feeling suddenly nervous.

They sat on opposite ends of the bench and Joanna looked out at the view for a moment before speaking.

'I used to come here with your dad, you know. He always moaned that there was nowhere to sit apart from on the beach or a hard rock, which he said we were getting too old to do, and when I came here after he'd passed, to spend some time with my memories, I decided that he was right. So, I commissioned the bench so that whenever I, or others who knew him, came here, we would have somewhere to sit and enjoy the view Stelios loved so much.'

'But why here? Why not back in Keriaphos, where he grew up and where my aunt still lives, and where Lena and I now live as well?'

'I knew how much he loved to come here to get away from everything, and I thought he'd like the fact that it's given a lot of pleasure to people that didn't even know him, as he always loved to help people, not just in big ways but also in little gestures.'

'Yes, he did like to look out for people, didn't he, especially here on the island. Can I ask, Joanna, were you one of the people he looked out for? What

I'm trying to say is ... were you and my father in love?'

There was a long silence and for the first time Joanna looked nervous. *No,* Callisto thought, *she's not nervous, she's ... sad, very sad.*

'Your father cared for me, that's true, but though he was very much in love, it wasn't with me. It was nice to see you again,' Joanna said, rising to her feet. 'I hope you get some peace and enjoy some nice memories sitting on this bench. I know I do. Goodbye.'

There was nothing more Callisto could do here in Thagistri; it was time to go back to the studio, pick up her case, and get a taxi back to Keriaphos. But first she would sit here a while longer. Pulling her phone out of her bag she was surprised to find that she had a signal. As there were no new messages or emails she tried the land registry site again and in a few minutes the information she had been looking for popped up. The land that her father had bought was sold to him by the Bouras family.

As in ... *Joanna Bouras*? Callisto was shocked. Joanna didn't just have a connection to the bench, she had a connection to the old house and everything else here as well!

Chapter 19

Trisha was up early and yet again she was preparing herself for the inevitable visit from Callisto. She had seen her come back late last night in a taxi and, to be honest, she was at the stage now that she just wanted to get it over with. Sitting here on her roof terrace just waiting for a knock on the door was not the way to be living her life, a life which should be happy and stress-free now she was retired, but was so far decidedly neither. She knew she was in no position to be complaining about anything, she had a beautiful home here on Vekianos, lots of new friends whose company she really enjoyed, and a home back in England, but for some reason she felt so lonely and sad.

She was just about to make another coffee to take out onto the terrace but she changed her mind. She was going to shake this feeling off and she would do so by going down to the pool to give Callisto the opportunity to approach her. It was time to get this meeting over with. She quickly got her things together and changed, and after filling her water bottle she was feeling confident and ready for a day down at the pool, no matter what it might bring.

After turning the sun lounger to a position where she could see both the main gate and the door into the apartment block, she decided to have a swim. She felt very blessed to have the pool, and just like the apartment, she didn't take it for granted at all.

After she'd completed twenty lengths it was time to enjoy the sunshine. As she was stepping out of the pool she noticed the gate opening, but it was Fotini, not Callisto.

'Morning, Fotini!'

'Hi, Trisha. Are you in the mood for some company?'

'To be honest, I would welcome it as really all I'm doing is waiting for the showdown with Callisto. I just want to get it over with.'

'Oh, me, too. I have a few words to say to that niece of mine and I have to speak with her about the refurbishment. Tassos called me yesterday to say that the funds are now in place to get started on the villa.'

'I presume you haven't spoken to her since she asked you to postpone it?'

'No, I haven't and now I've found out – and please promise me that you won't say anything – that Callisto has asked Lena for money, claiming the company needs it because Stelios misspent funds. Can you believe the nerve of her, blaming my brother for a mess of her own making? I am so mad. She's gone off somewhere but as soon as she's back she and I are going to have words.'

'I actually have an update on that – she came back last night. Poor Lena to be put in that position. Callisto must be desperate to ask her for funds. I don't imagine it's left her in the best mood.'

'Trisha, you are more than a match for Callisto. It will be like water off a duck's back for you.'

'That might be the impression I give, but I can assure you it's not how I'm feeling. Oh look, here comes Lena now.'

'I suppose you both know Callisto is back?' Lena asked glumly.

'Yes, darling, Trisha has just told me. But forget about her for now. How did yesterday go with Jacob? Did you have fun?'

'We did. We got one of the boats over to see the caves on Antipaxos and then over to Paxos. It was lovely and between just the three of us I'm really looking forward to spending more time and having more fun with Jacob. And on that note ... here he comes now! We're off out for a walk and some lunch.'

'Lovely weather for a pool day,' Jacob said as he joined them.

Trisha and Fotini waved the youngsters off and then shared a meaningful look.

'I reckon that fun with Jacob is just what Lena needs right now,' Trisha observed. 'I wish I felt like some fun.'

'What's got you in a muddle and upset, Trisha? You never know, I might be able to help.'

'I'll tell you, but first, why don't I go and grab us a cold drink?'

'That sounds the perfect idea.'

Trisha was only gone a minute or two and when she returned she found Fotini laughing. 'Today's not the day for your encounter with Callisto, it seems. She's just gone out and she looked like she was on a mission!'

Trisha was disappointed to have missed her opportunity but acknowledged that maybe it was for the best if Callisto was in a bad mood.

'Now, tell me what's going on with you,' Fotini urged.

'You make it sound like I'm in a therapist's chair!' Trisha laughed. 'But saying that, perhaps I should be. Here I am, a sixty-something-year-old woman, newly retired, just inherited a fabulous apartment on a Greek island, have a home in London and money in the bank. I should be happy but I'm just so sad.'

'Trisha, you've had a huge shock and you need time to adjust and get used to your new reality. Can I ask you something? If this had never happened – if you'd never received the apartment and you were instead back in London – do you think you would feel sad like you do now?'

Trisha didn't have to give that any thought as she knew the answer: of course she would be sad because for the first time in decades she didn't have a purpose anymore. She had gotten off the hamster wheel and didn't know what to do.

'Yes, I would be,' she admitted to Fotini. 'My job was my life, which meant I had no room in it for anything or anyone else, and now I feel my life's been taken away from me and there's a big void that I don't know what to do about.'

They sat there in silence for a few moments, Trisha not knowing what to say. She wished she hadn't put the job in the hotel first for so many years. She had been so consumed by it, and it was like a community – well, almost a family – in that they spent morning, noon, and night together. She had lived with colleagues, ate meals with colleagues, and rarely met people outside the hotel world, but it had all felt normal to her.

'If you had worked a nine to five job, what do you think you would have done with your evening and weekends off?' Fotini asked.

'I know what I *should* have been doing, though whether I would have, I don't know. I should have been spending time with my family, but I put the hotel before them every time.'

'From what I can see you put your work before yourself as well,' Fotini said gently. 'But surely now that's in the past it's time to move on? You can see your family; you have all the time in the world with them. Isn't that a good and happy prospect?'

'But you see, I think it's too late. They needed me then, not now. For one, my parents are no longer with us, and for another, my nephew and niece have already grown up without me being there to see it.'

'Did your parents ever complain they weren't

seeing you? Were they cross and upset with you?'

'Oh, no, never. If anything, they encouraged me with the job and when I had two days off together they said it was a long journey from London for just a few hours together so I was not to waste my time. Perhaps if they had been different and complained they didn't see me, life might have been different for all of us. Do you mind if we stop talking about this now? I'm starting to feel very emotional.'

'Of course not. I was just hoping I could help.'

'You have by just listening, so thank you.'

Trisha hopped back into the pool but instead of doing her lengths, this time she just floated around trying to clear her head. It had helped saying those words to Fotini, but it had also made her feel worse. She was riddled with guilt knowing she should have been there for her sister, helping with her children and then with their parents when they were getting older and were unable to do things. But no, everything was left for her sister. And the worst part? It was only now that any of this had even crossed her mind.

Once out of the pool both Trisha and Fotini lay out enjoying the sunshine.

A car pulled up a while later and Pavlos came through the gate looking very smart in a suit, carrying his briefcase, and with a huge grin on his face.

'Hello! How are you both today?' he called in greeting.

'Trisha and I are fine,' Fotini answered for them both. 'You look very smart, and also very happy. What's put that smile on your handsome face?'

'You two can be the first to know: I've just signed the lease on the restaurant overlooking the beach!'

Both Trisha and Fotini jumped up off their loungers to give Pavlos hugs and congratulate him.

'Thank you! I am so excited and can't wait to get stuck in. There's so much I want to change but I think perhaps I'll wait until the end of the season for the bigger renovations. For now, I'll just open it as-is so I can start to earn some money. Right, I'd best go and get out of these clothes and head down to get stuck into the cleaning. The place is very dusty as it's been shut up for so long.' He waved as he headed inside.

'It's so nice to see one of our fellow residents happy … actually, make that two, because I'm sure Jacob is as well given he's spending time with Lena. It's just us old women that need cheering up and sorting our lives out. I think I'll make a start by sitting down with my niece and putting our differences behind us.'

Trisha nodded but remained silent.

'For what it's worth, if I was in your shoes, the first thing I would do is speak to my sister, because it's high time you were back in one another's lives. I know how much I treasured my time with Sergio. We had always spent time together but when he was told the cancer was incurable, we started spending twenty-four-seven together. You need to spend what time together you can before it's too late.'

Chapter 20

Lena and Jacob had said goodbye to Trisha and Fotini and they were now heading a little distance up the hill to the turning where everyone came down to Keriaphos. Neither had done this walk before, which would take them to a coastal path that basically went all around the island, so it was something new and different for both of them. They had their backpacks with towels and water in so if they came across a nice bay they could have a swim, but hopefully there would also be somewhere on the walk that they could get something to eat.

'There we go, Lena,' Jacob said, pointing up ahead. 'That's the start of the path there. This is exciting, isn't it? It feels like we're explorers.'

'Aren't explorers people that discover places though? We have a map so that means someone must have discovered it already,' Lena joked. 'I'm kidding, you're right, this is exciting. Though we need to make sure to remember that however far we walk, we'll have to walk the same distance back.'

'Not necessarily. We might discover a town that could be on a bus route, or a taxi. Who knows where the day will take us; it's one big adventure!'

'Aside from the fact that you've probably studied the map and worked out exactly where we can eat, swim, and get the bus back?'

They both laughed.

'All I want is for you to have a nice day out,' Jacob said, smiling at Lena. 'It will also be nice to visit somewhere different that we've never been before, and to do that together is lovely.'

Lena could see how happy he was and appreciated all of the effort he had gone to. It was clear that he just wanted to please her, knowing how all the trouble with Callisto had been weighing on her mind, and that he was making every effort to distract her for the day. As they started to walk along the coastal path she couldn't take her eyes off of him. She really liked Jacob, he made her happy in a way no one ever had before.

'We're really high up here, aren't we?' Jacob asked as they paused to take in the view. 'I can see another island over in the far distance... No, that's the mainland. I think it's Parga? It would be nice to go there for the day sometime. I've been before and there's an old ruined castle on a hill, and a lovely harbour with fabulous restaurants. It's a lot bigger than the harbour here in Vekianos. I think we must be half an hour from a little beach that's up ahead,' Jacob said as they continued on their way, this time heading inland.

'I thought it was all meant to be a surprise!' Lena laughed. 'Don't spoil it by telling me.'

'Don't worry, there will still be a surprise. I promise you we're in for a real treat – the perfect day out.'

A short while later the path curved and they could see the sea again. They were headed downhill and the path was a little wider, and every now and then they passed other people, many with professional hiking gear.

'I think we're a little underdressed, Jacob! They must be laughing at us as they walk past.'

'No, we're fine. They're probably walking around the whole island, which is why they're all geared up. Now, I think that path up there, the one that stems off the main one, is where we need to go.'

'You're so organised.'

'Is that a problem?'

'Not at all. Oh, look! I can see a beach in the distance.'

With that the path came to a stop overlooking a little cove with not a single person or building in sight. It looked gorgeous and so romantic, just like in a film.

'This is so lovely! Thank you so much for bringing us here.'

'I thought you would like it,' Jacob said, smiling as he led her down the side of the hill towards the cove. 'I was hoping it would be quiet as you can only get here by foot or boat, and it looks like we're in luck. You can pick your spot, though I'm sorry there are no sun loungers. We'll have to make do with towels on the sand.'

'That's not a problem at all. To think, we get a whole beach to ourselves! You did say there would be a surprise and this is a really special one. It's hard to believe this is less than an hour from Keriaphos, and I didn't have a clue it was here.'

They settled for a spot near the rocks and both decided a swim was needed as they were hot from the walk. The water was so clear, just like when they went over to Antipaxos, and you could see the sand and pebbles underneath. They noticed the odd little boat passing and Lena hoped that was all the boats would do as she really didn't want anyone else coming onto the beach. As she floated around she couldn't stop thinking about how romantic this was, a private beach for just the two of them.

'You're very quiet over there. Are you ok?' Jacob asked a few moments later.

'Very ok, thank you. I was just thinking that this is so lovely. How did you know it was here? Have you been before?'

'No, never, but with the help of the internet and a map I've found out a lot about Vekianos. Ready to have a lie in the sun?'

'Yes, that's a good idea,' she said, following him towards the shore.

As they spread their towels on the golden sand and started to put on a fresh coat of suntan lotion there was an awkward silence. It was something that was new to Lena; she hadn't felt like this before with Jacob and though she knew she needed to say something, she didn't know what that should be. Maybe she should ask him about himself? She really didn't know that much about him beyond the fact that he illustrated books, his dad was an accountant, and his parents had split up, with his mum now living in England. She felt bad that she hadn't asked him more about his life before now. She had been so focused on her family drama and the apartment block with all of its secrets.

'So Jacob,' she began, 'have you decided if you're going to be staying here on the island full time?'

'I haven't decided yet, but as I can work from anywhere really it's definitely possible. And I have to admit that since being here I've done a lot more work than usual as I don't get distracted by all the noise like in Athens or in the UK.'

'That's good. So how does it work? You spend time with both your parents? That must make them happy.'

'Yes and no. I get on better with my mum than my dad because he's still disappointed I didn't train to be an accountant. He was expecting me to work with him and eventually take over the business, but I knew I wasn't clever enough to do that. Also, it just never interested me. I love to be creative, there's nothing better for me than having a sketch pad and filling a blank page with drawings, seeing characters coming alive makes me so happy, and of course the bonus to that is I can earn a living from doing it. I consider myself luckier than most.'

'But surely that all must make your dad happy? What more can a parent want than to see their children make money doing something they love?'

'Yes and no. He doesn't understand the freelance lifestyle as, to him, there's no guarantee another job will come along, and there's no regular income. I have been very lucky these last couple of years because what I do is popular at the moment, but I do realise taste and what's fashionable now will change at some point, and I will have to adapt. I know I can do it but I also know it worries my dad.'

'So that's your dad, how about your mum? How does she feel about it?'

'My mum is the complete opposite to my dad. Some would call her a free spirit whereas my dad would say she's, to use an English word, "scatty", which means all over the place. And he would be right because she flits from one thing to the next.'

'What do you mean by that?'

'She's really creative – that's where I get it from –and from a very early age she encouraged me, and I will always be thankful to her for that. But over the years she has gone from one thing to another. It could be making clothes and then it could be designing jewellery, or she will wake up one morning and decide to do pottery. Over the years there have been so many hobbies and projects. I suppose she just gets bored and to be honest whatever she turns her hand to she's ok at it. None of her ventures are disastrous but my dad couldn't cope with all the change. I think all he wanted was a wife who was at home to take care of the family. Of course, when I was a young child, that was the case, but when I got to the teenage years, and she didn't need to be doing everything for me, that's when she became restless ... and that was the start of the end of their marriage. She wanted more out of life and sadly he couldn't appreciate that. He thought she should be content with what she had.'

'Is that when she moved to England?'

'No, she waited until I got a bit older and was ready to leave school. Those were difficult years and I would probably say the worst. My dad wanted me to go to university and study to be an accountant, and my mum wanted me to go to art school because she saw potential in me and knew it would make me happy, which was all that she wanted. And as far as she was concerned, if I was, at some point, able to earn a living from it then that would be a bonus.'

'I suppose they both just wanted what they saw as the best for you. They cared and that's a good thing – a wonderful thing, actually. So what happened next?'

'My parents decided to separate. I think it was a relief to both of them and it should have happened years before, but it hadn't because of me, something I've struggled to make peace with. That was when my mum made the decision to go back to her family in England. It was a much needed new start and very exciting for her. While planning for her move she also researched art colleges that would suit my needs the most and put together a proposal to present to my father for how they could share custody but also give me the education I wanted and needed to fulfil my dreams. He didn't really put up any objection so a month before the course started my mum and I went back and moved in with my grandfather. He has a lovely big house just outside of London that's near a direct train line into the city.'

'Did you miss Greece and your life in Athens?'

'I definitely missed the sunshine. Oh my goodness the winters are *so cold* in the United Kingdom! Early mornings and late nights waiting for the train were horrible and my mum kept saying I would get used to it eventually, but I never did.'

'How about your dad, did you miss him?'

'Yes, I did. Every opportunity there was I flew

back and the nice thing is the time we spent together helped us to become closer. Ok, he never got over the disappointment of me not training to be an accountant, and for a few years I felt guilty that I had let him down, but not anymore. I am my own boss and I pay my own way. I don't need his money... Though, saying that, I suppose I kind of do since I'm currently living rent-free in his apartment. I've offered to pay him but he refuses to take anything off me.'

'Is your mum ok with you settling here in Greece for now? You must miss her.'

'I do, but I know she's happy for me and she's having too much of a good time in London and living a very fulfilled life. I'm pleased for her and of course she is so pleased I'm doing well with my art. There aren't that many people who can make a living from drawing,' he said, justifiably proudly.

'It sounds like everything has turned out well for all three of you.'

'Yes, but I have to say my dad's not the same since Stelios died. He misses him. They both had the same goals and they shared the excitement with all the projects. My dad has other clients he gets on well with, but the bond he and your dad had was very special and I can tell he misses that. And, of course, it goes without saying that he doesn't have that with your sister. On that note, enough about me and my family. How about another swim?'

As they swam around Lena thought how lucky Jacob was. She was also realising just how fond of him she was becoming; they were getting closer and for once it didn't scare her. She was ready to embrace wherever things were going with him.

After the swim they lay on the beach enjoying the sunshine and the peace and quiet, both commenting on how surprised they were that no one else had arrived.

'This has been such a lovely day,' Lena said with a happy sigh.

'Yes, but it's not over yet. Are you hungry?'

'Are you going to tell me you have a secret picnic in your backpack?'

'No, sorry, but I do know where we can get something to eat. We'll have to walk a little way, and I'm not sure if the food is any good, but I'm keeping my fingers crossed it will be. We can head off whenever you're ready.'

'I'm ready whenever you are. Lead me to the food!' she said happily.

As they headed off the beach and back onto the path Lena realised this had been her favourite day so far on Vekianos and she didn't want it to end.

Jacob led the way, checking the map on his phone every so often, and after a short while the path started to go inland. For the first time since when they started out this morning Lena could hear cars. Looking at the time she saw it was now six-thirty – where had the day gone? Smiling to herself she knew the time had flown because she had spent it with someone very special.

'We're nearly there now and hopefully it will be open,' Jacob said.

The coastal path led to a quiet road and in the distance they could see lots of roofs all together that had to be the village. It only took a few more minutes and then they were there and the first thing they saw was the restaurant, and it was open.

'There are quite a few cars parked outside. That's a good sign! If it's busy the food must be good,' Lena said with a smile.

'Yes, hopefully.'

As they got closer they could see people sat on tables and chairs at the side of the building and then the smell of the food hit them and they smiled at each other. It looked like they were in for a lovely meal. Once they were settled at one of the tables the waiter brought them menus and they ordered a large carafe of red wine.

'Do you fancy some tzatziki to start?' Jacob asked.

'Yes, with lots of warm bread, and then I think I will go for the moussaka. My dad always said the best moussaka was found in the little villages and towns, not the big cities or tourist areas.'

'Well if that's the case I will have the same. It's really lovely here and it's on a bus route so we won't have to walk all the way back. Win-win!'

'Thank you for all the research and planning you did to make this day special,' Lena said shyly.

'I've really enjoyed it and I'm even more pleased you have, too. It was good to get away from Keriaphos. I know we had that afternoon boat trip to Paxos but I think we were both a little on edge and nervous, whereas today there has been none of that.'

'I feel the same; we've really gelled.'

They shared a loaded look and at the same time stretched their hands across the table. As Jacob put his hand on top of hers Lena felt tingling go right through her body, a feeling she had never experienced before.

'Here comes the tzatziki,' she said a moment later.

'That's a shame.'

'What do you mean?'

'It means I'll need my hand back and at the moment I just want to keep it where it is.'

The tzatziki was lovely and the bread was so fresh, the perfect starter. The wine was also going down a treat and Lena felt so relaxed and comfortable as the waiter delivered the moussaka.

'Your dad was right, Lena, this is so moist. I think this will become one of my favourite places to eat, though I don't think I will be walking here every time.'

'I agree—' Lena began, but was cut off by the sound of her phone ringing. 'Sorry, I'll just ignore it.'

The phone rang off but then it went again.

'Perhaps you should answer it. You never know, it could be urgent,' Jacob said.

'Hello?' Lena answered.

'Hey, it's Pavlos. I have exciting news: I've taken over the lease of the restaurant down on the beach!'

'Congratulations, Pavlos! That's really exciting! I'm so happy for you.'

'Thank you but that's not the only news. I think it would make everything perfect if you came and worked with me. I know before you went to work in the banking industry you were a waitress so how about a full circle moment? You said you needed to find a job on the island so please say yes!'

'I ... don't know what to say. I'm taken by surprise and I need to think about it. Look, I can't talk at the moment,' Lena said, shooting a look at Jacob, whose smile had gone. 'Could I call you back later?'

'Of course, but I'm really hoping you'll say yes. You can choose your own hours and what days you want to work and we'll be the perfect team, I just know it.'

'I'll call you back,' Lena said, anxious to end the call and recover the peace she had been feeling with Jacob before her phone rang.

Lena came off the phone and could see from the look on Jacob's face that the call had spoiled their special day, and that was before she even told him about the job offer. Pavlos' timing couldn't be any worse, but there was no denying that she needed a job, and this would be the perfect solution. Surely Jacob would understand that?

Chapter 21

As Trisha came down the stairs from her apartment she bumped into Lena in the corridor. As they were both headed to see Fotini at the villa for coffee, they walked together.

'Do you think your aunt is ok?' Trisha asked as they left through the outside gate. 'She seemed a little strange when she called and invited me over.'

'I thought the same. No doubt it has something to do with Callisto and the refurbishment.'

'That's what I was thinking. Hopefully we can help her feel better. Did you and Jacob have a nice day yesterday?' Trisha asked, changing the subject.

'We did, thank you. When we get to Fotini's I'll tell you all about it. I also have some very exciting news: I got a job!'

'Congratulations! I can't wait to hear all about it!' Trisha quickly put two and two together and thought that the job must be working in the beach restaurant with Pavlos, but she wouldn't spoil Lena's surprise, she would wait until she shared her news.

Fotini was at the door of the villa waiting for them with a coffee pot in hand.

'The coffee is made and I thought we would go onto the back terrace. How are you both?'

'Lena has exciting news,' Trisha shared.

'How thrilling! Come through, come through,' Fotini said, ushering them inside.

They walked through to the back of the villa where there were cups and a plate of biscuits already waiting on the table. Fotini poured the coffee.

'Now, Lena, tell us all about your day out with Jacob.'

'First you tell us what's so urgent that you needed us to come around right away. Does it involve my sister?' Lena asked warily.

'Yes, it does, I had a call from her about an hour ago saying she wants to meet up with me here at twelve o'clock to discuss the revised plans for the refurbishment.'

'So that must mean she's given up on trying to persuade you to put everything on hold.'

'Yes, and I think that's all down to Tassos. He's obviously made it clear to her it had to go ahead because that is what your father set the money aside for, but it's the bit about the revised plans that concerns me. What if everything Stelios had put in place now isn't happening? I only know in my head what he told me he was going to have done, but I've nothing on paper, no drawings or costings. Do I call her bluff and pretend I do?'

'It's difficult, Fotini, but I think you're right to call her bluff. I would sit with her at a table all official and slowly go through her plans. I also wouldn't be afraid to push back if she tries to rush you or skips over anything.'

'Trisha is right,' Lena agreed. 'You're more than a match for her; she should be the one that's nervous, not you. And she's already lost one battle trying to persuade you to postpone doing it, so the ball is in your court.'

'Thank you both so much. That's helped. I think I was just panicking and overthinking everything. Now, that's my news done. I want to hear all about your day out with Jacob.'

'Jacob found this little beach that was empty and we swam and lay in the sun. It was lovely and gave us a chance to get to know one another better, and then we walked to a nice restaurant and had a gorgeous meal. It was the perfect day out until I got a phone call and the atmosphere changed. It was

Pavlos telling me he's taking over the restaurant down by the beach, and he was offering me a job!'

'How exciting! Trisha and I saw him yesterday and he told us the restaurant news but didn't mention he was going to ask you to work with him. What perfect timing as you were looking for a job. Have you already said yes?'

'Of course, though not at the time. I played it down in front of Jacob because you know how he was when I was spending time with Pavlos. After I hung up I explained that Pavlos had called about a job and he seemed sort of ok about it, but I'm worried Jacob was only saying he's happy for me because he knows that's what I want to hear. I want him to be genuinely happy for me as I'm really starting to fall for him.'

'I'm happy for you, Lena – and I'm sure Jacob is, too – but I'm also sad. Who will I have to lay around the pool with?' Trisha joked. 'So what happens next? When do you start work?'

'Tomorrow. Pavlos and I are going to clean the place out. Apparently it's very dusty. Today he's gone over to Corfu to sort out some equipment. But don't worry, we will still have time by the pool as I won't be working twenty-four-seven, and anyway, it won't be long before Fotini has moved into the apartment, with the refurbishment starting soon.'

'That's right,' Fotini agreed. 'I'm planning on staying away from the villa until it's finished and ready for holiday makers. I want the results to be a surprise.'

'I agree the last thing you need is to be having to make decisions and dealing with the builders. That can be left to Callisto. Speaking of, Trisha and I had best head off before she arrives. The last thing we need is for her to think we're ganging up on her.'

'I'll fill you both in on how everything goes later today. Thank you for coming around, I feel a lot better and less panicky now we've chatted.'

Callisto was ready. She had the plans for the villa, she had her notes, but more importantly, she was ready for any questions Fotini would throw at her. But the villa wasn't the only topic on her list, she also wanted to know more about Patricia and Joanna, and Fotini was the best person to ask.

As she took one last look in the mirror she thought about the fact that this meeting would be a completely different approach from usual. This was a family project, something special an aunt and a niece could do together, if they could work together. Only time would tell if that was possible.

Picking up her briefcase she suddenly felt too formal, and so she quickly changed into a pair of shorts and a t-shirt and fished just the file she needed out of the briefcase. Now the bit she hated: walking down the path to the main gate. Every time she did so she wanted to turn around and look at the apartment Patricia was in and shout out 'that's mine, I should be living there!' but she refrained, doing what she always did by keeping her eyes forward.

As she walked through the villa gate her heart was racing and she kept telling herself to calm down and play it casual. It was so obvious the villa needed a fresh coat of paint but there were other areas where she could save big money on the refurbishment if Fotini was willing to work with her.

Fotini greeted her levelly and led her out onto the back terrace.

'As it's lunch time I have prepared a few nibbles and opened a bottle of wine,' Fotini said. 'If you want to take a seat at the table I will fetch the tray of snacks.'

As Callisto walked to the table she saw it looked very official as there was a file and a notepad and pen sat ready and waiting. Her aunt was taking this all very seriously.

'There we go. Help yourself and I will pour the wine. It's very exciting we're getting the refurbishment set in motion but also a bit of a surprise after our last chat when you said everything might have to be put on hold for a while because of the finances.'

'That's all sorted, I'm glad to say. It was a temporary cash flow problem that is now in the past.'

'Oh good, so you won't need the money you asked to borrow from Lena? That will be a relief for her.'

Callisto was momentarily taken aback, but she shouldn't have been surprised as obviously Lena would have mentioned it to their aunt. It seemed Fotini wanted to make it clear that there would be no wool being pulled over her eyes. No, her aunt was on the case.

'Yes, the company won't need to borrow any money from Lena, or anyone else, come to that. Now, shall we get down to business as no doubt you have a busy day ahead?'

'Oh, no, dear, I have all the time in the world. This is all very important so I'm prepared whether it takes one hour or five. The last thing we want to do is upset the plans your father put in place.'

Fotini had done it again, got one over on her. This wasn't going to be the walk in the park Callisto had anticipated. She had to change tactics.

'Before we get on to that, can first I ask you about Joanna Bouras, the lawyer that dealt with the apartment block? Did you know her before all of this started?'

'Yes, I knew her family well and she and your father were friends before he went to England. She has done very well for herself. Why do you ask?'

'Because I met her the other day, by accident, somewhere unexpected. There's a plot of land in Thagistri that my dad bought that's been a problem for lots of reasons. I went over to see if I could sort it out and while I was there I noticed a bench nearby, which has an inscription on it to Dad. I felt it was a strange part of Vekianos to erect a memorial to him and, cutting a long story short, she had it put there.'

'What a lovely thing for her to do. I must go over and take a look.'

'But don't you find it odd, Fotini?'

'Not really because that's where her family came from, and I know she works and lives in Athens, but I presume if she came back to the island that's where she would go.'

'Still, it made me wonder if perhaps she and Dad were a couple at some point?'

'Even if they were, you know your father, he wouldn't have talked about it as he liked to keep those things to himself.'

'You say that, but that clearly wasn't the case with Patricia as he always talked about her, even when I was very young. I always used to think it was just because he worked with her in England and we all know how much he loved to reminisce about his years in London, but I am beginning to think, now she's here living in one of the apartments, that she was a bigger part of his life over there than he let on.'

'I guess we'll never know,' Fotini said with a shrug. 'Now, can we talk about the refurbishment?'

Fotini wouldn't talk about Joanna or Patricia. This wasn't going the way Callisto had hoped and that was before they'd even started to discuss the villa. She would just have to try to turn the tables on Fotini; if her aunt wanted to be in control of this meeting, then she would let her lead it.

'I see you have your file and notebook ready, so

let's get started. As you and Dad planned things together, which part would you like to talk about first? The outside of the building, the decoration of the rooms, fixtures and fittings, the new bathrooms, the kitchen design...?'

'It's so long since Stelios and I talked about it that I've probably forgotten a lot of the details,' Fotini said smoothly.

Callisto smiled to herself. She suspected her aunt hadn't a clue what had been outlined, which would make it easier to save money. And if she saved money on this project there was no way Tassos could complain. This was it, she was on the way to getting her old life back.

Chapter 22

Lena was up early because she was excited for her first day at the new job. She knew it likely wouldn't be an easy day as there was a lot of cleaning to be done as the building had been closed up for quite a while, but she was ready for the challenge, and the sooner it was looking good the nearer it would be to opening up and serving customers. Looking at the time she saw she had half an hour before she had to meet Pavlos down at the restaurant. That would give her enough time to quickly nip into the villa and see Fotini, and find out how yesterday's meeting with Callisto had gone. Fotini had sent her a short text the night before saying she thought things would be ok, but Lena wanted more details of what had been discussed.

'Do you have time for a coffee before you meet Pavlos?' Fotini asked as she answered the door at the villa.

Lena agreed and the women sat down with their drinks in the kitchen.

'Are you excited to get started?' Fotini asked.

'Absolutely! And I'm looking forward to going out with Jacob after to celebrate. How did it go yesterday? She didn't ask to borrow money, I hope?'

'No, not at all, apparently the cash flow problem, as she called it, is now over and in the past so I don't think she will be knocking at your door again.'

'That's good news! And the refurbishment? Are you happy with the plans and when does it start?'

'She had some excellent points about how I have to look at the villa as a rental and as the biggest part of that will be the cleaning, everything should be simple and very straightforward, definitely not cluttered. She also suggested that rather than going for expensive pieces of furniture it was better to have things that wouldn't cost too much to replace if they got damaged or were broken, which makes sense to me. We talked about freshening up the outside with a coat of paint and painting all the rooms inside white as that way it would be cheap to touch up everything when things got marked.'

'Dad really thought of everything, didn't he?'

'Well, actually, I think they were all Callisto's ideas. You see, my darling, when your dad used to talk about his plans for the villa I didn't really pay a lot of attention because I didn't really want it to happen, because if it did, it would mean your dad would be gone, and that wasn't something I could face thinking about. So I blocked it out, pretended nothing was wrong and he wasn't ill and life was just going to carry on as normal. I just said yes and no in the right places as he talked me through his plans. But one thing I do remember was that he wanted to knock walls down and put a little extension on the back of the villa, and there was no mention of that when Callisto explained everything. The way she talked about it, the refurbishment isn't much more than a refresh, whereas your dad described it as a complete remodel.'

'That's interesting, Fotini, did you mention that to her?'

'No, I didn't. To be honest, by that point I was quite tired and my head was ready to explode with all the different rooms we'd covered. But as I sat pondering it last night I started to wonder if perhaps she has toned everything down so she can save money.'

'You may be right, but if you're happy with what she's described then won't that be ok? Something for you to think about. For now, I'm afraid I need to be going. I can't be late on my first day!'

'Of course, you head on your way and have fun. It's very exciting and not just for you but also for the whole town; we're getting the old beach café back!'

'Thank you, Fotini, it is. And remember, you don't have to do anything with the villa until you're ready. See you later!'

As Lena found herself almost running down the hill she thought back to that first day when she'd arrived back here on the island and saw the restaurant was all locked up. She had felt so sad, like her comfort blanket had been taken away from her, but now she was going to be part of the reopening.

The shutters on the side windows were still closed but the door on the decking overlooking the beach was open. She was bursting with excitement that turned into shock and horror when she stepped inside. What had happened to the inside of this beautiful café? All the character had disappeared and it looked like a hospital with its shiny white walls.

'You look like you've seen a ghost,' said Pavlos. 'I have to admit I did, too, when I first came to view the café. It was such a shock to see the building I had loved gone, disappeared behind all these white walls, but once I calmed down and looked a little closer I realised it didn't have to stay like this.'

'What do you mean?'

'Let's open the side windows and get some light and air into the place and then I'll tell you what I have planned.'

Between them they got the shutters open and then came back in and swung the windows wide. Lena thought it actually looked worse in the daylight, just a mass of white where all the old wood walls and shelves had been. The only thing she recognised was the flooring and that made her stop and take a deep breath. This was the floor she and her dad had walked on, played on, and when she was very small, danced together on.

'No sad faces allowed!' Pavlos called over to her. 'I know what will make you smile, come over here with me. I have a surprise for you and I think you will like it, at least I hope so. I need you to put your hand on this piece of wood and don't let it fall forward; you don't have to lift it, just support it, and it might help if you cross your fingers as well.'

'Pavlos, why am I supporting a wall and how can crossing my fingers help?'

'It's not a wall, just some white board hiding the wall, and I'm hoping once I unscrew it behind it will be those gorgeous walls covered in the old planks... Right, here goes. It looks like there are only eight screws so it shouldn't take long.'

Lena had her fingers and her legs crossed. She really wanted everything behind the boards to be just how she remembered it.

'I just need to get these last two screws out, are you still ok supporting it?'

'Yes, fine, can you see anything yet? Is everything as it should be back there?'

'I won't be sure until I come down the steps and slide the board out the way... Here we go, are you ready?'

Pavlos moved the steps and slid the board away from the wall and they both stood there, amazed. It was just as they remembered, the walls were full of character ... but also very dirty and dusty.

'Why do you think they covered up these gorgeous walls?' she asked.

'Because they wanted a modern restaurant, which would have been fine and successful somewhere else, but not here; that's why it didn't work. This needs to be a beach bar with snacks, not high quality cuisine, but hopefully now we can restore it to its former splendour and make it a success. But first we need to unscrew the rest of the boards and then start the huge task of cleaning. But I'd say it's looking better already, what do you think?'

'Absolutely! It's now getting exciting.'

The rest of the day was taken up removing all the false walls as some were easy to unscrew but others were a right pain and the job took a lot longer than they'd thought, but they both agreed they would stay until every single one was down so that they could get stuck into the cleaning straight away the next morning.

'Are you sure you don't mind staying to help?' Pavlos asked as the day wore on.

'No, it's not a problem. I'll just have to give Jacob a call and tell him I'll be late meeting him tonight.'

'Oh dear, he won't be happy.'

'Don't worry, he won't have a problem with it. Now, which board next?'

Lena could tell Pavlos was getting very frustrated with how long it was taking but the more he was trying to rush the slower it went. She glanced at the time and saw it was now nearly six o'clock. As she was meant to be meeting Jacob at seven-thirty she thought it best to give him a call. She went out onto the decking to do it, grateful for the fresh air. With all the dust in the restaurant it was so stuffy.

'Hi, Jacob, how are you? Have you had a good day?'

'I have, thanks, I'm ahead with my work so hopefully I'll be able to take a couple of days off in the next few weeks so we'll be able to go out, perhaps to Corfu or over to Parga. For tonight, I just need a shower and I'll be ready. Sorry, I haven't asked, how has your first day gone?'

'That's actually why I'm calling. We've had a bad day and we haven't got on as far as we thought we would have, so we're going to work a bit longer to get it all finished. Would you mind terribly if we rescheduled our dinner?'

There was a silence at the end of the phone. Lena had known Jacob would be disappointed but what else could she do? The work had to be finished by the morning.

'I'm really sorry,' she said, when it appeared no answer was forthcoming. 'Look, I need to be getting back inside as the job we're doing with the walls takes both of us and the quicker we get it done, the better. I'll give you a call tomorrow.'

She hung up, stepped back inside, and asked Pavlos where they would be tackling next.

'The electric screwdriver is dead,' Pavlos announced several hours later. 'It needs recharging before we can get the last two walls down so why don't I plug it in and then nip and get us some gyros from the restaurant up the road? Also, beer or wine?'

'Beer, please, and while you're gone I'll start brushing down the walls that we've uncovered. Thank goodness I'm not afraid of creepy crawlies!'

Pavlos was back within twenty minutes and they pulled two chairs out onto the decking to sit and eat their food.

'I can see why this didn't do very well as an evening restaurant. There's no one around. It's a shame for them, really, with all the work they put into it, but saying that it's to your advantage now.'

'Not just me, Lena, you as well. I know this beach café means as much to you as it does to me.'

They picked up their beer bottles and clinked them just as someone walked down the boardwalk, Pavlos saying, 'To our future! We have so much to look forward to, you and I. Oh, hi, Jacob! Come and join us. Can I get you a beer?'

'No, I'm ok, thanks. I just brought some food

down for Lena. I thought she might be hungry but it looks like she isn't... I'd best be going.'

Without waiting for a reply Jacob turned and left.

Chapter 23

Callisto was feeling pleased with herself. Fotini had agreed with the new plans Callisto had outlined for the villa, but saying that, they really were good and the villa would look fabulous and be the perfect holiday rental. The best part was that it would only cost slightly under two thirds of the original budget, which was a massive win for Callisto. She hoped today would herald another success as she was on a mission to discover if Joanna's family had sold Stelios the piece of land over in Thagistri.

First, she called Santiago to tell him it was full steam ahead with the villa project, letting him know that there would be some significant changes to the original plans. She also let him know she would be back in Athens the following week to go over everything, but in the meantime she wanted him to concentrate on sourcing material for the kitchen and two bathrooms that was fresh, contemporary, and most importantly, cheap. She was hoping some of their suppliers might have end-of-range stock that they wanted to shift.

She finally felt as though she had the fire back in her and she was moving back up that ladder.

She got the taxi to drop her right down next to the beach and she arranged to be picked up in three hours. As she stood looking out to sea the first thing that caught her eye was the bench, but she needed to block it out; today was business, there was no room for sentimental thoughts. She needed to be on her game.

Within minutes a truck pulled up and the chap got out and walked towards her.

'Hello, are you Callisto Drakos?'

'Yes, and you must be Sabbas. If you'd like to follow me?' She led him towards the tomato fields. 'Out of curiosity, did you notice the house on the road as you came down?'

'Yes, why?'

'That's where the nearest water and drainage pipes are, and so the quotes to get the services to this plot of land are eye-watering, but I think I have another solution and I wondered if you think it might be viable and at what cost. We need to just walk up this track a little bit, it's not too far.'

They eventually got to the old polytunnel and the fallen down house. Callisto turned to look at Sabbas. 'I know there are services to this house and the fields, and there will be water and drainage here somewhere, so I would like you to quote me for directing all the services from here down to the plot of land we've just come from.'

'It should just be a matter of finding the mains,' Sabbas said, nodding casually, as if he hadn't just said the magic words that could turn this entire project around for Callisto. 'I'll work out the exact cost and get it back to you within a couple of days. Was there anything else?'

'No, that was all for now,' she said.

Sabbas took his leave then, heading back down the track to where he'd parked, and Callisto stood in shocked silence for some time. In less than fifteen minutes she had found a solution to the biggest obstacle this project had faced, and now had at least two hours to kill before her taxi came back for her. She decided to pass the time by going back to the little street with the restaurant and shops, thinking perhaps she could get a coffee and a cake in at Makis' café.

'Welcome back!' he greeted her warmly as she stepped inside a short while later. 'Take a seat, what can I get you?'

'Just a coffee and a piece of your delicious spinach pie, if you have any.'

'Of course! If it wasn't for that pie I wouldn't have any customers.' He laughed. 'Are you here on business? I'm sorry to say that the studio has someone in it this week.'

'No, I'm just here for a few hours before heading back to Keriaphos.'

'I'm glad you popped in. The last time you were here you asked me about the old house and the tomato fields?'

'That's right,' Callisto agreed.

'Well then, you might be interested to know that they've been put on the market.'

'The land is up for sale?'

'Yes, the lady that owns it, Joanna Bouras, was here from Athens to sort it out right around the same time you were. Hold on, I'll just grab that pie for you.'

Now *this* was interesting...

Callisto had no interest in purchasing the old house or the land as it wouldn't be a good investment, but this could cause hiccups with getting the services she needed to her father's land. And Joanna was the owner? It looked like it wouldn't just be Tassos she needed to have a meeting with when she next visited Athens...

Back home later on, she kicked her shoes off and poured a glass of wine, thinking about how she was going to approach Joanna. Originally, she'd thought because the house was crumbling down and the land was empty that a token financial gesture would be all that was needed to connect to the services, but if Joanna was looking to get rid of the land altogether, that wouldn't be sufficient anymore. It really was one step forward and two back with every project she tried to fix!

Picking up her phone she saw she had an email from Tassos telling her he was coming to Vekianos to see his son and meet with her and Fotini about the villa refurbishment. Had she said two steps back? This felt more like ten! Having undoubtedly seen the original plans, Tassos would know how much she had changed them, and he wasn't likely to be happy with her. It was bad enough knowing he was keeping an eye on things from Athens, now he would be in the apartment above her!

Two hours – and more than a few glasses of wine – later she was feeling very sorry for herself. Moving to top up her glass, her eyes caught the mirror and for a brief second she thought she saw her dad looking back at her. And then she heard her dad's voice in her head saying, 'You've messed up, Callisto, but don't worry, you can sort it out.'

'No, I can't,' she answered aloud. 'What do I do, Dad? I've ruined everything you worked so hard for.'

But no answer was forthcoming.

Back on the balcony she felt drained. Her dream of successfully carrying on her father's dream was over. But that was the thing – all of this was Stelios' dream, not Callisto's. Thinking back over her life, all the way back to when she was at school, she couldn't remember having a dream for her life that was truly her own. Her teenage years had been focused on parties and boys and after leaving school she had gone to work with her dad because it was the easy option; she knew he wouldn't be strict and she could take time off when she wanted. As long as she looked like she was interested that would keep him happy and in his eyes she could do no wrong. Even when Tassos tried to tell him she was a burden on the business, Stelios would always take her side.

But all that freedom had come at a cost. It had

made her someone who was snappy and bossy, bluffing her way through meetings without ever actually taking the time to learn the business or take pride in her work.

Given that her dad was now gone, taking all of his years of expertise and wisdom with him, she was hit with an intense regret for the time she had wasted. It was certainly coming back to bite her now, where it seemed like nothing would ever go right again.

And now Tassos was on his way to the island. No doubt he had copies of the original plans and he would be determined to fulfil Stelios' wishes and protect Fotini from the evil niece. But Callisto wasn't evil, she was just... She couldn't think of a word to describe herself – well, not a nice one.

As dejection and shame washed over her, Callisto heard her dad's voice again, Stelios telling her that she was special, and she would come through this battle victorious.

'I'm with you,' he seemed to whisper.

'But I'm not special, Dad,' she whispered to the sky. 'I stopped being special the day you left us. I miss you so much and I'm so sorry.'

Chapter 24

As Lena made her way down to the restaurant in the early morning light, passing through the quiet town and greeting the few locals who were also up and about, she yawned and stretched. Her body was aching; she hadn't done so much physical work in years and there was still so much more to do to get the restaurant ready to open.

'How on earth did I think I could turn this restaurant around in just a couple of days?' Pavlos announced with a sigh as she walked through the door, not even pausing to greet her. 'I really feel like giving up. I thought it would be a simple case of taking those white false walls down and then behind it everything would be fine but instead we have old wooden walls that need to be cleaned and varnished and ... why are you laughing?' he asked.

'For a start, they don't need varnish, they need to be stained. Secondly, I was thinking the exact same! Well, I did until I walked through the door. I don't know, once in here I feel different. It's this place, this building, it has a draw to it, though I don't know if it's memories from my past or excitement for the future or some combination of the two. But regardless, there's no going back. It's time to get scrubbing so we can get this place looking a million dollars ... or at least looking a hundred euros.'

'That much, you think?' Pavlos joked.

'Come on, boss, less of the talk, more of the action.'

'Boss? Definitely not. If we do manage to get the place open I think we should be more of a partnership.'

'That would be great,' Lena said, grinning. 'Now, what's the plan for today? I had a thought that we should start at the back and work forward, clearing rubbish and cleaning, rather than going from one part of the building to the next with no real plan.'

'I think you're absolutely right.'

They quickly got started by moving all the tables and chairs to the very front of the building and piling them on top of each other. This left the rest of the restaurant empty so they could see exactly what they had to do. The kitchen area was fine, though in need of a deep clean, so the main task for the day would be the walls, brushing them down, washing them, sanding where necessary and then adding the stain.

Five hours later they were amazed at how much they had achieved.

'What a difference!' Pavlos said, looking around happily. 'I know we still have so much to do but we can finally see what we're working with. Are you as pleased as I am?'

'Yes, I'm feeling a lot better than I did earlier today. We'll need to scrub the floors next but first ... caffeine! Coffee will help get the job moving faster.'

'I can take a hint.' Pavlos laughed. 'I'll go grab some. Do you think a couple of pastries with the coffee would help us move even faster?'

'One hundred percent.'

'Right, give me five minutes and I'll nip to the bakery.'

Once Pavlos had gone Lena pulled up a chair and admired what they had done. For the first time she could see a light at the end of the tunnel, and she was feeling so much better.

'I've brought you one coffee, two pastries, and a visitor!' Pavlos said jovially, jolting Lena from her thoughts. She turned to see him stepping inside alongside her aunt.

'Fotini! What brings you down here?'

Fotini glanced around her warily. 'Oh my goodness, you both have so much to do.'

'Yes, but we're slowly getting there and once the coffee is drunk I will be like a whirlwind.' Lena and Pavlos shared a laugh.

'Well, I won't hold you up. I've just popped down to invite you both to the villa tonight. I'm having a little get-together before I move into the apartment. I know you're both so busy here so would around eight-thirty be ok for dinner? Trisha and Jacob are both coming as well. I also invited Callisto, but she said she was busy.'

'A party! That will be lovely, Fotini, and by that time Lena and I will be glad to be able to stop,' Pavlos said.

'You said Jacob will be joining?' Lena asked. 'Did you have to persuade him or was he keen? Never mind,' she hastily added. 'That look on your face says it all. You had to twist his arm, didn't you?'

'Nothing of the sort! Actually, I didn't give him the opportunity to say no. I told him he would be there and he would enjoy himself!' Fotini laughed. 'I'd better head off now. I'm stopping the both of you working. See you tonight and please don't worry, Lena, everything will be fine.'

With that Fotini was gone and once the coffee had been drunk it was right back to the work.

The shower she'd had as soon as she arrived home had woken Lena up and helped with her aching bones. Now she was ready to party and she was looking forward to seeing Jacob.

As she walked down the path away from the apartment building she glanced back and saw that Callisto's light was on. Did that mean she wasn't busy and might decide to pop over to the villa after all? If so, it could make for an uncomfortable evening...

'Hold the gate!' she heard someone call and she turned to find Jacob walking towards her. He looked happy and the sight instantly brought a smile to her face.

'I can't wait to hear all about the restaurant,' he said as he fell into step next to her and they made their way to Fotini's villa. 'How are things going?'

'One word, Jacob: slowly. But I can tell you more about it at the party.'

'Party? I just thought it was a little get-together.'

'It is, but I thought "party" sounded better, more exciting.'

'Come in, you two,' Fotini greeted them warmly. 'Head out onto the patio. Trisha and Pavlos are already out there. Can I get either of you wine or beer?'

Lena and Jacob said wine and walked around the villa to the patio, Lena wondering how Jacob would be with Pavlos.

'Hello, you two!' Trisha smiled. 'Pavlos has been telling me all about the restaurant. It sounds like it's been quite the undertaking with all that dust behind the walls.'

'Dust isn't a strong enough word for it, Trisha. I promise you've never seen anything like it! But we have made a lot of progress today, haven't we, Pavlos?'

'A bit, but another dozen pairs of hands would come in handy. So if you happen to know of a dozen people looking to do some gruelling manual labour, send them my way,' Pavlos joked.

'I can lend you one pair of hands, if you like,' Jacob offered.

'Are you serious?' Pavlos asked.

'Yep. I need to finish off something tomorrow but the day after I'm free because I've not received my next project. As I'm at a loose end until it arrives I would be more than happy to help you both.'

Lena was taken aback. Where had this Jacob turned up from? One day he's jealous of her being with Pavlos and now he's offering Pavlos his services!

Pavlos enthusiastically thanked Jacob as Fotini joined them and passed out wine.

'Who's hungry?' she asked. 'I have tzatziki, fresh bread, and salad, and then to follow I've made a spanakopita. Trisha, would you be kind enough to give me a hand to bring it out please?'

Trisha nodded and followed Fotini back into the villa.

'I'm glad the lads seem to be getting along ok,' Fotini said once they were alone.

'Me too,' Trisha agreed. 'I thought there might have been a bit of friction but Jacob has offered to go and help with getting the restaurant ready.'

'Oh that's good news! I'm glad that's one worry ticked off the list.'

'I presume another is moving into the apartment?' Trisha offered gently.

'That will be quite straightforward to be honest. All I have to do is fill the fridge as everything else I'll need is already there. The thing is, all my friends keep asking if I'm upset or worried about moving, to the point that I'm starting to wonder if I should be. Life is going to be so much easier as I'll have less to worry about and – best of all – more time on my hands because there won't be so much cleaning to do.'

Trisha could see Fotini's point but she found herself wondering who the other woman was trying to convince: Trisha ... or herself? Something told Trisha that Fotini was possibly not as happy about the move as she was claiming.

'You really do have a good attitude to life,

Fotini,' she hedged, trusting that Fotini would open up to her when she felt ready to do so. 'A young outlook. I was a lot like that when I was working in the hotel. For more years than I can remember I was always the oldest member of the team, but I was never made to feel I was, and I certainly didn't act like it!' Trisha laughed. 'It's the same here with Lena and the lads. I'm comfortable.'

'So does that mean you're staying instead of moving back to London?'

'I think so. One thing that needs ticking off my list first is talking to Callisto and clearing the air. I've done nothing wrong.'

'Of course you haven't! I'm glad you're starting to think like that and I'll be over the moon if you do stay. As for Callisto, I suspect she has a lot more on her mind at the moment than who got which apartment.'

'What do you mean?'

'I've had a phone call from Tassos to say he's coming over to make sure Stelios' plans are carried out exactly as he wanted them to be.'

'I got the impression from you and Jacob that Tassos was the company accountant. Why is he getting involved with the building work?'

'Reading between the lines, I suspect that he doesn't trust Callisto, and sadly I have to agree. But before it all kicks off I need to move into the new apartment. That way I'll have somewhere to escape to when the shouting and arguing starts!'

Chapter 25

Callisto hadn't been out of the apartment for a couple of days, but it was getting to the point where she needed to buy milk and some food. The one thing she *wouldn't* be buying was wine. After the other night she never wanted to drink again; she was still feeling the after effects and it hadn't solved any of her problems. Her life was still a mess and it was on the way to getting worse with Tassos' imminent arrival.

As if she'd summoned him with her thoughts, her phone beeped and Tassos' name flashed up on the screen. She knew there was no point putting off speaking with him, and that he probably just wanted to arrange a day and time to meet at the villa, so she needed to ignore her unease and get it over with. The sooner it was sorted the better.

'Hi, Tassos, how can I help you?' she answered.

'Hello, Callisto. I wanted to let you know I will be on Vekianos the day after tomorrow and I'm staying for a few days so I can fit around your schedule for the site meeting. Jacob told me Fotini is moving into the apartment today so hopefully we can start quickly. Secondly, I've been contacted by a company that is interested in buying the apartment in central Athens.'

'But it's not finished and not even on the market yet.'

'Apparently they're willing to take it as-is. I'm as shocked as you are, but it should just be a case of working out if it will be more profitable to hold on to it and finish the project, or get shot of it. I'll email you all the details and you can look over what's been spent so far and then we can talk it over when I get to Vekianos. If they want it that badly they can wait a few days.'

'Thank you, Tassos, I'll review the numbers and will get working on a spreadsheet. I have nothing planned for the days you're here so whenever you want to discuss the villa I can be available.'

Unloading the central Athens apartment would certainly put money back into the bank account right away but was that a good business move? Surely the company would make more by finishing it and – hopefully – prompting a bidding war between prospective buyers? She was glad of the distraction she knew the work would provide as it gave her something to focus on and would help to fill her day. Before she started, though, she really needed to go and buy some food ... but that would mean braving that Patricia woman and her aunt as she'd seen them chatting down by the pool earlier, in between Fotini's trips back and forth to the villa. She needed to pick her moment carefully and she needed to make herself look half decent.

Showered and dressed and looking out the balcony doors a short while later, she saw she was in luck as there was no one down at the pool. This was her opportunity.

Once outside and walking down the lane she breathed a sigh of relief. It felt so good to be out in the fresh air and not stuck in the apartment.

A while later, she had managed to get everything she needed and had carried it back up the hill. Now came the dangerous part: getting through the gate without bumping into anyone. She placed some of her shopping on the ground so that she could get her key out of her bag and unlock the gate, but before she had time to think it swung open and Patricia was stood before her.

'Would you like a hand with your shopping?' she

offered.

'No, I'm fine, thank you,' Callisto said guardedly.

'You must be Callisto. I'm Trisha, but then I suspect you already knew that.'

Callisto wasn't sure how to respond and she couldn't make a quick escape because of all her shopping bags. She decided to try and calm the tension with humour.

'And no doubt you've heard all about me: the evil daughter.'

'I don't think anyone thinks you're evil. Perhaps "misunderstood" is a better word for it? How about you let me make up my own mind for myself? Shall we say around seven o'clock, up in my apartment over a glass of wine?'

'I'm sorry but I can't make tonight—'

'Well then how about tomorrow or the following day?' Trisha interrupted. 'I think we need to talk because this avoidance game we're playing is starting to screw me up a little and I don't like that feeling.'

Callisto knew Trisha was right. They did need to have a conversation at some point, and there was no denying she had an awful lot of questions for this woman.

'Ok, seven o'clock tonight it is. But I won't be able to stay very long.'

'I'll look forward to seeing you then,' Trisha said happily.

As she struggled to her apartment with the shopping, Callisto couldn't really grasp what had just happened. This Patricia woman had said she was screwed up about their situation? Well, that made two of them. Hopefully their chat tonight would help clear some things up.

Shopping packed away, it was time to run the numbers on the Athens apartment to see whether their best option was to sell now or later, but it didn't take long for her to realise that she was out of her depth and she needed Tassos' advice.

Switching off her laptop it was time to focus on the other matter in hand – her meeting with Patricia. Thinking about the older woman and the fact that she had been given the apartment that Callisto had thought she would be living in, she had a sudden thought: no one could sell their apartments because of the stipulations in her dad's will, but as far as she knew there was nothing saying they couldn't swap around. And if Patricia was only using it as a holiday home, she really didn't need such a big apartment. Perhaps that could be the answer?

Taking a deep breath Callisto knocked on Patricia's door and was greeted warmly.

'Come in! I thought we could sit out on the roof terrace. Would you like red or white wine?' Trisha asked.

'I'm ok, thank you, nothing for me.'

'But you must; I've invited you for a drink after all! Please have something.'

'Ok, red then,' Callisto acquiesced.

Before she knew it they were out the door and onto the terrace and she hadn't really had any chance to see anything of the apartment.

'You've made it lovely out here with the furniture and the plants. Last time I was here it was still just the concrete roof.'

'I've actually done nothing; this is how I found it, and it shocks me every day how perfect everything is. In fact, the only thing I've added to the apartment at all is what I brought with me in my suitcase. It really is completely my taste.'

'Yes, mine is the same. It's just how I would have furnished it myself, right down to the china and the glassware.'

'Callisto, I think we need to address the elephant in the room and get it over with. It was a complete shock to me to learn Stelios had gifted this flat to me. I feel very uncomfortable about it and I've been told how much you wanted to be up here so I'm sorry. The only reason I keep coming up with is that he chose this one for me because he didn't want to favour you over Lena or vice versa.'

'I suspect it's his way of showing me he's still the boss even though he's not here. I'm sure he's having a good laugh about it wherever he is,' Callisto said, though more to herself than to Trisha.

'I couldn't begin to imagine what his thought process was. I hadn't seen him for many years, sadly.'

'I'm surprised you'd lost touch. He always talked about you, your name turning up in conversation whenever he talked about his time working in London, and the frequency of his reminiscing increased after he became ill. That said, I hadn't realised how much he really must have loved you until I found out you were here.'

Trisha teared up and Callisto rushed to apologise.

'I'm sorry, I didn't mean to upset you! The whole situation is all very strange. Who builds an apartment block and then gifts the units to their family and friends? It's bonkers! Now you're stuck with an apartment in a foreign country, and to make it worse, none of us can do anything about it for ten years as he has stated we can't sell the apartments. The whole thing is crazy and very stupid.'

'It's not that crazy to do something nice for people though, is it? I know I'm conflicted about it but from what I've seen and been told, Pavlos is very excited about being here as he can now open the beach restaurant, Fotini has said she will be happy not having a large villa to look after as she's getting older, and Lena, well ... she is young and the apartment has given her independence, which I believe is a good thing.'

'How about you, Trisha? You said you're conflicted? Has this situation caused you problems?'

'It's messed my head up for sure as I've had my past come back – all my mistakes, my selfishness... To be truthful, all I've thought about for the last forty plus years has been myself, and it was only when I came here that I realised how many people I've hurt by doing so.'

Callisto was shocked. This wasn't the woman she had thought Trisha would be.

'When you said you upset people, was one of those people my dad?'

'I suspect so. He wanted me to stay here with him on Vekianos, but I ask myself: would he have been happy and so successful if I had? There's a part of me that feels I should have stayed, but then, if I had, you and your sister wouldn't have been born and the two of you were a big part of his life. I just know you brought him every happiness.'

'Not *every* happiness, I don't think. He wasn't that happy with my mum or Lena's mum, and then there's whatever he did or didn't have with Joanna. No, I think we both know there was only one love of my dad's life and that was you, Trisha.'

Before Trisha could respond, Callisto rose to her feet. 'Thank you for the drink but I need to be getting off as I have some business things to tie up. I'm glad we've chatted though, and I really hope you manage to come to terms with everything.'

'No, thank you, Callisto. I know this wouldn't have been easy for you so I really appreciate you coming up and chatting with me. If it's ok, I'd like to offer you some advice. Don't end up like me, sacrificing family and friends for a career. If you do, you'll come to find that, in the end, it really wasn't worth all those wasted years that could have been spent with the people you love and cared about.'

Chapter 26

Lena was smiling to herself as she came in from the balcony. She couldn't believe what she had just seen: Jacob and Pavlos walking out the gate together, on their way down to the restaurant. Perhaps today was the day *she* would be the one in the way, she thought wryly.

Before she followed them down the hill she popped upstairs to have a coffee with Trisha.

'Come in!' Trisha greeted her warmly. 'Can I get you something? Coffee or juice?'

'Coffee, please,' Lena said gratefully. 'I can't stay long as I need to get down to the restaurant, but I wanted to hear how your meeting went with Callisto.'

'Let's sit inside so that we won't have to whisper,' Trisha said as she ushered Lena to one of the plush sofas. 'Not that I think she would hear us from up here, but you never know.'

'I wouldn't be surprised if she's got all the apartments bugged!' Lena said, only half joking.

'I doubt it. To be honest, in the short time we spent together I felt a little sorry for her ... actually, more than a little. She's definitely hurt from all the business with the apartment block, and I can understand that. There she is running her dad's company and she comes to find he kept all of this a secret from her.'

'I'm shocked you've fallen for her sob story, Trisha. She's coming across like that on purpose so you'll feel sorry for her, and then she'll go in for the kill and ask if she can swap apartments with you.'

'Well, she can ask, but she won't be getting it.'

'So you're here to stay?' Lena asked, knowing

hope was evident in her tone.

'I think so, but I have a lot to sort out first. But before I get into all that I'm looking forward to my sister coming to stay for a couple of weeks. She hasn't agreed just yet but we spoke on the phone yesterday and I'm sure with another few conversations like that I can persuade her to come for a little holiday.'

'That would be lovely! Now I best get a move on or else the boys will think I'm slacking and I can't have that.'

Lena rushed down the hill, stopping at the bakery for takeaway coffees and a few pastries for the lads. Her theory was that if they were full of sugar they would work faster and get more done. It helped that there was now an extra pair of hands to make everything a lot quicker.

'Sorry I'm late! I had some family business to—' Lena stopped in shock. 'Oh my goodness! You've got on so well. I can't believe how fast you've put the stain on; it really brings out the grain in the walls.'

'You and Pavlos did the hard work of preparing the wood so my bit has been easy,' Jacob said with a shrug.

'Are you pleased, Pavlos? Is it the look you wanted?' Lena asked.

'Definitely. It looks so natural and once it's done it will look like it's been like this for years. Do I smell coffee?' Pavlos asked hopefully.

'Yes, you do, and pastries, too. That sounds like your phone beeping, Jacob.'

'It is. I've been waiting for a message from my dad to let me know what time he's arriving... Looks like he's catching the five o'clock boat from Corfu so he won't be at the apartment until going on for seven-thirty. I was going to ask, Lena, would you like to join us for dinner? You would be doing me a huge favour.'

'I'd love to. And if we need to be gone from here by six-thirty, I best get some work done. Where do you want me to start, Pavlos?'

'There's a brush over there and another pot of stain. You could start by the door and work your way in so that we meet in the middle before the end of the day.'

Lena grabbed the supplies and got to work.

Lena was rushing to get ready. She had stayed down at the restaurant longer than she had intended, but it was worth it considering how much they'd achieved. The walls would likely be finished tomorrow and the place was really starting to look like the restaurant Pavlos envisioned.

As she took a quick shower she thought about the fact that she wasn't really looking forward to the evening. She knew Tassos and Jacob didn't get on that well and she would probably have to keep the conversation going. Thankfully she had the new restaurant to talk about, and the apartment.

She was trying to think of when, apart from her dad's funeral, she had last seen Tassos. It must have been in Athens, that time when he came to her dad's office while she was visiting him.

She made her way to Jacob's apartment – Tassos' apartment, technically speaking – and Tassos and Jacob greeted her warmly.

'Where are we going to eat?' she asked.

'There's a pasta restaurant down the hill, just past the beach, that Dad says he remembers from years ago. Would that be ok?'

'Oh yes! That sounds great to me. You must have gone there with my dad; he loved it,' she said to Tassos. 'Shall we get going?'

Lena and Tassos chatted as they made the short walk to the restaurant and she couldn't help but notice that Jacob seemed completely different to the man she had come to know. He looked uncomfortable and was so quiet as they sat down at the table.

Lena ordered wine for the group and they all looked at the menu in silence. Once the food was ordered – each chose a pasta with garlic bread – Lena tried to get the conversation going.

'So, Tassos, what do you think of the apartments? Did my dad do a good job?'

'He did and I know he threw everything he had at them and enjoyed the process so much, from the very beginning right until the end.'

'I'm just so sorry he didn't get to see the final result with all the furniture and bits and pieces he chose. Did you feel when you walked into your flat that the furnishings were all things you would have chosen for yourself?'

'Yes, I did, especially the artwork. It's all spot on, he knew me so well.'

'I felt the same way when I first saw mine. Have you decided how long you're going to be staying? I know Fotini is very excited you're here.'

'I'm looking forward to seeing her. I'm not sure how long just yet. It will depend on work.'

'Did Jacob tell you I got a job in a restaurant? I'm going to be working for Pavlos, my dad's godson, and we've been busy getting the place ready. Jacob's been a big help with all his hard work.'

'So Jacob has actually done some physical labour? That's a first.'

She decided to ignore the barb for now, but if Tassos kept having a go at his son she wouldn't be able to stop herself from speaking up for Jacob, who didn't look keen to do it for himself.

'What role will you be undertaking at the restaurant?' Tassos asked.

'I'll be a waitress, serving drinks and snacks to the visitors.'

'Just a waitress?' Tassos blurted, then immediately looked apologetic. 'Sorry, that wasn't meant to come out like that. I just think you're capable of a lot more than that. I know your dad was so proud of what you achieved in your role at the bank.'

Tassos' judgement took her by surprise and she realised it wasn't just Jacob who needed to be wary of the older man's opinions. But if he was going to have a go at her, she wasn't going to keep her thoughts to herself.

'Yes, *just* a waitress, though a very happy one. And isn't that the most important thing? To enjoy what you're doing?'

'It's nice, for sure, but you also need to have ambition and challenge yourself. Do you not have any interest in getting involved with your dad's company? You could work alongside Callisto.'

'From what I can see, there isn't much of a company left if she's having to ask me for money and trying to put off doing the refurbishment of the villa.'

'It's merely a cash flow problem that will soon be sorted. Your sister has grand ambitions and isn't afraid to do whatever is necessary to achieve her goals.'

Lena was shocked. Was he defending Callisto? And was she mistaken or did his face sort of light up when he said her half-sister's name?

'If that's the case, then why have you had to come and make sure she's doing what my dad had planned for the villa? I got the impression from Fotini you were here because Callisto isn't to be trusted.'

'Stelios asked me to oversee things so that's what I'm doing. Oh look, here comes the food,' Tassos said, clearly eager to end this line of questioning.

Lena could see Jacob looked uncomfortable and to be honest she wasn't feeling that great herself anymore. Thankfully they could now concentrate on the food and take a break from the conversation.

'Is it as good as you remember?' Lena asked, after a while.

'Absolutely.'

'There was something I wanted to ask, do you have any thoughts on who might have been gifted the final apartment? Fotini and I are both very intrigued to know who my dad would have given it to. I think it's Joanna, the lawyer, but have you any thoughts?'

'No, not at all, but it's strange it's still empty after all these weeks. Perhaps I could ask if I can use it while I'm here,' he said thoughtfully, almost to himself. 'It would give me more space as you can't move in mine at present, with all of Jacob's stuff everywhere.'

'That's just how it is when you work from home. I'm sure if you didn't have your office you would be like Jacob and have to have "stuff", as you call it, piled up in your home.'

'Work from home? What Jacob does isn't work, it's a hobby. Pens, pencils, paper everywhere... It's like a classroom in that apartment.'

'Dad, I need all of that to do my job and earn my living.'

'Your living? That's pocket money, Jacob. You live rent free in my apartment, you don't pay bills ... no, your so-called wage is nothing more than pin money.'

Lena had had enough.

'I have to disagree with you, Tassos,' she said as she grabbed her phone. 'Let's put Jacob's name into the search engine, shall we?' She pulled up the results and showed them to Tassos and Jacob. 'Congratulations, Jacob, you've risen to number four on the bestsellers chart.'

'What is this?' Tassos asked, clearly confused.

'I would think that, what with being Jacob's dad, you would have been checking his progress with his books.'

Lena could see Jacob was embarrassed but she was on a roll now and she was determined to make her point.

'How about we look at the US charts? Here they are ... not one, not two, but *three* of Jacob's books in the top one hundred children's books. Can you believe it? Out of all the millions of books available in America, Jacob has three of the top one hundred bestsellers. That's such a huge achievement and so exciting! No wonder so many authors want you to illustrate their work,' she said to Jacob, smiling supportively.

She was pleased to see that she had put Tassos in his place.

'You've never mentioned any of this, Jacob,' he said to his son, looking visibly uncomfortable.

'Oh, it's nothing,' Jacob said, as though trying to shrug off Lena's praise. 'You could look again tomorrow and they will have fallen out of the charts. It's probably just a one-off that I happen to have three listed right now.'

'He's being modest, Tassos,' Lena argued. 'The books stay there for weeks. All those years of hard work have paid off and you should be proud of what your son has accomplished. Now, I hope you both won't mind but I don't think I'll stay for dessert or another drink. I'm exhausted and have another busy day tomorrow.'

As she kissed both Jacob and Tassos goodbye, she hoped she had laid the necessary groundwork for a conversation that would carry on well into the night. There was much the two men needed to say to one another.

Chapter 27

Callisto took a deep breath as she stood outside Fotini's villa. She was as ready as she ever would be to meet Tassos and her aunt, but she wasn't looking forward to it.

Fotini answered Callisto's knock with a wary smile and the two women stepped inside to wait for Tassos to join them.

'I met Trisha yesterday,' Callisto blurted into the awkward silence that had quickly settled over them. 'She seems nice, not at all like I imagined she would be.'

'What did you imagine?' Fotini asked.

'To be honest I'm not really sure. Have you seen much of Lena? I saw her heading out with Jacob earlier. Are they a couple then? I've been so busy I haven't had time to catch up with her.'

'I think they are. You likely saw them headed down to the beach café. Pavlos has bought it and they're all working together to do it up. That sounds like the gate,' Fotini said, a look of relief washing over her face. 'It must be Tassos.'

Fotini ushered Tassos inside and offered him a coffee, which he gratefully accepted.

Callisto took a deep breath, prepared for Tassos to make a point of putting her in her place in front of Fotini, likely with a big smile on his face.

'So,' Tassos began, once they were all settled. 'Let's talk through Stelios' plans for the villa.'

'Do we need to walk around and go through each room?' Fotini asked.

'I don't think so. I have the plans Stelios drew up so we can just go through them and check each item off so the three of us know we're all on the same page.'

Tassos laid out the plans so everyone could see them.

'Let's start with the big things first. Can you see ok from there, Fotini?' he checked.

'Yes, I'm fine, thank you.'

'Now, the major work will be taking these two big walls down to make one big space for the new kitchen and dining area.'

'Oh no, Tassos, I'm not getting rid of walls,' Fotini announced.

'But that's what Stelios wanted.'

'He might have, but it's not happening. No, the walls will not be coming down.'

Callisto was stunned. She had never seen her aunt like this before, so in control.

'But why not? It's what's best for the villa,' Tassos argued.

'Says who? I'm the one who will have to keep it clean between visitors and it will be far easier with individual rooms rather than one big space. I know my brother was right most of the time, but he isn't in this situation. I'm happy to see the plumbing, electrics, and decoration modernised, but the walls are staying where they are.'

'Please help me here, Callisto,' Tassos entreated. 'You know your dad's vision for the villa was right.'

'My dad was right most of the time, yes, but on this occasion perhaps he wasn't. I think if he was here now and Fotini put this argument to him he would have to agree with her that a rental property has different needs than a family home.'

'I still think Stelios knew what he was doing. Perhaps if I run through the plans in a little more detail you'll be able to better see the big picture, Fotini.'

Callisto could see he wasn't prepared to back down but she knew from years of experience that her aunt wasn't one to lose. She wanted to smile at the fact that her day had suddenly been turned around completely.

After about half an hour Callisto could see Tassos was ready to give up and concede.

'Look, Fotini, why don't I leave the plans here and you can take your time looking at them? I don't expect you to change your mind, but I want you to make sure you make the right decision for the villa, and more importantly, for you.'

'Ok, it's a deal. I will take the decision very seriously, I promise you.'

'I just want you to be happy,' Tassos said kindly. 'Now', he added, turning to Callisto, 'we need to get down to business with the Athens offer and the Thagistri plot. Where would you like to chat about it? Shall we walk down into the town, have a little lunch, and figure out our next move?'

'Actually, Tassos, do you like spinach pie? Because if you do, we could get a taxi over to Thagistri to eat and then see that bit of land, killing two birds with one stone. Also, you might be interested to hear what I've recently found out about it.'

'That sounds a good plan, but before we go, is there anything else you wanted to ask, Fotini?'

'No, I don't think so. Go off and have fun, the two of you.'

Fun wasn't the word Callisto would use and looking at Tassos she saw that he was embarrassed by the suggestion as well.

They said goodbye to Fotini and waited outside for the taxi. Callisto was hoping it wouldn't be too long as once the car arrived the taxi driver would likely not stop talking, which would make things a lot easier.

Thankfully, Callisto was right and the taxi driver

– who remembered picking Tassos up from the harbour yesterday – didn't stop chatting the whole way to Thagistri.

Once they'd arrived she paid the taxi driver and they headed into Makis' café and found a corner table.

'Hello again, Callisto,' Makis greeted her. 'Nice to have you back.'

'I've made an excuse just to come over here for the spinach pie, and of course your gorgeous coffee.' She smiled.

'I'll have the same, please,' Tassos chimed in.

'Great! I wish all customers were as straightforward as you two.'

As Makis went off to get everything Callisto got out a file from her bag.

'Now, Tassos, what are we going to do about the Athens apartment? I would value your advice.'

'I do think that as long as it doesn't look like you'll be making a loss, it would be good to offload it now. The buyer is very keen so I just need to go through your figures to work out the legal fees and taxes associated with the sale. By the end of today, or early tomorrow at the latest, we'll have a clearer picture of the total financial impact.'

'There you go, two coffees and two pies. Enjoy!' Makis said, delivering the food with a flourish.

'If you don't enjoy this, Tassos, I will … well, I don't know exactly. But I'm sure you'll like it. Go on, dive in and tell me how good it is.'

She waited for him to bite into the piece of pie.

'You're right,' he announced a moment later. 'This is so tasty! What a find. How did you stumble across this place?'

'By chance. I came over for a couple of days to assess the land and came across the restaurant by accident.'

'So what was it you wanted to tell me about the

land?'

'It was Joanna Bouras' family's land. I think my dad bought it through her, and I think it might be because they had some kind of relationship.'

'I don't know a lot about the relationship but Stelios did mention that she'd lost her parents. Maybe he was just helping her out financially after that happened?'

'Maybe. I've got good news though. I think there could be a solution to our water and drainage problem that doesn't involve having to close roads and go through other properties, but it will mean getting permission from Joanna or whoever she sells the rest of her land to. It'll be easiest for me to show you but there's no rush, we can have another coffee first.'

Sitting there, enjoying their lunch, Callisto felt she was looking at a different Tassos. Was it because they weren't in an office, or was it something to do with being away from Athens and here on Vekianos?

Not wanting to dwell on it, she asked him about his dinner with Jacob and Lena the night before. She'd seen them all leaving together.

'Your sister put me in my place!' he said, though he was smiling. 'I deserved it. You see, I'm a little like you in a way. I'm snappy and think I always know best, but your sister pointed out I was wrong about something important. I've always said that Jacob was wasting his time drawing when he could follow me into the business, and last night over dinner I was having the odd dig at him about it when Lena, shall we say ... took the bull by the horns and made me feel the size of an ant. She didn't mince her words as she pointed out that Jacob's work was in the list of top selling children's books all around the world.'

'Oh my goodness. You must be so proud.'

'Yes, I am very proud ... now. But the sad thing

is that I didn't know, I had to have it pointed out to me. I've never recognised the success my son was having because I always thought I knew best. I was far too much up myself to even ask about his work – or life, come to that.'

'Oh dear, but at least you know now, and all the not knowing can be put behind you. Bridges can be built.'

'Yes, and we have started ... all thanks to your sister. She walked out the restaurant after putting me in my place, and Jacob and I talked – really talked – for the first time in years. I asked questions, and even more importantly, I listened. We were actually up until three o'clock this morning looking at Jacob's work online. To think my son has his name on the front of bestselling books... It's incredible.'

'I'm very happy for you both,' Callisto said, finding she really meant it. Seeing that Tassos looked like he could use a minute to compose himself, she suggested they walk the long way around on the road before she showed him her potential solution, to give Tassos a full overview of the situation.

As they got to the front of the house on the road they both looked over the little wall.

'This is where the initial research said that the water and drainage pipes for our property would have to come from, which would mean cutting across part of their land.'

'Do you know who owns the house?' Tassos asked.

'No, the land the house is built on was sold by Joanna's family many years ago. If it had still been owned by Joanna things could possibly be a lot easier.'

They carried on a little further until they crossed into the car park and then stepped onto the beach.

'What a view! It really is stunning.'

'It is,' Callisto agreed as she led him towards the four posts that marked their plot of land. 'Shall we head back to where I think the solution to the problem is?'

'Lead on,' he said.

They started up the track and before long they came to the old polytunnels.

'Here we are. It's all fallen down now but the fact the building was here means there is definitely water and drainage running to this plot that we could tap into. I've spoken to a local specialist and he should be coming back to me with a quote any day now.'

'If the utilities for our land could be connected here that would save a small fortune,' Tassos agreed, 'but that would depend on getting the necessary permissions. How far up this path do we have to go until we're back in the town?'

'It takes less than ten minutes. Come, I'll show you,' she said, leading the way.

'What are you thinking, Tassos?' she asked as they walked. She could see him thinking it through critically.

'Lots of things. One being that perhaps not listening to my son wasn't the only mistake I've made. Perhaps I also should have listened to your father. I don't think this was the spur of the moment purchase I always thought it was. I think he knew exactly what he was doing.'

Chapter 28

Callisto was up early having a coffee in front of her laptop. She was still trying to figure out what she should do with the Athens apartment. She was also thinking back to yesterday over in Thagistri with Tassos. The biggest shock to her was how much she had enjoyed spending the day with him, the one person she had never seen eye to eye with. It made it hard to remember why she didn't like him, after all, they had never had a specific argument or a falling out that she could name as being significant enough to cause a rift, and they were of a similar age – he was just five years older than her – so they had plenty in common.

She switched the laptop off. One of the first things she had planned for the day was to go over to see Fotini, to see if she had any questions – or second thoughts – now that she had had time to study Stelios' plans for the renovation.

When Fotini greeted her at the villa's door by announcing that she hadn't changed her mind about not having any walls knocked down, Callisto breathed a sigh of relief.

Even though she had her answer, she found herself agreeing when her aunt offered her a coffee, and in no time at all the two women were settled outside on the terrace.

'Did you have fun yesterday?' Fotini asked.

'You mean my meeting with Tassos? I wouldn't say it was "fun", exactly, but we did have some lovely spinach pie and made steps forward on a couple of projects. How are you feeling about the villa project? Are you ready to move out for good now that you've made your decision about the work you want done?'

Callisto could see she had caught her aunt off guard as she looked a little panicky.

Before Fotini could respond they heard a voice calling out a greeting, and Lena stepped outside to join them. Fotini took the opportunity to escape by offering to make Lena a coffee, and Lena settled in the chair next to Callisto.

'I hear you've been busy with Pavlos' new restaurant,' Callisto said cordially. 'It sounds very exciting. I'm really pleased for you.'

'Thank you! I think I'll enjoy it and Pavlos and I seem to get on well together in a professional capacity.'

'It seems it's given you new confidence. Tassos thought he'd met the wrong sister the other night. I hear you put him in his place and good on you for doing so. I know that, in the end, he was very grateful you did it.'

'I just hate seeing people getting put down for no reason and though Jacob is doing so well with his work, he would be the last person to sing his own praises, so I had to do it for him.'

'There you go, Lena,' Fotini said as she carefully handed over a very full mug. 'I hope the coffee is strong enough for you.'

'It will be, thank you, Fotini. I called in to see if you needed any help taking the last of your bits over to the apartment.'

'No, I'm fine, it's only a few bits of clothing and what food I have left in the fridge and cupboard. I'll probably do that tomorrow. Now, isn't this nice? The three of us together? I wonder what your father would say. I often thought it was so strange we were all kept separate, not so much when he was well and working in different places, but certainly when he started to get ill. It should have been a time when we were all together with him.'

'That would have been nice, don't you think, Callisto? Since being here, I have to admit I've wondered what it would have been like to grow up with you in my life. Why do you think he kept us so separate from one another?'

'I don't know. And I do see your point, Fotini, but I think it's kind of nice that we all got to spend quality time alone with him while he was ill, don't you?'

'I must admit it was so lovely having him here at the villa, very special. We had happy times talking about our childhood here and growing up together on the island. Those conversations are special memories that I cherish.'

Callisto sensed there was something not quite right. From the way Fotini spoke about the villa it seemed like she was dreading leaving it. She needed to find out for sure how her aunt felt but she knew she couldn't go in all guns blazing. This was a sensitive situation, and needed to be eased into.

'And now, with the apartments he's left us, it's like he's encouraging us to make new memories, isn't it? Though how he knew this would all work out the way he'd planned, I'll never know. If I'm honest, if it wasn't for a few problems with the company I wouldn't be here at all. And I still don't understand why he thought you would want to move from this gorgeous villa into an apartment, Aunt Fotini. This has been your home for so many years and, like you said, it holds so many memories.' She could see she had hit the nail on the head because Fotini looked like she was going to burst into tears.

Callisto found herself rushing to try and make her feel better.

'It would have made more sense if he just updated the villa to make it easier for you to live in, just like what's going to happen shortly, and then left you the apartment to rent out and bring in an income. Or am I just being silly thinking like that?'

That was it, the tears started to come.

'I'm sorry, I don't mean to get upset, but you're right. I should have said something at the time, but your father was ill and I didn't want to upset him. I'm not saying the apartment isn't beautiful, he put so much care and love into it, but this is my home and it has been since the day I was born. I don't want to leave it, I really don't.'

Lena got up and went and put her arms around Fotini and the three women lapsed into silence for a few minutes. Each one wanted to ask Stelios why he had done it but that wasn't a possibility anymore.

'Aunt Fotini, you shouldn't have to move out of the villa if you don't want to. Why not rent the apartment out, like Callisto suggested? It doesn't have to be to holiday makers, it could be to someone who already lives here on Vekianos. That way you wouldn't need to be cleaning it and turning it around every week for different visitors.'

'That's a great idea, Lena,' Callisto agreed. 'The money is there to refurbish the villa, Fotini, so why not move into the apartment while the work is being done and then come back here to live? This is your home and should be for as long as you want it to be.'

'Oh, girls, do you really think that would be ok? I just feel I'm going against Stelios' wishes. He put everything into that apartment block.'

'You have to do what's best for you,' Lena said gently. 'Why not think about it for a bit? There's no rush—' Lena was interrupted by her phone ringing, and she was surprised to see that it was a call from Joanna Bouras. She apologised to Fotini and Callisto for the interruption and stepped away to answer.

'Hello?'

'Hi, Lena, it's Joanna Bouras.'

'Hello, how are you?'

'I'm fine, thank you. I was hoping I could meet up with you at the apartment block the day after tomorrow? There's something I'd like to talk to you about. Would eleven o'clock be ok?'

'Yes, of course. Is it anything I should worry about?'

'Not at all. I'll look forward to seeing you then. Goodbye.'

Before Lena could say anything to Callisto or Fotini, another phone rang. This time it was Callisto's, and Lena and Fotini watched on as she had an identical conversation with Joanna to the one Lena had just had.

Callisto came off the phone looking puzzled and confused.

'Do you think this means what I have been saying all along is right? That Dad left her the other apartment? It seems like the only reason she would be coming to tell us both,' Lena said.

'It would make sense given she's selling her family's land over in Thagistri. What do you think, Fotini, would Dad have left her an apartment?'

'I want to say yes as Stelios was very fond of Joanna, but something tells me no. I think this meeting is something else, though don't ask me what because I don't have a clue. But surely it must have something to do with the empty apartment.'

'It does seem the most obvious answer,' Callisto agreed as all three women nodded in unison.

Lena laughed. 'You know, one thing Dad did do right was to bring the three of us back into each other's lives. I'm looking forward to getting closer to you both, the way it always should have been.'

Even Callisto found she had tears in her eyes. This really was a new start for the Drakos family.

Chapter 29

Looking at the time Trisha could see she had half an hour before she had to be over at Fotini's. She was tempted to show up early because ever since Fotini's phone call last night she had been wondering what it was that she needed to discuss so urgently.

As she got herself ready she checked her phone, hoping for a text from her sister Julie. She had promised to get back to Trisha about a date for coming to visit, but nothing had come through yet, and she was beginning to think Julie had changed her mind. She hoped that wasn't the case.

When she arrived at Fotini's she was greeted warmly and ushered through to the terrace, where coffee and biscuits were waiting. Settling into her seat she couldn't help but notice that Fotini seemed more bubbly than usual. She got her answer for the reason when Fotini suddenly announced, 'I'm not moving. I have decided to stay here in the villa.'

'Oh my goodness, that's a shock! I thought you were excited about it? You said the apartment would be less hassle as you got older.'

'I said a lot of things that I thought people would like to hear, but deep down I knew I didn't mean them. This is my home and I have loved it as far back as I can remember. It's where I belong.'

'Good for you! I can see in your face how happy the decision makes you.'

'It really does. I'm also looking forward to a little modernisation, a new kitchen, updated bathrooms, and fresh decoration right through the whole villa. I might even treat myself to some new furniture.'

'Can I ask what Callisto has to say about it?'

'She's happy and so is Lena. They were actually

the ones that suggested it. They showed me I had a choice when I really didn't think I did.'

'So what will happen to your apartment?'

'I'm going to rent it out, though I'm not sure yet if it will be a holiday let or a long-term one. To be honest, since I sat down with Lena and Callisto all I've focused on is how the villa is going to look when the refurbishment is done. I'm properly excited now!'

'Fotini?' a voice called from the direction of the gate.

'Tassos! Come through, we're on the back terrace,' Fotini replied.

'Sorry, I didn't realise you had company,' Tassos said, starting to turn back.

'Come and join us! Have you met Trisha?'

'Not officially, but I think I've seen you by the pool next door,' Tassos said to Trisha as he shook her hand. 'I've heard a lot about you over the years. Stelios mentioned you frequently.'

'All in a good way I hope. It's nice to meet you, Tassos. You have a very helpful, pleasant son. You must be so proud of him and all he's accomplished. Jacob really has a gift.'

'He does, and yes, I am very proud. And don't worry, Stelios only ever had good things to say about you.'

'As it's nearly lunchtime I insist you both stay. I'll leave you two to entertain each other while I go and prepare a few snacks.'

'So, Tassos, do you think Fotini is doing the right thing staying here in the villa?' Trisha asked.

'If that's what she wants and it makes her happy then yes, I do. I know Stelios thought he was doing the best thing for her but perhaps on this occasion he was wrong. I think there's something about this island that makes people reflect. I suspect it made Stelios want to right perceived wrongs from the past, and I've only been back here a couple of days and already my mind has wandered to places it hasn't in a long time, made me rethink previous judgements,' he said, looking thoughtful.

'For me it's brought up regrets. But I suspect I'm starting to sound like a broken record as I've talked about them so much, so I'll save you my musings.' She laughed.

'I understand what you mean about regrets. Losing Stelios has made me do a lot of looking back. I do miss him and of course I have so much to thank him for. When we first met I was very young and had only just qualified as an accountant, and he gave me my first break. He always said he saw the hunger in my eyes and that because he always went with his heart, he needed someone like me to bring him down to earth when he had decisions to make. It worked well and even though we both looked at potential projects differently, we always managed to meet in the middle. I don't have that kind of relationship with any of my other clients.'

'And now you're working with Callisto, which must be very different.'

'It is, but things are different between us since Stelios died. No, that's not quite right. I think it's since we've been here on Vekianos. I've seen a different side to her these last couple of days.'

'I brought a red and a white,' Fotini announced as she returned. 'Lunch won't be long. What are you both chatting about?'

'The usual subject: Callisto,' Trisha joked.

'Did you and Callisto have fun when you went over to Thagistri?' Fotini asked, a gleam in her eye that Trisha couldn't quite decipher until she noticed Tassos' blush.

'It was fine,' he mumbled, avoiding eye contact.

'By the way, when Lena and Callisto were here yesterday they both had a phone call from Joanna

Bouras. Apparently she's coming here tomorrow to meet them.'

'And you've not been asked to join?' Tassos asked Fotini.

'No,' Fotini said with a shrug. 'I'm just going to check on the food. Won't be long!'

Chapter 30

Lena was excited, the mystery of the empty apartment would at last come to a conclusion. She suspected that Joanna would sit them down and tell them their dad had left it to her because they had been in a relationship for many years. There was no other explanation that Lena could fathom. Before the meeting she nipped down to the restaurant to see how Pavlos and Jacob were getting on.

'Hi, Pavlos, is Jacob not here yet?'

'He's coming a bit later as he had a work meeting on Zoom, but it's not a problem as we're well ahead now. I thought you had a meeting with Callisto and Joanna?'

'I do, but not for another hour or so. Jacob didn't say he had work to do today. I hope everything's ok.'

'Apparently it was last minute and he only found out about it this morning. Right, we need a plan of action. The equipment isn't arriving until later today so I thought as I was here by myself I would concentrate on the kitchen area, making sure all the work surfaces are sealed properly and there is one little bit of grouting to finish on the backsplash tiles, and then tomorrow we can set all the tables and chairs in place. We just need to sort out an official opening day and then I can start to order food and drink to come in. Can you believe how far the place has come on in such a short time?'

'I know! To think how disappointed we were when we saw how much work was needed on the original walls.'

'If it wasn't for Jacob's help we would still be in the process of putting them right. He's been a huge help. But then, he had an incentive,' Pavlos said with a wink.

'Sorry?'

'You, Lena! He's besotted with you. You make the perfect couple, probably because you're like the male and female version of one another.'

'I sort of know what you mean. We get on so well together. I'm looking forward to getting into a routine with the restaurant so that Jacob and I can spend more time together.'

'It sounds like everything is falling into place and we have Stelios to thank for all of it. I will be forever grateful to him.'

'So will I. I kind of feel like my dad knew by giving Tassos the apartment that Jacob would live there. It's like he was saying "I'm going, but now you have Jacob".' Lena teared up at the thought and fought to compose herself. 'Before I burst into tears I best get going!' she said, and Pavlos laughed, pulling her into a quick hug.

As Lena walked back up the hill to the apartments she was so happy. She just knew that she and Pavlos were going to get along so well. Working together on the beach restaurant was going to be such a happy experience and then, when she had finished in the evenings, she would be able to spend the time with Jacob.

Walking through the gate she was pleased to note that she was on time, but then she realised she didn't know where they would have this little meeting. Would it be in her apartment or Callisto's? Or maybe it would be in the empty one? Looking over to the patio she saw Callisto at one of the tables, so headed over to join her.

'Been out for a walk?' Callisto asked.

'Yes, I nipped down to see Pavlos who is very excited about the way everything is coming together at the restaurant.'

'I'm pleased for him, and for you. A new home, a new job ... and possibly a new man? I've noticed you and Jacob spend a lot of time together.'

'I'm really happy,' Lena said, her face breaking into an involuntary smile. 'The first few weeks I was here on Vekianos I really didn't want to be, but so much has changed since then. I think it's been like that for most of us. What about you? How are you feeling?'

'My life is ok. There are a few business issues that still need ironing out but Fotini seems happy I'm here, which was one of my biggest concerns initially, and I've appreciated the chance to enjoy spending time with you both. I hope we get more of it.'

'I'm looking forward to spending more time with you, too, and once you and Tassos get it together the four of us can all hang out together!' Lena said happily.

'Sorry?' Callisto asked, completely flummoxed. 'You've got the wrong end of the stick there, Lena. Tassos and I would never get together; we can barely stand each other!'

'Well that might be how you feel ... but I know he feels differently. Every time your name is mentioned he has this strange look on his face.'

'I'm sure you're just imagining that.'

'No I'm not! Tassos is holding a flame for you—' Lena was cut off by the arrival of Joanna.

As Lena welcomed the lawyer and offered her something to drink, Callisto's mind was whirling. Lena's claim had really thrown her. Of course it was a load of rubbish, just some romantic notion in Lena's head. Callisto knew Tassos had no time for her.

'How are you, Callisto?'

Joanna's question roused Callisto from her thoughts and she realised they were alone. Lena must have gone inside to get the drinks.

'Did you say something, Joanna? I was miles away...'

Before Joanna could respond, Lena was back and handing round the waters.

'Are we ok to sit here?' Lena asked and Joanna and Callisto both nodded.

'I know you're both intrigued about why I called this meeting, and I suspect it will come as no surprise that your father is behind it.'

Callisto was the first to answer.

'Not more surprises! Please just put us out of our misery.'

'The empty apartment has been left that way on purpose. Stelios wanted you both to get settled in and start to get to know each other better before explaining what he envisioned for it.'

'I don't understand,' Lena interjected.

'He has left the remaining apartment jointly to you as he thought it would be a nice rental income for you both. I also think he wanted a means of ensuring that you stayed in one another's lives.'

Lena and Callisto sat dumbfounded while Joanna handed them the paperwork and the three keys for the apartment.

'I know this is a shock for both of you but the paperwork will explain everything and I'm available to answer any questions you may have once the two of you have chatted things over. I know your father has done this out of love and a desire to bring you closer, and I hope you have fun together. And, of course, make a nice income out of the apartment.'

With that Joanna stood and walked down the path and out through the gate.

'So what do we do now?' Lena asked. 'I'm completely thrown and confused.'

'Me too, but like everything that's happened since our father's death, I'm sure it will all become clear in time. For now, why don't we both go off and think about what's happened and then meet up again in the next few days and put a plan together? I'll also put some figures together and see what this new business venture could earn us.'

Two hours later Lena was still in shock and jumped when her phone rang. She was pleased to see it was Jacob calling and eagerly answered, asking him how his day had gone.

'I was wondering if we could meet up and have a drink or something to eat tonight,' Jacob said, not really answering her question.

'Please! I have so much to tell you, I really don't know where to start. Where do you want to go? Just down in the town or further afield?'

'Let's take a walk to clear our heads and see where it takes us. Is that all right for you?'

'A walk will be great.'

'Shall we meet in about an hour down by the gate?'

'Ok, see you soon.'

As she had some time to kill, she took a look on one of the holiday letting sites to see how much an apartment might let out for here in Keriaphos. Within minutes she was sucked into all the different websites and she was shocked at her findings. From May until early October they could earn a *lot* of money. Ok, they would have bills and costs, but still, they would both get a nice little income from it. Even in the winter months, when most of the island closed down to the main tourist business, they could still make a little each month as there were lots of walkers and visitors who preferred to come in the cooler months.

Hearing a knock at her door she checked the time on her phone and realised she was at least fifteen minutes late to meet Jacob. She hadn't even changed yet.

'I'm so sorry, Jacob,' she said as soon as she opened the door. 'I just went down a rabbit hole on my phone and completely lost track of the time. Come in, I won't be a minute getting changed.'

'It's not a problem. I was just worried something had happened. You don't need to rush on my account. We have the rest of the day, that is, if you haven't got anything planned?'

'Oh no, nothing, I will be as quick as I can. Go sit down.'

He looked sad as she left the room and she wondered what was weighing on him. Was it still to do with her working with Pavlos? Or maybe it was to do with his dad being here? Something was definitely wrong and she had to do something about it. She couldn't stand to see him hurting and wanted him to feel comfortable opening up to her. She wanted to prove to him she was there for him and would be for a long time to come.

One final look in the mirror told her she was ready. It was a lovely feeling getting dressed up for someone else and not just herself. She hoped he would like the effort she had gone to, but more importantly, she was ready and excited to ask Jacob to take their relationship to a new level.

'Sorry again! I just need my bag and phone and then I'm ready. Lead the way,' she said cheerfully.

Jacob didn't answer, only smiled and opened the door. They walked down to the gate in silence and were nearly at the end of the lane before either spoke.

'Up the hill or down?' Jacob asked.

'You choose.'

'Ok, shall we go where we went last time? It shouldn't take that long and the walk's nice and we know the food at the end of it is a treat.'

'Works for me,' Lena agreed.

They got to the top of the hill and then turned on to the coastal path, Lena filling Jacob in on Joanna's news and updating him on Fotini's decision to stay in the villa. She happily babbled until all of a sudden Jacob stopped walking and took both of her hands in his.

'I'm so sorry,' she apologised. 'I haven't stopped talking since we started on the path.'

'Don't apologise. It's just ... there's something I have to tell you and if I don't do it now, I know I'll lose my nerve.'

'What is it you want to say?' she asked warily.

'I'm not sure where to start. I had a Zoom meeting today with a company that has seen my work and they really like it... Actually, I've never had anyone so enthusiastic about it before.'

'How exciting! Tell me more.'

'They want me to work with them on some projects, unbelievable commissions that I have never ever even dreamt about.'

'Congratulations! How exciting. But something tells me you aren't happy for some reason. Is there a catch?'

'Not a catch, per se. The work and the job would be brilliant and challenging, but I wouldn't be able to work from Vekianos. The job would be office based ... in America.'

Chapter 31

As she walked to the restaurant the following morning, Lena's head felt like it was about to explode. So much for Jacob being her happy ending; within a short time he would be out of her life forever.

She didn't want him to go, but of course that wasn't what she'd told him yesterday. No, she had put on an act and said what she suspected he wanted to hear, that this was a huge opportunity for him, and he would be silly to turn it down because a job offer like this only comes once in a lifetime.

Lena knew the only thing that would make her feel better was a pastry so she popped into the bakery on the way. She wasn't all that surprised to run into Trisha, but she *was* surprised when Trisha's simple 'are you ok?' set her off.

Lena erupted in tears and Trisha instantly put her arms around her and ushered her outside.

'Whatever is wrong?' Trisha asked, concerned. 'Come on, let's sit on the wall here. Take a deep breath and tell me what has upset you.'

'Jacob is leaving me and I don't want him to go,' Lena managed to get out between hiccupping sobs.

'Oh dear, so you've had a fallout? Try not to worry, Lena, these things happen. You just need to talk over whatever the problem is. I'm sure everything will be ok.'

'No, we haven't fallen out. Jacob's been offered a job in America. It's huge, a massive opportunity for him, the chance of a lifetime, and I don't want him to go but I can't stand in his way.'

'I don't know what to say.'

'There's nothing to say. I just need to get over it,

pull myself together, and pretend I'm happy for him. I should really be getting to the restaurant now but thank you for listening,' Lena said as she pulled herself together.

'When you've finished for the day, why not pop up to my apartment and we can chat about it?'

Lena thanked Trisha and after buying two coffees and some pastries, she headed on to the restaurant, apologising to Pavlos for being late.

'I can smell the coffee,' she said. 'Does that mean the new machine is up and running? Are you happy with it?'

'Yes, very happy, but then I've worked with this model before and already know it's very straightforward to operate. As long as we buy the right coffee beans it will be a success. Now, let me show you what I did yesterday,' he said as he led her into the kitchen. 'The backsplash and the work surfaces are finished, and the fridges and the freezers are in, though they won't need to be switched on until twenty-four hours before we open. We're still waiting for the industrial vinyl to go down but that should happen before the end of the week. I also sorted out artwork for the walls. I know an artist over on Corfu who is going to provide us with paintings that will be for sale. When we sell one we'll get ten percent of the sale price, and she'll then replace it with another, which means the art will be frequently changing to give our customers something new to admire. It's win-win! We just need to choose which ones we want to display first. But before that, let's have some coffee and pastries. Do you know if Jacob will be popping down today?'

'I'm not sure. He has a lot to sort at the moment with his job, and also his dad is still here.'

After fuelling up they played around with the tables and chairs, making sure customers and wait staff alike could move easily between them. They also looked through the potential paintings to display. As the walls were a darkish stain they decided that the pictures had to be full of colour to really lift the room.

When Pavlos got a text a while later to say the china, cutlery, and glasses had arrived at the harbour, he suggested calling it a day.

'We've sorted a lot today and you seem to have a lot on your mind, so why don't you head off a bit early?' Pavlos suggested.

'That would actually be great. If you're sure you can manage all the boxes yourself?'

Pavlos rolled his eyes at her and flexed his muscles jokingly.

'Ok, I'll be off then. I'll look forward to seeing all the dishes tomorrow.'

'It's going to be great. Lena, please stop worrying, everything will be ok, you mark my words.'

As she headed back up the hill she couldn't help thinking that everything would *not* be ok because Jacob would be leaving. Before she got to the gate she texted Jacob to say she had finished early at the restaurant and she was just popping in to see Trisha for an hour, and to ask if he would like to meet up after. Within seconds he texted back a 'yes' and said she could take as long as she liked as he didn't mind waiting.

She was still smiling about his message as she knocked on Trisha's door.

'You look like you're feeling better!' Trisha said warmly.

'I am, a bit. I'm going to meet up with Jacob later and hopefully we can talk about his job. I want him to do what's best for him, but it will be hard to see him go. I feel like we were only just getting to know one another but I really like him.'

'I have a feeling things will work out the way

they're supposed to,' Trisha said sagely.

'Have you been having a nice day?' Lena asked, keen to change the subject before she got teary again.

'Yes, I've been lying in the sun and doing some pottering. I spoke with Fotini earlier and she mentioned she was going to rent out her apartment. I was thinking perhaps that's what I should do with mine, rent it out while I go back to London and carry on my life there.'

'But ... you didn't really have a life there, did you?' Lena asked gently. 'I'm sorry, that sounded really horrible and I didn't mean it like that. What I meant was since you've retired you don't have any responsibilities in London anymore, so there's nothing keeping you there.'

'Yes, but I'm getting bored here. I know that's an awful thing to say but I'm the type of person who needs to be doing something. I need a bit more structure to my life and back in London I could get a little part-time job, say two days a week, something to occupy my time.'

'But you could do that here on Vekianos! Why don't you come work in the beach restaurant with me and Pavlos?' Lena said, getting excited by the idea. 'He would jump at the chance to have you there and it wouldn't have to be long days. Perhaps you could just come in for the lunchtime trade. It will be fun and you know you can do it stood on your head. Please don't leave, Trisha.'

'That does sound fun, but I was also thinking I should go back to sort out my relationship with my sister.'

'I thought that was going ok.'

'It is, in a way, but I keep inviting her and her husband to come and stay and she keeps making excuses. I need to go back and clear the air with her, talk about the things that should have been mentioned years ago.'

'But you don't have to go back and live in the UK to do that. Why not just call your sister and tell her how upset you feel and ask her why she won't come for a holiday?'

'I'll think about it. You'd better go though, before you're late to meet Jacob.'

They shared a hug before Lena went down to her apartment to get ready.

Lena beat Jacob to the gate.

'Not just on time but also early! I'm impressed.' Jacob smiled.

'I didn't want to let you down again.'

'You could never do that. How about we catch the bus over to the harbour? It would make a change.'

'That sounds nice.'

The bus wasn't that busy and it didn't take long to get to the harbour, which was bustling with holiday makers. Lena suggested a lovely little restaurant overlooking the water. They settled at one of the outdoor tables and ordered two large beers and two plates of gyros and chips.

'It's not until I come over here that I realise how much I've missed it,' Lena said with a contented sigh. 'I need to come here more often, especially once I start working in the restaurant as the last thing I'll want to do is spend my time down in the restaurants in Keriaphos.'

'I came over here the other day with my dad and we went to one of the restaurants in the side streets that he used to go to with Stelios.'

'How is your dad? He's obviously in no hurry to get back to Athens.'

'He's ok. He's been working on his laptop from the apartment and has had some meetings with Fotini and Callisto.'

'What does he think of Callisto? ...Why are you laughing?'

'I think he might *like* her,' Jacob said, emphasising the word 'like' while wiggling his eyebrows. 'When he says her name his face lights up.'

'You know, I noticed that, too, and when I mentioned it to Callisto she was very defensive. Maybe he's not the only one who is feeling something?'

While they ate they laughed and joked about what would happen if Tassos and Callisto got together, and when they were done they decided to take a walk along the harbour.

'What a view,' Jacob said. 'Miles and miles of ocean in front of us. This island is very special. Do you think you would miss it if you weren't living here on Vekianos?'

'Now I've been here for so many weeks I think I really would.'

'So you wouldn't consider leaving?' Jacob pressed.

'That's an odd question. Why would I leave?'

'Maybe to ... move to the US?'

'What?' Lena asked, confused. Was he asking her what she thought he was asking her?

'Lena, I really like you, and I think there's something special between us. I know that this job offer has come at the worst time, but what if it's actually an opportunity for both of us? An opportunity to take the next step. What I'm trying to say is, would you consider ... coming with me?'

Chapter 32

After speaking with Lena, Trisha decided that there was no time like the present to phone her sister Julie and was just in the midst of dialling when a recognisable knock came at her door.

'Hi, Fotini,' she greeted her friend. 'You have perfect timing as I'm just making coffee.'

'I wish I could stay and enjoy it but I want to get the final packing done and sorted. The reason I'm here is I was sorting out Stelios' room and I found some old photo albums and I thought you might like to have a look before I give them to the girls,' she said as she handed them over.

'No, no,' Trisha said as she tried to hand them back. 'I don't need to see them as I already have all those memories in my head. Please give them straight to Lena instead. I know she'll enjoy looking through them.'

'Trisha, I think you *do* need to look at them. It might help you to come to terms with where you are in your life right now. There's no rush, you can open them in your own time, when the mood takes you.'

'Ok,' Trisha agreed, reluctantly giving in. 'Thank you, Fotini.'

Closing the door, Trisha placed the albums on the table in the hall, determined to leave them there until she next saw Lena and could hand them over.

She picked up her phone again and called her sister.

'Hi, Julie, are you free for a chat?' she asked.

'Sorry, I'm driving at the moment. Can I call you back when I get home?'

'Of course. I'm free for the rest of the day so call any time. Drive carefully.'

*

Trisha had been on the terrace for about an hour and there had still been no call back from Julie. Heading inside to grab a snack, she passed the photo albums and thought that perhaps it wouldn't hurt to have a little look, so she grabbed them and took them back outside.

As she opened the cover of the first one, she found pictures of Buckingham Palace, the Tower of London, and Marble Arch. It took her right back to the early days in London when she and Stelios had spent their days off as tourists. Their excitement at seeing all the famous landmarks for the very first time had been palpable, they were literally like two kids in a sweet shop. They really must have walked miles and miles that first month, everything was new, fresh, and exciting, and they had wanted to see it all.

Turning another page, her heart sank. Oh no. She knew she should have left these albums alone! She had known that diving into these memories would bring up so many emotions. Stelios looked so handsome and so happy in the snaps. She had been so lucky to have him in her life, he had helped her to believe in herself.

Trisha decided it was time for wine and headed into the kitchen to pour herself a glass. She knew the combination of wine, memories, and emotions would likely add up to a lot of tears, but the floodgates were already open and there was no stopping it now. She decided to risk it and reached for the second album.

Opening the cover she laughed out loud. Oh dear, here were the funny photos – parties, nights out in clubs, and so many people, most of whom she didn't recognise anymore. She wondered where the photos had all come from and who had taken them. She should have known as she was in so many of them, but as she thought back over all those nights out, she couldn't be sure.

As she put the second album down a while later, something told her the last one could be different and bring on very different emotions. She decided to leave it for now and cook herself a little pasta before Julie called back.

As she waited for the water to boil she asked her smart speaker to play some music from the early seventies, songs that would have been in the charts when those photos were taken. As she cooked and then ate, songs she had forgotten about filled the room and even more memories flooded back. She was genuinely happy and wished this side of herself was on display more often, not the 'woe is me' Patricia.

She had just placed her empty pasta bowl in the dishwasher when her phone rang. Perfect timing.

'Thanks for calling back,' she said to her sister. 'I'm just walking back onto the roof terrace so excuse me for a moment. Juggling a phone in one hand and a glass of wine in the other requires a little bit of balancing, especially when it isn't the first glass of the evening.' She laughed. 'Right, I'm sat down.'

'It's cold and dark here. Aren't you lucky to still be outside at this time of night,' Julie said.

'Yes, it's dark as well but very warm. Now, the reason I called you was I wanted to sort a date out for your visit. You and Keith deserve a holiday and I'm not coming off the phone until we set something in stone.'

'Well, I'm not sure, really, if we can make it this year,' Julie said evasively.

'Why not? Is it that you don't want to spend time with me? Please, Julie, be honest with me. Let's clear the air once and for all.'

'It's nothing to do with spending time with you,

Patricia; I would really enjoy that. It's ... well ... you lead such a glamorous life! I don't own the right clothes and I could never hold a conversation with the type of people you mix with. I worry I would struggle so much with everything.'

'Julie, oh my goodness, there is nothing glamorous about the way I live here! I mix with down to earth people who go out and do normal everyday jobs. Ok, before I retired I came in contact with famous, well known, and very glamorous people all the time, but that was only at work. I never socialised with them, only waited on them, making sure the service in the restaurant was right. My life here is very down to earth and calm. Please tell me you believe me. I really want you to come and stay. We don't have to go anywhere if you don't want to, we could just stay here on the roof terrace drinking wine and eating crisps. I promise there will be no getting dressed up.'

'I'm sorry, I can tell I've upset you. It's just that when you sent me photos of your apartment it looked like, well ... like something I see in films!'

'The apartment *is* glamorous, yes, but that's as far as it goes. To be completely honest, I can't even remember when I have had a pair of proper shoes on, let alone high heels. My life is sandals, shorts, and t-shirts. Now about that date. I'm free for you to stay whenever you want.'

'I promise you I will get back to you with options before the end of the week. I'm sorry I've been so silly.'

'You haven't!' Trisha rushed to reassure her. 'It's all been my fault.'

'Not at all. I hope you have a lovely rest of your evening. I'm really looking forward to coming to stay now. It will be wonderful to enjoy that heat and the view from the terrace with you.'

Once off the phone Trisha really didn't know

what to think. Had she been giving her family the impression all these years that her life was too glamorous for them to be a part of? Did they think she thought she was better than them? She sincerely hoped not! She was so happy Julie had finally agreed to come to stay, and she was determined to make things right while she was here.

What a strange old day it had been. Gathering her things from the terrace she headed inside, placing the photo albums back in the hall, all ready to give to Lena.

But after walking into the lounge, she stopped. Perhaps she should look at the last album? She suspected what it was going to hold, and she knew that if she was right, it would cause her to cry, but if she didn't do it now she probably never would, and that would be something she would likely regret for years to come.

Making herself comfortable on the sofa she took a deep breath before opening the cover of the album. She was right, it was what she had been expecting: photos of her visit to Vekianos. The first page showed her with Stelios' parents in the garden of the villa next door. She was so young and had a huge smile on her face, her happiness so clear for all to see. It had been her first time abroad and to come to such a beautiful place had felt like a dream.

Turning the pages she was confronted with so many photos of herself, all taken by Stelios over the two weeks she had visited. They had travelled to so many different parts of the island. She could remember being on the back of his old scooter as they raced around, Stelios determined to show her everywhere and introduce her to everyone, friends he had been to school with, relations, neighbours... Stelios had been so proud to show off his island.

Coming across pictures of her and Stelios together she could clearly hear him say to people, 'could you take a photo of me and my girlfriend?' She had loved being called his girlfriend, it made her feel so special, so lucky. Feeling overwhelmed, she closed the album and placed it on the sofa. She got up and walked outside, looking out to sea in silence.

Even though decades had passed, her holiday here with Stelios was as clear as if it had been last week, and one day was clearer than all the rest –the day she made her greatest mistake, the day she said 'no' to Stelios.

The day had started like all the others, they got up to a breakfast feast – Stelios' mum wasn't happy unless they were eating her specially prepared food – and then they had grabbed their beach things and headed off to have a day in the sun. Before they left, Stelios' mum had asked him if he could pick up a box of tomatoes from a friend on the other side of the island. She suggested they could make a day of it as just in front of where the tomatoes were grown was a beautiful, quiet beach.

Thoughts of that beach drove Trisha back inside and she picked up the album from where she'd left it. Turning back to the page she'd left off at, she found funny snaps that she and Stelios had taken in amongst all the tomato plants. Pictures of the beautiful beach where they had spent the day followed and she remembered how magical it had felt. They'd laughed, kissed, and hugged the whole day, and Stelios had insisted they wait for the sun to set. He'd said it would be like the sun was dropping into the sea and making a splash, and he was right.

What had happened next had been a shock, and closing her eyes now she was transported right back to that moment. She could hear Stelios start to talk, his voice nervous, as he said, 'Patricia, will you marry me? I want to live every day like this one, here on Vekianos with you. I know we'll be so happy here together.'

As tears started to fall down her cheeks in the present, she remembered looking at Stelios in disbelief and uttering just that one word: 'no'.

She hadn't even given it any real thought, she'd rejected him because she felt they were too young and she had her career to focus on. Marriage was way down her list of things she wanted to accomplish. He had looked at her in silence with tears in his eyes and though she'd known then that he was upset, it was only now that she realised how deeply it had hurt him.

'Oh, why were you so stupid, Trisha?' she muttered to herself. 'If only you had known then how much he loved you, because it's so obvious he never stopped.'

Chapter 33

After a busy day yesterday unpacking and washing all the china and glasses down in the restaurant, today was completely different for Lena. She was meeting up with Callisto to talk about the apartment they apparently jointly owned. But before that she had to arrange a meeting with Jacob, the one that she had been putting off since he had asked her to go to America with him. She hoped they could meet up later today to talk about it and was pleased when he quickly responded to say yes.

Looking at the time she saw she should be heading next door. She let herself in and found Callisto had already arrived.

'This is different, isn't it?' she asked as she looked around. 'I had thought all the apartments would be the same but this looks a lot plainer, not so homey.'

'I think the fixture and fittings are a little less grand because Dad wanted to use practical things in here as it's a holiday apartment rather than a home.'

'He really did think of everything and everybody, don't you think?'

'It seems he did. Have you had a chance to think about what you want to do? Which road would you like to go down – the short-term holiday rental market or the yearly lease? The holiday let could bring in more money, but there's no guarantee we can rent it out fifty-two weeks of the year, and we would need to factor in the cost of cleaning.'

'I really don't know.' Lena shrugged. 'You're the business professional, what would you do? Come to that, what would *Dad* do if he was in this situation?'

'Oh I know exactly what he would do. There

would be someone here in Keriaphos that needed a home and he would feel sorry for them and let them have it rent-free. He had a big heart but thank goodness he always had Tassos to see sense and point out he wasn't a charity, otherwise he likely would have gone broke years ago! He was always so kind to everyone.'

'Yes, and thoughtful. Look at how everything worked out here with the apartments.'

'You certainly seem very settled with a new job and a boyfriend.'

'Well, perhaps not that settled... The boyfriend bit could be changing as Jacob has been offered a fabulous job in America, which he would be very silly to turn down given it's what he has been working towards ever since he started. I'm really happy for him but it will be sad to see him go.'

'So where does that leave you two?'

'He's asked me to go with him, but I don't think I can.'

'You'd turn down the chance to be with the bloke you want to be with and start a new life in the states? How come? That's such an exciting prospect.'

'For some people, maybe, but I love it here. How about you, Callisto? What does the future have in store for you? Will you go back to Athens? I would think there's not enough life here on Vekianos for you, and with Tassos and the business based there it would seem to make sense.'

'I do miss Athens, but as for Tassos, you really have got it all wrong. He doesn't like me in the way you're thinking, I can assure you, though it has been nice to see we're getting on better recently. He hasn't had his guard up as much and I've seen a different, more relaxed, side to him. Anyway, that's not why we're here. We need to figure out what we're doing with this place,' Callisto said brusquely, getting back to business.

'I have to admit, I thought you'd have all this sussed out and be dictating the plan of action.'

'I want you to have your say, Lena. If it was left to you alone, what would you do?'

'That's simple. I would ask Tassos! He's the money man.'

'You might be onto something. I'm meeting him tomorrow as it's the start of the villa works, so I'll ask him what he thinks... You're smiling again. What have I said that's funny?' Callisto asked warily.

'Nothing. It's just ... I never thought we would ever really get on, especially after that first day when you came to my apartment, but you've changed, Callisto, you're more mellow. That's what this island does to people.' Lena smiled as Callisto broke into a grin of her own.

'I know I've changed. I've had a big kick up the backside, going from thinking I was the bee's knees to, well ... the bottom of the pack. But do you know something? I'm glad it's happened. I feel more grounded and I've learned I have to keep my eye on the ball more.'

'What do you think has made the difference?'

'Finding a solution to the problem out at Thagistri has been a real turning point. I looked at it practically and figured out a solution where other people couldn't. I suppose that it means even more because it's the first thing I've ever achieved without Dad or Tassos' advice. I did it all by myself.'

'I sort of get that. Since being back on the island I've been able to make my own decisions, rather than having to listen to my mum, and I think that's been a good thing. You know, we should go out for dinner one night and get to know each other a little better.'

'That sounds great.' Callisto beamed. 'I'm really looking forward to having you in my life. We have so many years to catch up on and so much to enjoy together in the future.'

'Me too. It's honestly one of the main reasons I don't want to go to America with Jacob. I want to spend the time I have with you and Fotini. We are a family and we should have all been together many years ago. Now, speaking of Jacob, I need to get going. I have the horrible task of telling him I won't be going to America with him.'

Lena moved to give Callisto a hug, and the response was not what she was expecting as her sister held her like she didn't want to let go.

As Lena headed back to her apartment she called Jacob to ask what the plan for the afternoon was.

'Perhaps we could catch the bus down to the harbour and get the boat over to Corfu?' Jacob suggested. 'No, I know what would be nice, how about if we got a boat over to Parga? We could climb the hill to the old castle and have a meal looking down over the harbour.'

'That sounds lovely! It's been a long time since I've been there and I remember there are so many gorgeous shops leading up the hill. I can be ready in ten minutes. Shall I meet you by the gate?'

'Sounds good! See you in a bit.'

They caught the bus to the harbour and killed time waiting for the next boat by going for a coffee.

'I noticed your dad's still here,' Lena observed. 'I thought he would have gone back to Athens by now.'

'Me, too, but he seems to be enjoying himself here on the island. He's done a lot of walking, which is something I have never known him do before, and he's really relaxed. The biggest shock though is that we've been getting on really well together. He's asked a lot of questions about my work and he seems genuinely interested.'

'That's wonderful! Has he mentioned Callisto at all?' Lena couldn't help asking.

'He hasn't really mentioned your sister but that's probably a good thing.'

'What do you mean by that?'

'Well, in the past he was always saying how she was lazy and didn't understand the job she was supposed to be doing, and that Stelios let her get away with everything. But now I think he's actually enjoying working with her and that's why the complaints have stopped. I think we'd best make a move; we don't want to miss the boat.'

The journey over to Parga town didn't take that long and as the boat was pulling into the little harbour they could see it wasn't that busy as everyone was still on the beaches.

'Food first, Jacob. I'm starving!'

'Definitely. Are you still sure you want to go up the hill to the castle?'

'Oh yes, but I'll pre-warn you that when we come back down I'll be looking in all the little clothes shops.'

'That's fine by me.'

They turned left and walked along a little pathway until they emerged at the bottom of the steep, narrow hill.

'When I was really young and came here with my dad, I used to moan that it was too steep but he always encouraged me on by saying there was an ice cream stand at the very top, before you got to the gate into the castle. But saying that, he used the same carrot when coming down as there's another ice cream shop opposite the harbour wall. What can I say? I was highly motivated by ice cream at that age!' Lena laughed.

'Well, this time there's a whole meal at the top of the hill so let's see how fast you can get up there.'

'You are on.'

Before Jacob could reply Lena was off; she was on a mission to get there first. She was hungry and the sooner they ate the quicker she would be able to go into the shops on the way back down.

'You win,' Jacob panted as they reached the summit. 'Is that the ice cream kiosk you were on about?' he asked.

Lena nodded.

'Do you fancy one?'

'Not right now. I want a big bowl of pasta first. Do we want a harbour view restaurant or one looking down the opposite side, towards Valtos Beach? You choose.'

'I really don't mind.' Jacob shrugged.

'Let's do the beach view. The harbour view is better at night when it's dark and everything is lit up with all the twinkly lights.'

Within minutes they had found a restaurant with some outside seating with the view they were hoping for. They ordered two large beers, two pastas, and spanakopita with garlic bread, without even looking at the menu.

'This is lovely. I like discovering new places together,' Lena said, realising this was a good way into what she needed to say. 'Jacob, we need to talk about America.'

'Yes, we do. I have some news on that subject, just let me get my phone out and I can show you...' He swiped on his phone to pull up the surprise and then turned the screen towards her. 'What do you think of this?'

'What is it?'

'It's the apartment I'll be living in when I move over. I contacted the people who I'm going to be working for, mentioned I needed somewhere to live, and they sorted it out for me! What do you think? It's only a ten minute walk from the office where I'll be working.'

'It's lovely and looks so big compared to what we're both living in now.'

Lena was given a reprieve as the beers arrived and they both took grateful sips, still warm from the climb up the hill.

The apartment did look lovely but it still wasn't enough to convince Lena she wanted to go. She knew she needed to be honest with Jacob, but she was reluctant to ruin their day when it had only just begun, so she took the easy way out and changed the subject.

'Tell me about the job! Do you know what you will be working on yet?' she asked eagerly.

Jacob looked thrown by the abrupt subject change, and Lena could sense that he realised the photos of the apartment hadn't won her over. A mask slipped over his features and he answered coolly.

'They've not said yet. Apparently they want me to meet up with the design team to talk about what area of speciality would work best. Here comes the waiter with the food.'

As they started to eat a silence settled over their table as neither of them knew what to say.

Lena finally ventured, 'Isn't it great that we can just hop on a boat and go to another island any time we'd like? We're very lucky.'

Lena just about got a smile from Jacob so she continued; talking about the view, all the people on Valtos Beach, the boats moored out to sea... But Jacob stayed resolutely silent.

What a sad end to the day, she thought.

'Was everything ok for you?' the waiter asked as he collected their empty plates. 'Can I get you a dessert or something else to drink?'

'It was really good, thank you. No dessert for me but if you want something, Lena, you go ahead,' Jacob said, finally meeting her eye.

'No, I'm fine, thank you. Just the bill, please,' she said to the waiter.

'Ok, one minute.'

'This is my treat,' Lena insisted as soon as the waiter had gone.

'Thank you,' was all Jacob said.

Leaving the restaurant Jacob asked if she still wanted to visit the shops.

'I'm not in the mood, thank you,' she said. Two could play at this cold shoulder game.

'Right, so shall we go down to the harbour for an ice cream then?'

'Actually, I think I've eaten enough for one day. Let's get the boat back home to Vekianos. Because Keriaphos *is* my home, Jacob,' she said, finally finding the nerve to say what she needed to say. 'I'm sorry but I can't come to the US with you. You need to throw yourself into this job one hundred and fifty percent and that wouldn't happen if I was there. And as for me, I need to spend time getting to know my sister. A few weeks ago I couldn't have dreamt of ever saying that, but Callisto and I have come a long way and I want to keep building my relationship with her, especially now my dad is gone. No one else knew him the way Callisto and I did.'

'I understand,' Jacob said glumly. 'Let's go and get the boat back to Vekianos.'

Chapter 34

Trisha hadn't felt this dreadful for years. It was nearly ten-thirty and she had only just woken up. She was feeling very sorry for herself but she also knew she had only herself to blame as she had drunk two bottles of wine last night while reminiscing and poring over the photographs. She had just kept coming back to how much Stelios must have loved her, and what could have been if she hadn't rejected his proposal. She knew she needed to get away from the apartment today or else she would continue moping around, and she knew exactly where she wanted to go, but couldn't remember what the place was called. Fotini would know it. She just had to ask where her parents used to buy the tomatoes. She decided to ask over a quick call rather than going around to the villa. The last thing she needed was Fotini to see her looking like she did today.

A few minutes later she had her answer: Thagistri.

Trisha was pleased Fotini had known exactly what she was talking about, and she had also helpfully shared that Trisha could get a bus there from the stop at the top of the road.

Now to get ready.

An hour later she was on the bus. There weren't many other passengers so she had a window seat where she could look out towards the sea, and the driver, who understood English, had promised he would tell her when they reached her stop. She didn't know how long the journey would take, as she hadn't asked Fotini, but it didn't matter. She was happy for the time alone with her thoughts. She found herself mulling over something Fotini had mentioned in their brief chat – that Stelios owned some land in Thagistri. She wasn't all that surprised though, as it was a lovely place and she could understand wanting to own a piece of it.

'Excuse me, madam, this is Thagistri,' the driver called, as promised.

As she got up and went to the door, the driver helpfully pointed out that if she turned right it would head into the little town, and if she turned left, the road would take her to the beach. She thanked him and got off the bus, taking note of the bus stop on the other side of the road, where she would need to catch a bus back. She got her bearings and decided she would head down to the beach first.

The walk wasn't a bit familiar, but given that it was decades since she had visited, that wasn't surprising. She knew she would remember the tomato field though, and the old house on the dirt track.

At one point she wondered if she was going the right way as the road seemed to go backwards, away from the ocean in the distance, but she could see up ahead that it turned back after a while. When she reached the car park she stopped and had a drink of her water before walking down to the beach.

As she stepped onto the sand, all of a sudden her heart raced as so many memories flooded back. It was as if she and Stelios had been here only yesterday.

It really hadn't crossed her mind how she might feel being back here. All she had thought about was what a beautiful place it had been and how she'd like to see it again. But this was so much more emotional than she'd expected.

She was a fool. This was where Stelios had asked her to marry him and stay on the island. It was where she had said no. It was where things between them had ended for good. *Of course* it would be emotional!

She took a few minutes to compose herself, taking another swig of water, and eventually she made her way further onto the beach. Apart from a group of three people, the little beach was empty as she made her way to the end where there were a few rocks – including the rock she had sat on with Stelios.

'Come on, Trisha, pull yourself together,' she told herself.

Taking her towel out of her bag and placing it on the sand she made herself comfortable leaning against the rock. She got her book out of her bag and settled in for a few hours of reading and enjoying the gorgeous Greek sunshine.

After a few minutes she realised she had been crazy to think she would be able to switch off and read. Putting the book back in her bag she decided it was time for a swim.

Even though she had been here in Greece all these weeks, this would be the first time she went into the sea. She loved the pool, which was so convenient, but this was different, and suddenly she was glad she had waited until now to dip her toes in. It meant something to do it here, surrounded by so many memories. This was special.

Over the next five hours she went in and out of the sea multiple times, but drying off after the last time she realised she was starting to feel thirsty, and as she had drunk all her water it was time to pack up and stop in the town before getting the bus back to Keriaphos. She sorted herself out and then looked for a place to sit where she could get the sand off of her feet before putting her sandals back on. She noticed a bench just off the beach and headed towards it.

She reached it and was just about to sit down when she read the little plaque and did a double take.

In memory of Stelios Drakos, a man that was loved by so many.

Her legs turned to jelly and she burst into tears as she sat down.

She had gone from feeling so happy to now desperately wanting to turn back the clock.

'Oh, Stelios, why did you have to die without telling me how you still felt? And why did I say no to you all those years ago? We both missed out on so much time together. I'm so sorry.'

Trisha really didn't know what to do. Her thoughts were racing and she wished she had never come to this beach.

'Excuse me, do you mind if I sit here?' a gentle voice asked.

'I'm sorry?' Trisha asked, startled and embarrassed to find she wasn't alone.

'I asked if it was ok to sit down.'

'Of course, sorry, I'll move up.'

'No, it's ok. I have plenty of room here,' the woman said as she settled in next to Trisha. 'The view is magnificent isn't it?'

This was the last thing Trisha needed or wanted, a strange woman starting a conversation, but thankfully the woman didn't say anything else and they sat in silence, both looking out to sea.

Trisha wondered who had put the bench here. Was it Fotini? Was this Stelios' land that she had mentioned on the phone earlier?

'I never get fed up with this view even though I was born and grew up here. I think I appreciate it more now because I don't live here anymore,' the woman said, interrupting Trisha's thoughts.

'It's very special. I forgot how much until today.

It's been many years since I've been here but it feels like it was just yesterday. A very good friend brought me here so it's very nice to revisit it.'

'That's lovely that you were able to come back. Are you having a nice holiday?'

'I'm not on holiday...' Trisha began. 'Well, in a way I am, and in a way I'm not. I've been given an opportunity to move here but for lots of reasons I've not yet made my mind up about whether I'm going to stay.'

'Well, there are a lot worse places to live!' the woman said with a chuckle. 'I'm based in Athens but I keep coming back. I don't have relations here anymore, but I do have memories, and it's nice to revisit them when I can.'

'I live in London but I've been staying in Keriaphos for a few weeks now.'

The woman didn't respond and Trisha was surprised to see she was staring at her, a look of contemplation on her face. Feeling a bit uncomfortable, Trisha looked away and got ready to leave. Putting her sandals on and picking up her bag, she was just about to say goodbye when the woman spoke.

'I hope you don't mind me asking, but your name wouldn't be Patricia, by any chance, would it?'

'Yes, it is,' Trisha responded, surprised. 'Should I know you?'

'No, but I suspect you've probably heard about me. My name is Joanna Bouras,' she said, holding out her hand.

Trisha shook it, saying, 'Oh yes, Stelios' lawyer ... and the person we all thought was going to move into the empty apartment. It's nice to finally meet you.'

'You, too. So, you haven't decided if you're staying here on the island or going back to England. What would help you to make up your mind, do you think?'

'I don't really know. Can I ask you something? Did Stelios ever tell you why he left me an apartment? And why is it the biggest?'

Trisha could see Joanna wanted to say something, but that she didn't seem sure of how to say it. She was about to offer her an out when the lawyer spoke.

'Planning, designing, and watching the apartment project come to life gave Stelios so much pleasure, and it kept him going during the final months of his life. Facing his impending death, he had a lot of things he wanted to sort out. For one, he wanted to bring Lena and Callisto home, and he also wanted to bring them together, hence their each receiving an apartment as well as being granted joint ownership of a third apartment. He liked the idea of giving them a project they could work on together, hopefully growing closer in the process. With Fotini, he wanted her to be comfortable so gave her the ground floor space that would make for easy living in her later years, and he wanted her to be financially secure for the rest of her life, so he made the plan for the villa to become a vacation rental. He took being Pavlos' godfather very seriously and wanted to ensure his godson had a base to start his adult life from. As for Tassos, Stelios knew he wouldn't have ever been as successful as he was without him, and he wanted to reward him not just for his service, but also for his friendship, which Stelios valued greatly.'

There was a long silence. Trisha wanted to ask so many questions but somehow none of them would come out of her mouth. Was that because she really didn't want to hear the answers?

Finally, she couldn't help but blurt, 'But what about me? How did I fit into all of this?'

'Patricia, Stelios never stopped loving you. You

were the love of his life and I don't think he would have considered, even for a second, giving that apartment to anyone else. He wanted you here, even if it wasn't with him, because he genuinely felt like this is where you belong.'

Trisha was stunned into silence.

'It's been so lovely meeting you after all these years,' Joanna said as she stood, readying to leave. 'All Stelios ever wanted was for you to be happy. So I hope you find that happiness here, in the place he loved.'

As Joanna walked away, Trisha fell back against the bench, lost in thoughts, memories, and so many regrets...

Chapter 35

The day had finally arrived and the villa refurbishment was set to begin. Callisto was headed over to the villa to meet with Fotini, Tassos, and the building team, when she met Fotini coming through the gates with two big bags.

'Hi, Aunt Fotini, let me help you with those,' she offered.

'You're ok, they aren't that heavy. It's just the last of the things out of the refrigerator. I'm officially handing the villa over to you to create some magic for me. And talking of magic ... I think you are in for a nice surprise. Tassos smells gorgeous and I know it's not for me or the builders.'

'Fotini, you are as bad as Lena! There's nothing between me and Tassos.'

'Mark my words, there will be,' Fotini said with a wink. 'Now, I need to get these things into the fridge. Have fun,' she called over her shoulder as she headed into the apartment complex.

Callisto shook off Fotini's insinuations as she headed over to the villa. Of course Tassos would smell nice. It was early morning and he would have only just showered and put his aftershave on. She had just sprayed some perfume on herself. It was just what people did!

Stepping into the villa she greeted Tassos and he asked where they should start.

'This is all new ground to me,' he added. 'I'm not usually on site but I'm looking forward to seeing how it all comes together.'

'It's the boring stuff first, I'm afraid. We rip out the kitchen, bathrooms, old shelves, and light fittings. Then we can start on the rewiring and checking the plumbing.' Callisto broke off to introduce Tassos to the builder.

'I think we have everything we need,' the man said, after introductions had been made. 'I'll hopefully have an update for you on the electrics and the plumping in a few days. It was nice to meet you, Tassos, I hope you're planning to stick around on Vekianos so you can see the villa finished.'

'I am, and I'm looking forward to seeing the villa in all its glory.'

It was news to Callisto that Tassos was planning on staying on, even after Jacob went to America, and she tried not to let her surprise show.

Business sorted, she tried to make a quick exit from the villa but Tassos caught up with her at the gate.

'Do you have any plans for the rest of the day?' he asked casually.

'Paperwork and more paperwork,' she said, forcing a laugh.

'Could that wait until tomorrow? I wondered if you might fancy going out for lunch. I could drive us over to the harbour?'

'Drive?'

'Yes, I've rented a car for my stay as I thought it would be nice to have freedom to explore the island on my own schedule. If you're feeling guilty about taking time off we could call it a business lunch,' he offered. 'To be honest, that's one of the things I miss about Stelios. We used to have some great lunches.'

Callisto was reminded again that she wasn't the only one who had lost Stelios, and she softened.

'Ok,' she agreed. 'I can get the work done when I get back.'

'Great! Shall we meet back here in twenty minutes? My car is parked just over there,' he said, pointing it out.

Callisto took in the Porsche as she nodded.

Heading back to her apartment she realised she'd need to dress up a bit if they were going to be riding around in a sports car. Perhaps a summer dress? She laughed out loud. The last thing she ever thought she would be doing here on Vekianos was dressing up to go out with Tassos!

A few minutes later, she peeped out the window and saw Tassos heading to the car. She locked her apartment door and headed out, running into Lena at the gate.

'You look lovely!' Lena enthused. 'Are you off somewhere nice?' A gleam entered her eye. 'And does it have anything to do with Tassos, who I've just seen looking smart and all dressed up as well?' she asked playfully.

'We have a ... business meeting,' Callisto said stiffly.

'If that's the case, I think you've forgotten something.'

Callisto looked at her sister questioningly.

'Your briefcase! You can't have a meeting without all your paperwork. But then ... if it was a date, you wouldn't need that, would you?'

'Lena, it's not a date!' Callisto let out an exasperated sigh as Lena laughed and headed on up the path.

As she closed the gate behind her Tassos opened the passenger door for her. When was the last time a man had opened a car door for her? It felt good to be treated like a lady.

'You look very nice,' Tassos said, giving her an appreciative look.

'Thank you.'

'Is the harbour still ok with you for lunch, or do you fancy somewhere else?'

'The harbour is fine. I'll enjoy arriving in this beautiful car. The locals will no doubt have a field day with the gossip when they see us.'

As Tassos headed down the lane and then up the hill Callisto started to relax.

'Where do you fancy eating?' Tassos asked as he navigated the narrow roads with ease. 'You know the island and the restaurants better than me. Whenever I came here with your dad we always ate in that local restaurant behind the main street in Keriaphos. It always made me smile the way you ordered by telling the people on the next table and then they passed it on. In a place like that it's easy to see why your dad was happiest here.'

'I think if he could have made a living here without having to do projects in Athens he would have been so happy. Talking of Athens, have you had a chance to look at whether we should take the offer on the partially completed apartment?'

'I really don't know. I think it comes down to what you want to do as things have changed a bit. There was a big chunk of money that was set aside to do up Fotini's villa but the new plan will cost much less than what was initially anticipated, so the financial situation is better than it was, meaning you don't have to rush into decisions. On that note, we have arrived,' Tassos said as he pulled up at the side of the road a little bit back from the harbour.

'Come on, Callisto, switch off from the business stuff for a while. Show me your favourite places.'

As they walked towards the harbour she wondered where they should go for lunch. She wanted it to be outdoors as it was such a beautiful day.

'I know a little shortcut avoiding the main street,' she said as they got closer. 'There's a little restaurant tucked away down it that would be good for lunch. There's no sea view but there will be plenty of beautiful bougainvillaea.'

'Sounds nice,' Tassos said as they made their way to the quiet little square and took their seats at the restaurant.

They ordered two glasses of wine and the waiter left them the menu while he fetched the drinks.

'So much has changed in the past few months, for all of us, hasn't it?' Tassos said thoughtfully, breaking the comfortable silence that had settled over them. 'Being back here on Vekianos feels so different without your dad, and my life has changed so much since I was last here with him. I still have other clients and I'm always busy but I'm not enjoying my job as much as I did. Working with your dad ... he made me feel needed, special. I don't get that with my other clients, I don't get a buzz from the work, the way I always have with Stelios' company.'

'I know what you mean. It feels like there isn't any buzz with the company now he's gone,' Callisto said.

The conversation paused while they looked at the menu.

'I think it's swordfish and a Greek salad for me,' Tassos announced.

'Yes, I think I'll have the same, and some warm bread.'

The waiter took the order and the atmosphere felt a little awkward. Here they were sat opposite each other in a gorgeous setting, and they were both lost for words.

Callisto decided a change of subject was in order.

'By the way, you must be so proud of Jacob. To be offered that job in America is huge. This opportunity could change his life forever.'

'Yes, I'm very proud and excited for him, but also disappointed in myself. I never took his drawing seriously before now. I'm lucky he's very forgiving.'

'It sounds like it's all worked out ok in the end.

He'll be able to go off knowing you are one hundred percent behind him, which is all that matters.'

'I hope so. It's a shame he's not going away entirely happy. He'd hoped Lena would consider going with him but she told him she needed to stay here.'

'They're still young. Once he starts working, he'll start moving on.'

'I hope so,' Tassos said as the waiter set their food in front of them.

'I know I said we should leave the business talk for another day but I'm curious to know if you've had any news back from the chap about the water situation at the plot of land over in Thagistri.'

'Yes, and surprisingly it's good. The quote is less expensive than I thought it would be.'

'That's great news. You don't seem that excited though. How come?'

'It would be a major project so I think I'm going to sit on it for a while. To be completely honest, I want to get back to Athens and take time to find the buzz the company has lost since my dad's passing. Why are you smiling?'

'Strangely – and it's a shock to me as much as it will be for you – I feel the complete opposite. I really don't want to go back to Athens even though I know I have to. How weird is that?'

They finished their meal and decided on a little walk along the side of the harbour.

'This is so lovely. I really get why your dad was at his happiest when he was here. There's something about this island that is very captivating. Shall we get some dessert?' he asked, nodding to the nearby ice cream parlour.

'Yes, but it's my treat as you paid for lunch.'

Callisto joined the queue while Tassos wandered over to look in an estate agents' window. As she shuffled slowly forward she reflected on what a lovely day this was turning out to be. She was very surprised by how honest she and Tassos had both been, letting their respective guards down. But was that a good thing or a bad thing? She wasn't sure just yet.

She bought the ice creams and headed over to join Tassos.

'There you go. I thought lemon sorbet would be perfect after the fish we have just had. Tassos?' she asked when he didn't respond.

'Sorry, I was away in my head, but I didn't go far … just around to the other side of the island. Look what's up for sale – the house near to your bit of land. The one on the road with the swimming pool.'

'Oh yes, and the price isn't that bad either.'

'You know, if you were to combine your bit of land, with the bit Joanna is selling, and now this property, which backs onto Joanna's land, it would make a really good development. What would you say to taking on a new project … together? Do you think that could give us the buzz we're both looking for?'

Chapter 36

It had been two days since Callisto and Tassos had been out for lunch together and they had both been looking into the sale of the two pieces of land in Thagistri. Today they were off to meet up with the agent selling the house, and then Joanna later on.

Every time Callisto stopped to think of the big picture she felt very overwhelmed but Tassos' excitement was infectious.

When she went downstairs to meet him she had to laugh. He was almost vibrating with energy and enthusiasm.

'You're the money man,' she pointed out. 'Shouldn't you be the one that's cautious and reining me back in? It seems like it's going to be the other way around.'

'Come on, let's go and have some fun,' he said, brushing off her hesitance. 'I've had a good look at the area on a map and there's tons of potential to do something really unique and special.'

'I think you're forgetting that the company doesn't have the best relationship with the bank at the moment. It's going to cost a lot of money to buy the two pieces of land and then there's the development cost on top of that.'

'Come on, Callisto, where's your fighting spirit?'

'I'm just stating the facts, that's all,' she said, raising her hands in surrender.

They drove in silence and the nearer they got to Thagistri the more she started going off the idea of the project.

The agent was already waiting for them when they arrived at the house.

'Good morning and welcome to Vekianos! My

name's Dina.'

'Hello, Dina. Thank you for the warm welcome but neither of us is actually new to the island. My father was Stelios Drakos.'

'Oh, I'm so sorry I didn't realise. I was very sorry to hear he'd died. He did a lot for the island and many people earned a living from the developments he worked on. Are you and your husband looking to move back? Because if so, this is the perfect house!'

'Oh, we aren't husband and wife,' Callisto rushed to correct the woman. 'We work together.'

'My mistake. You just looked like the perfect couple.' The woman smiled apologetically.

Tassos was smiling but Callisto was keen to move on.

'We have a busy day ahead of us so if we could start the tour?' she prompted.

Dina led them into the grounds, which featured a pool and an outside eating area. Stepping into the house Callisto's first reaction was that it felt like the holiday home it was, all very basic and nothing homely about it. Looking around, she could see it wasn't the type of property her dad would have taken on because it needed a lot of investment to do it up, and she reckoned the return just wouldn't be worth the cost. Ok, it was near the beach, but it didn't have a view of the water, so the asking price seemed high to her.

'Do you have any questions?' Dina asked once they had toured all of the rooms.

'No, I think we've seen everything we need, don't you, Tassos?'

'Actually, I'd like to walk around the grounds. I think we have time before our next appointment.'

Dina led the way with Tassos right behind her and Callisto trailing them.

'I'll wait for you by the car, Tassos,' she said as they stepped outside.

He didn't reply, just nodded. This was the business Tassos she knew of old, and as she stood waiting she tried to figure out what she was missing with all of this. What had he seen that she hadn't? What did he know that he wasn't telling her?

'Sorry to keep you waiting. How long have we got before we meet Joanna?' Tassos asked as he joined her.

'About three hours.'

'Shall we go and have some spinach pie then?'

'Fine with me,' she agreed.

They drove up to Makis' restaurant and ordered their pies. While they waited for the food, Callisto wanted to take the opportunity to grill Tassos but he got his phone out and started typing furiously so she'd have to wait.

'Enjoy your lunch!' Makis said as he delivered the pies a short while later.

'Is it mostly locals and people who live on the island who come here?' Tassos asked Makis before he could walk away. 'Do you get many holidaymakers? Are there places for them to stay around here?'

'A mixture. I think if we had more holiday accommodation it would be easy to rent out, no problem, but most of the new villas are being built nearer to the bigger towns, not here.'

'Villas, you say? Not apartments?'

'Yes, that's what visitors want now – private villas with a pool. Nothing grand, just modern and clean. Please excuse me. I just need to see to those people at the door.' Makis rushed off.

'So, Callisto, what was your opinion on the house? Did you like it? Could you see its potential?'

'I think it would take a lot of money to make anything out of it. The chic new look Makis mentioned wouldn't come cheap.'

'Fair enough. But say there were no walls

knocked down and we focused on adding new, modern bathrooms and kitchen, like what you're doing at Fotini's place. Would that make it a more attractive prospect?'

'I don't know, most buyers are looking for big, open plan living spaces.'

'Never mind what most buyers want. Would *you* like it if it was approached the same way as Fotini's villa?'

'Ok, yes, I think that would be nice. But I don't understand what you're getting at.'

'I'm not getting at anything,' Tassos said with a shrug. 'I just wanted your opinion on the place.'

With that the restaurant door opened and Joanna appeared.

'I see you both had the same idea as me,' she said, nodding to the pies on their plates.

'Would you like to join us?' Tassos offered.

'Thank you.'

Joanna ordered from Makis and then turned back to Tassos. 'So, what's keeping you here on the island? I would have thought you would be itching to get back to Athens after just a few days.'

'Actually it's the complete opposite. I'm enjoying being here and I'm shocked at how much work I'm able to get done. I think it's because at the office the phone is going all the time and my secretary always needs an answer to something, whereas here I just need to see to a couple of emails a day and client meetings are easily accomplished on Zoom. It also means they last a lot less time!' He laughed.

'That's where we differ. I really enjoy the energy of the office and am looking forward to getting back. I rented a little studio here in Thagistri and will leave for Athens as soon as I decide what to do about the family plot. How about you, Callisto, are you enjoying island life, or would you sooner be back in the big city?'

'I have to admit that I miss Athens, as it's all been very different here on Vekianos. Would you both mind if I nipped off for a bit?' Callisto asked, needing some space. 'There are a few things I need to sort and then I could meet you where we planned?'

Callisto headed out before Tassos could say he would come with her. She hadn't a clue where she was going but found herself wandering down the street towards the track to the beach. She decided to go and sit on her dad's bench and wait until it was time for the meeting.

After half an hour of her head being all over the place, she knew she had to switch into businesswoman mode. Walking back up the track she could see Tassos and Joanna coming towards her.

'Did you get everything done that you needed to, Callisto?' Tassos asked amiably.

'Yes, thank you, all sorted.'

'I was just saying to Joanna that our main objective for this visit is to take in the area of land and establish the boundary lines.'

'Follow me and I'll show you, but be careful as it's a bit up and down, very uneven,' Joanna said.

They walked for about five minutes and eventually came to a fence that had seen better days as big parts of it were missing.

'I think if we walk to the far corner, nearest to the road, and then follow the fence down to the beach, that will give you the best overview of the land and boundaries.'

Callisto nodded and thought to herself that Tassos was very quiet. She had expected that he would be asking Joanna hundreds of questions but no, he stayed silent. He did stop and take a few photos though, and she could see he was making notes on his phone. Eventually they got to the end of the plot of land and there was the beach in front of them.

'Has this helped you to get a better understanding of the size of everything?' Joanna asked.

'Yes, it's all very clear now. It's one thing looking at a map but walking the land gives you a completely different perspective, doesn't it? Thank you,' Tassos replied.

They all walked back up the track into the town where the car was parked. Callisto was breathing a sigh of relief it was all over and she could not wait to get back to Keriaphos.

When they got to the car they said goodbye to Joanna and Tassos thanked her and said they would be in contact.

As Tassos and Callisto got into the Porsche, he asked if he could show her something at Zagandros beach.

'Sure. It's years since I've been there but my dad always loved that beach. I remember there was a very old beach bar – it was a shack, really – and they served the best gyros on the island.'

'Sounds great. Just let me get my bearings. I think we go this way,' Tassos said as he pulled out of the parking spot.

When they arrived at the beach Tassos parked the car and led the way towards a nearby street, but Callisto paused.

'Tassos, that sign says the road is private. We can't go down there.'

'It leads to the beach though. Come on, we'll just pretend we haven't seen the sign. Follow me.'

They started walking and before very long they came across a fence and gates, behind which they glimpsed a large villa. They passed several more along the way and when they finally arrived at the beach the little beach bar looked nothing like she remembered it – it was a lot bigger and more substantial than it had seemed when she was a little girl.

'Is it like you remember?' Tassos asked.

'No, it's very different. The beach has been tidied up and I can't remember ever seeing sun loungers here. The big test will be the gyros. Lead the way.'

Food ordered, along with two small beers, they sat at a little table and took in the view.

'I'm surprised, Tassos, I thought you would be throwing hundreds of questions at me after today.'

'I only have one question actually: what did you think of the walk down here to the beach?'

'It was ok, though we probably shouldn't have done it as it was a private road.'

'Yes, I know, but the walk? The villas? Did you count them?'

'Not consciously but I suppose there must have been ... five or so?'

'Seven. All with pools, all extremely private, and all a stone's throw from the beach.'

It clicked for Callisto.

'So that's what you think we should do over in Thagistri?'

'Yes. We buy up the two pieces of land that are on offer and do something similar.'

'I have to agree it would be brilliant and exciting, but with the way things are at present we could never raise the type of money needed to accomplish that before the land is sold off to other interested buyers.'

'But what if we could?'

'I'm sorry, I don't follow.'

'What if I invested in the company?'

'What?'

'I think we should become equal partners in your dad's company. Well ... *your* company.'

Callisto was frozen. Tassos wanted to become business partners? Was this why he'd been so nice to her these last few days? A wave of anger rose within her.

'You expect me to hand over half of my company just like that, do you? It's not happening. I am the boss and you are the accountant and that's how it's going to stay. Now, if you don't mind, I would like to go back to Keriaphos. This business meeting is over.'

Chapter 37

Trisha headed out onto the roof terrace with a coffee and her notepad. She just wanted to take five minutes to check she had done everything, although she already knew she had. Everything had been ticked off, and so the only thing that was left to do was to shower and head over to the harbour to meet her sister. She was excited but also nervous as she couldn't remember when they'd had so much time to spend together just the two of them. It would be very odd, but saying that, her whole life had been odd since arriving here on Vekianos.

There was a knock at her door and she recognised Fotini's unique cadence. Her knock always managed to sound happy somehow.

'You're just in time for a coffee!' she greeted her friend warmly.

'I won't stop as I know you've been busy getting ready for your sister's visit and I'll likely only be in the way.'

'No, you're fine. I still have five hours before she arrives. Come and tell me all about the villa.'

'Actually, that's why I'm here. Something's happened but I'm not sure what.'

'Sounds ominous! You go out on the terrace and I'll make the coffee and then you can explain.'

Trisha wondered briefly if this might have something to do with Callisto. She'd seen her and Tassos come back in his car yesterday and the minute it stopped Callisto was out and slamming the door. Completely different from the other day when the two of them had been laughing and giggling after their meeting over at Fotini's.

Fotini launched into her story as soon as they

were both seated. 'Late last night I had a call from Callisto asking if I could meet her early this morning at the villa just to just talk over plug and light sockets, which wasn't a problem. That's where I've just come from and it's all sorted, but while I was there, she told me she's going back to Athens today. I asked for how long and she said she didn't know, which was fine as the builders know what they have to be getting on with, but then I mentioned Tassos because I know they have been spending time together.'

'Yes, I saw them together the other day. I suspect I know what you're going to say next: they've fallen out.'

'How did you know that?'

'When they came back yesterday she almost slammed the gate in Tassos' face before storming up to her apartment.'

'Ahh. Well, I said to her that it was nice that the two of them were getting on so well and that was it, she flew off on one saying the reason he was being nice was because he was buttering her up. She claimed he wants half of her company and I said she must be wrong but she was adamant it was true and she wasn't going to discuss it anymore.'

'Oh dear. That's two break-ups in one week.'

'Yes, and it's such a shame as I really believe Callisto and Tassos – and Lena and Jacob, for that matter – could be happy together. There are always two sides to every story though so I think I need to have a chat with Tassos. For now, I've kept you long enough. You have your sister to meet, and I really hope you both have a lovely time together. I know you're worried but I'm sure it will be fine.'

'I hope you're right. I'm looking forward to it but I would be lying if I said I wasn't also nervous.'

'You'll be fine,' Fotini reassured her before heading off.

*

Trisha arrived in the harbour almost two hours early but she was looking forward to distracting herself and killing time by grabbing a drink and then looking around the shops. There was always something new to browse and she loved the buzz of the harbour with all the boats bringing visitors from other islands for the day.

She stopped off for a cool drink in one of the cafés overlooking all the boats coming and going and as she was sat there her phone beeped with a text from Julie to say she had arrived at the harbour in Corfu and was waiting for the next boat over. She messaged back to say she would be waiting to meet her.

'Hi, it's Trisha, isn't it?'

'Hello, Tassos,' she said, trying to keep the surprise from her tone as she turned to face him.

'Do you mind if I join you?'

'Not at all. Take a seat. How are you?'

'I'm fine, thanks. Just having a day away from Keriaphos?'

'Yes and no. My sister's arriving from England today.'

'That's wonderful. Is it her first visit?'

'Yes. I'm looking forward to spending some quality time with her. How are you feeling about Jacob leaving?'

'I'll miss him when he's gone.'

'Will you be heading back to Athens then?'

'I don't know. I'm really enjoying my time here on the island, even though I never thought that would be the case.'

'That's good. I noticed you and Callisto have been able to unwind from all the work pressures and have some fun, that must be nice.'

Tassos laughed. 'I wouldn't call it "fun". Callisto is mad at me but she's just got the wrong end of the stick. You see, there's a project that could be very successful and I've come up with a solution to make it happen, but she's convinced I'm using the opportunity to take over her company. The problem with her is that she doesn't look at the big picture.'

'Hopefully you can sort out your differences,' Trisha offered. 'I'm sorry but I need to be going. I've got a few things to get before my sister's boat gets here.'

Errands complete, she found a spot in the shade to sit for the last fifteen minutes before the boat was due to arrive. Julie's holiday plan would kick into action with a taxi ride back to the apartment, and then they would have a few drinks on the roof terrace before dinner and get a chance to talk about the holiday and what Julie fancied doing. Trisha had done her research and she had a number of ideas about different places they could visit.

'Welcomes to Vekianos!' Trisha said the moment Julie stepped off the boat. 'You look wonderful! I love the hair.'

'Thank you and look at you! Your tan is amazing. Hopefully I'll have one, too, before I head home.'

'You will. It's so good to have you here. Let me take your case. We only have a short walk to the taxi rank. It looks like we're in luck,' she said as she caught sight of it in the distance. 'There are only two people in the queue.'

The journey back to Keriaphos was quite quick and Trisha used the time to point different sights out as they passed.

'Let me just get my keys out,' she said once they'd reached the apartment complex and hauled Julie's luggage out of the trunk of the taxi. 'Are you sure you're ok with that case? We have a couple of flights of stairs to climb.'

'I'll be fine,' Julie insisted.

Trisha led the way up the stairs and into the apartment and showed Julie her room first before taking her on a rapid-fire tour around the rest of the space and ending on the terrace.

'I'll get us a drink. I have wine, beer, gin... What would you prefer?'

'I'd prefer you slow down and take a breath!' Julie said, putting an arm around Trisha. 'You haven't stopped since I got off the boat. You've not even let me answer any of your questions. I would love a glass of wine but I will go and get it while you sit there, calm down, and pull yourself together. Count to ten or whatever number it takes for you to feel relaxed.'

Trisha did as she was told. She knew Julie was right; her heart was racing, her head was banging, and she felt like she might explode.

'Here we go,' Julie said as she returned. 'I brought the bottle and I found the glasses. I think that means I've settled in so you're officially off the clock. Your hostess responsibilities are done for the day.'

'Thank you.'

Julie poured the wine and for a brief few minutes they sat in companionable silence. Trisha knew she had to say something but what? She couldn't think straight; it felt as if everything that has been building up inside of her was ready to come flying out.

'I'm so sorry, Julie,' she finally blurted. 'I don't know what's come over me and I really didn't want you to see me like this. I've been so looking forward to us spending time together but actually seeing you here ... it's all a bit overwhelming. It feels too good to be true.'

'It does feel like a dream, doesn't it? The two of us here on this lovely island in your magnificent apartment.'

'Magnificent is the perfect word for it. Even after all these weeks of being here it hasn't sunk in that it's mine. But it's not just the apartment that I'm struggling with, it's also knowing how much Stelios really loved me, even after I let him down so terribly. It overwhelms me every time I think about it because I don't deserve this apartment or his love, I really don't.'

Chapter 38

As Lena threw everything she needed for the day in her bag she sent a quick text to Callisto to ask when she'd like to meet up to discuss things, and a response came through almost immediately.

In Athens on business. Will let you know when I'm back. C

Lena mulled over the message as she headed down the hill to the beach. It was strange that Callisto hadn't mentioned she had to go away on business. But Lena didn't have time to worry too much. Her priority for the day was the restaurant.

'Good morning, Pavlos,' she greeted him as she stepped inside.

'Hi, Lena. Raring to go?'

'Absolutely!'

'Good. I'm starting to feel really nervous and all these silly doubts are popping into my head. I keep finding myself wondering why I invested in this place when the last owners couldn't make a go of it. What makes me think I can?'

'For a start, they tried to turn a beach bar into a high end restaurant. They were pretty much doomed from the start. You, on the other hand, are doing what is needed for this location and space, so enough of all those thoughts. You've got this! What's the plan of action for today?'

'I don't actually have a plan. The big food and drink delivery is coming tomorrow and we've done everything else. Unless you can think of any jobs that need doing?'

'I don't think so, apart from a good wipe around. But I think it's best to leave that until the day before we open so that we don't have to do it multiple times.'

'Probably a good idea. I'm sorry I've dragged you down here when there's nothing to do. You should be spending time with Jacob before he leaves for America.'

'That would have been nice but sadly I'm not top of Jacob's "to spend time with" list. He's still upset I'm not going with him. Look, if there's nothing here to do, why don't we go off and cheer ourselves up by checking out the opposition? It will be fun as well as educational.'

'Educational seems an odd word choice,' Pavlos said with a laugh.

'No it's not. We need to find out what other businesses in the area are focusing on, sit and take a look at what customers are eating... We'll learn a lot from that.'

'Ok, sounds good to me.'

'So ... start in the harbour?'

'I don't think so. I'd like to go over to Zagandros. There's a lovely beach bar there that has recently been done up.'

'I think I know where you mean. When I used to go with my dad it was just an old shack.'

'Not a shack anymore.'

'Lead the way.'

They walked up to where Pavlos had parked his car and Lena started to feel better. It would be good to get away – both for her and for Pavlos. The only thing she was slightly worried about was that this outing would give him new ideas for what to serve. All the menus for the restaurant had now been printed so he wouldn't be able to change anything without them being redone, which could be costly.

'This is our first staff outing!' she said, trying to shake off her worries and buoy Pavlos up at the same time. 'I'm excited. Have you been to this place before?'

'Yes, several times. It's a bit different from our situation though because they're the only place to eat and drink on their beach. They have no competition whereas we have the restaurants behind us.'

'But what makes us unique in Keriaphos is that we're the only actual beach bar.'

'Very true. And like you said, it will be good to have had a day out, a staff bonding day.'

'As if we need that.'

They both laughed as they headed around the coast to Zagandros. Once there, they parked in the beach car park.

'A lot has changed since I was last here with my dad, but it still looks lovely. I can just about see the beach through the trees.'

They walked the short distance to the beach and found themselves in a gorgeous bay, which was so much bigger than the one back in Keriaphos.

As they took a seat and looked at the menu Lena looked around at the people drinking beers, and eating bowls of chips, Greek salads, and gyros.

'You're worse than me!' Pavlos said.

'What do you mean?'

'You're staring,' Pavlos said in a stage whisper.

'Sorry. I was only looking to see what I fancied ordering. I think I'll have a club sandwich with chips.'

'I'll have the same, I think, but then maybe I should have something different so we can get more insight into the menu.'

Once they'd ordered, Lena turned to Pavlos, all business. 'I've been thinking. I don't think you actually need to see what everyone else is doing. You have a brilliant vision for what you want to create and you've done a fantastic job bringing it to life. All we need to do is open the doors and let the customers in.'

'Thank you, Lena. You know, I couldn't have done any of this without you. When I'm down you pick me up and when I get over excited and too enthusiastic you rein me in. I do feel bad about one thing though: if it wasn't for my needing you at the restaurant you probably would have gone off to America with Jacob.'

'You haven't held me back at all. Going to America was never going to happen. It's a huge opportunity for Jacob to make a name for himself and I would have just distracted him. Without me he'll be able to give it one hundred percent of his focus.'

'That all sounds very practical, but I'm sure Jacob would find a way to make it work. He really cares about you. Anyone can see that.'

'I know. I really like him, too, and I feel bad about having upset him with my decision, but I meant what I told him. I need to be here right now, focusing on rebuilding my bonds with the only family I have left who knew my dad as well as I did.'

Their drinks arrived quickly and Lena used the distraction to steer the conversation away from her and Jacob and back to the beach bar, which carried them through their lunch.

When they finished Lena paid the bill while Pavlos discreetly took a couple of photos of the menu, and then they headed back across the beach to the car park.

'That was really nice. Thank you for treating me, Lena. It was supposed to be a staff day out and me being the boss I should have paid.'

'You can pay next time. This has been lovely.'

'Lena, can I ask you something?' Pavlos asked as he suddenly stopped walking, a serious look on his face. 'We've spent so much time talking about my dream over the past few weeks as we got everything ready, but what is *your* dream?'

They carried on walking across the beach as she mulled over what to say, and were nearly at the car before she stopped and faced him.

'To be honest, up until I came to Vekianos, I never had a dream. But then I met Jacob and I was struck by a desire to live and work here on the island ... with him. I had this vision of us being so happy together, but with him leaving... I guess I'll have to find a new dream.'

Chapter 39

Trisha was on the roof terrace with her first coffee of the day. Julie had said all the right things last night to make her feel better and they had spent the rest of the evening chatting about Stelios and their time together in London. She had even told Julie that he'd asked her to stay on the island with him. The one subject they hadn't broached was her lingering guilt for leaving her sister to do everything for their parents. She wasn't sure when the right time to bring that up would be.

'Good morning, Trish! I'm making a drink, can I get you another?'

'No, come sit down, Julie. You're the guest so I will get the coffees.'

'Don't be silly. You have been waiting on me hand and foot since I arrived. I can get them. I won't be a minute and then you can tell me what exciting things you have planned for us today.'

Trisha decided to suggest a few things and let Julie choose.

'We can have a day by the pool or on the beach, or we could take a walk, or catch the bus somewhere. There are lots of other lovely beaches around the island. Or we could get dressed up and go out for lunch, perhaps over in the harbour. There are some lovely restaurants to sit and enjoy a delicious meal while watching the world go by.'

'That sounds great!'

'What, all of them?' Trisha laughed.

'No, the lunch. I brought a nice new summer dress with me and that will be the perfect outing for it. We could also look around the shops. I can't remember when we last went shopping together.'

'I think it must be over forty years ago.'

'I know and now that we are older, time seems to fly even faster, doesn't it? Perhaps we could have a swim first, if we have time?'

'Of course! Don't worry about timings. You're on holiday and the restaurants are open all day so we don't need to be clock watching. Why don't you have another coffee and some toast before your swim and then we'll just go with the flow.'

'Are you coming down for a swim, too, Trisha?'

'No, I think I will give it a miss today. You go and have the pool to yourself. I've got a few things to do this morning.'

Trisha waved her sister off, pleased that she seemed really content with her life. She was happy and no one deserved to be happy more than Julie.

As Lena stepped outside she saw an unfamiliar face by the pool and realised this must be Trisha's sister, Julie. She eagerly took the chance to introduce herself.

'Is your holiday off to a lovely start?' Lena asked. 'I know Trisha has been so excited you were coming to stay. What do you think of her apartment?'

'It's been great so far and the apartment is gorgeous. You must feel so lucky to live here.'

'Yes, I'm very lucky. To be honest, it's been life changing for all of us here, being left these apartments. It's a lot to wrap your head around.'

'I understand that completely. I expect some have coped with it better than others.'

'I'd say so. Has Trisha mentioned how she's feeling about it?'

'I know she really doesn't feel she deserves the penthouse. I've tried telling her Stelios wouldn't have gifted it to her if he hadn't wanted to, but she still feels guilty.'

'We've all said the same to her at one point or another. I know she has good days and bad days and... Look, I'm not sure I should be saying this to you – and please don't tell her I mentioned it – but I think part of the reason she can't settle is because she feels so much guilt. She is really down on herself that she left you to care for your parents while she was away working and so to be left a reward like this, I think it just feels unearned, you know? I think if she could get all that out of her head she would be able to start enjoying her time here in Greece.'

'Thank you for your honesty, Lena. I'd best go and have my swim as Trisha and I are headed out for lunch shortly, but hopefully I will see you again before I leave.'

'I'd like that,' Lena said cheerfully as she waved goodbye and headed out through the gate.

'I'm back,' Julie called as she came through the door. 'That was lovely and it has set me up for the day. I bumped into Lena as well; she seems really nice.'

'If it wasn't for her and Fotini I don't know how I would have gotten on here.' Trisha smiled to herself. 'Take your time getting ready. I thought we could catch the bus as it goes into a few little villages, so you'll be able to see more of the island.'

'That'll be fun.'

While Julie went to get ready Trisha tidied everything up in the kitchen. She was looking forward to spending a few hours pretending to be a tourist and she knew Julie would really enjoy the shops and strolling around the harbour. Trisha really wanted her sister to enjoy herself.

Stepping off the bus into the glorious harbour was always a treat for Trisha and this time was no exception.

'That was so much fun!' Julie enthused. 'Because we were higher up in the bus than we would have been in a car, and with the stopping and starting, I could see and take in so much more than I expected. It's such a beautiful island and this harbour is stunning.'

'You see those five boats over there, with the tall masts and sails, the ones that are a lot older looking? They will have just brought day visitors over. They've most likely come via Paxos, which has beautiful clear blue sea, and they'll stop off here for two or three hours before heading off to secluded coves where the visitors can dive in and have a swim in the caves.'

'How lovely! Now, we need a plan of action. Food first, I think, as I'm really hungry, and then a little shopping before wine o'clock followed by dinner. Sound good?'

Trisha nodded.

'Great! Do you have a favourite lunch restaurant you want to go to?'

'Not really as they're all wonderful. Let's find somewhere where we can sit outside with a nice view. If we walk down here by the harbour wall we can see what jumps out at us. It's quite busy right now with all the day trippers but come four o'clock they all get on the boats and head back to where they came from and the little town turns into a much more laid back place. In the evening all the twinkly lights come on and the streets are full of families all dressed up, ready to go out for dinner. It really is a lovely atmosphere.'

'Look over there!' Julie said as she pointed. 'That restaurant looks busy, which is usually a good sign that the food is delicious, and there's a table outside under the canopy that would give us a perfect position to people watch.'

Trisha agreed and they went over and grabbed

the table before anyone else could. The waitress brought the menus and Julie ordered them a carafe of white wine.

'I really feel I'm in the holiday spirit now!' Julie said happily. 'This is such a beautiful place to be. I can see myself coming back again and again, and I'm looking forward to bringing Keith with me. I just know how much he'll enjoy the island as well. That is, if you're planning to stay? Here comes the wine,' she added before Trisha could respond.

'Sorry, we haven't looked at the menu yet. What would you recommend?' Julie asked the waitress.

'We're well known for our gyros and I can promise you, you won't be disappointed.'

'That sounds good to me, how about you, Trisha?'

'Perfect. But not too many fries for me, thanks.'

'No, she'll have the regular amount,' Julie said conspiratorially to the waitress. 'What my sister doesn't eat, I will!' she promised.

All three women laughed and the waitress headed off to place their order.

Julie turned back to Trisha. 'So, have you decided if you're staying or going back to London yet?'

'I'm not sure if I mentioned it, but the apartment came with a few rules. None of us are allowed to sell our units for a given number of years – Stelios stipulated that in the contracts – and obviously I can't afford to keep both my house in London and the apartment here, so if I decided to return to England I would have to rent out the apartment.'

'Well, as I see it, it's a no brainer! This should be your home. If it was, would you sell the UK one or rent it out?'

'I think I'd sell. I wouldn't want the worry of tenants and everything that goes with that. Life here *would* be a lot easier I think.'

'Then I think you have your answer. It's the one I was hoping for, and not just because I want to keep coming to visit!' Julie laughed. 'I honestly believe you'll be happy here, you just need to get over a few more hurdles in your head. Oh look, here comes the food. Those plates are very full, aren't they? Not that I'm complaining though!'

Trisha wondered what her sister had meant by "hurdles". Could she see through Trisha's act? Did she know what Trisha wanted to say but didn't know how to broach the subject?

'Come on, dive in before it gets cold,' Julie encouraged.

The lunch was delicious and so filling that Julie couldn't finish everything on her plate, let alone what was on Trisha's. They weren't in any rush though, so they sat back in their chairs and ordered more wine, enjoying looking out at the boats in the late afternoon sunshine.

'I can't believe we've been sat here for nearly two hours,' Julie said at last. 'I think we need to take a walk to help the lunch digest. By the way, this is my treat. I'm just going to pop to the bathroom and then I'll ask for the bill.'

While Trisha was waiting for Julie to come back she thought about what a lovely day it was turning out to be. She agreed with her sister, her life here on Vekianos could be fantastic. Ok, the sun wouldn't shine all twelve months of the year, and a lot of businesses on the island would partially close down in the winter, but it still wouldn't be as cold and wet as it would be in England, and having that view from her roof terrace every day really was so special.

'Are you ready to walk the meal off? I settled the bill so lead the way and show me what this town has to offer.' Julie smiled.

'Shall we carry on down by the sea wall and then

on to the shops? There are a few gorgeous properties along the way and a little pebble beach with four or five benches from which we'll hopefully be able to see the big tourist boats leaving. It's such a lovely sight watching them follow each other.'

They stopped and looked into the odd shop window as they walked, and Julie couldn't get over the beautiful one-off pieces for sale that you really wouldn't see anywhere else.

'With all this available to you, why would you ever want to live anywhere else?' Julie asked. 'I imagine it would be different in winter, of course, but it would undoubtedly still be fabulous.'

'You're right. I'm looking forward to seeing a different side to the island's tourist business. I imagine we'll get more walkers and explorers taking advantage of the cooler temperatures. These are the benches I mentioned. Shall we sit and take in the view? We've got perfect timing because here come the boats.'

They sat in companionable silence for what seemed ages and Trisha finally felt ready to explain to her sister what was eating her up inside.

'I know we spoke about this on the phone, but I need to say it again. I was so engrossed in my London work bubble I didn't stop to think about everything that fell on your shoulders when it came to caring for our parents as they got older. I really can't imagine what you had to go through and never once did you ask me for help or complain. I was so selfish and I'm sorry. I really let you down.'

'Let me stop you there. I didn't have it hard at all and do you know why that was? Because you bought Mum and Dad a car so they could keep their independence, because you sent them on countless holidays, because when they needed a little more help you paid for a cleaner to come in twice a week. Do you see a pattern emerging? Their last years were made so comfortable because of your generosity and that's something I will always be so grateful for. You gave them a quality of life they could never have dreamt of.'

'That's very kind of you to say but I wasn't there, hands on, day in and day out.'

'Neither was I. Mum would never let anyone cook in her kitchen and Dad wouldn't take any help in his garden. All I had to do most weeks was order their shopping online. I will admit some weeks it was a nightmare.' Julie laughed. 'Mum could never get her head around quantities – she was so used to pushing a trolley round the supermarket and grabbing things by hand – but it always turned into a laugh and we got there in the end. In short, there's nothing to be sorry for. We were a team between us and that's how it worked so well. I think instead of feeling so much guilt you should feel proud of yourself. How many children could do for their parents what you did?'

'Thank you. That really is so kind,' Trisha said, truly touched.

They sat in silence while Trisha looked at the whole situation in a different way, realising that perhaps her parents' life *had* been easier with the financial help she had given. The main takeaway, however, was that Julie didn't begrudge her any of it. Finally feeling free of the guilt that had weighed her down for so long, Trisha breathed a sigh of relief. She could move on with her life now, her new life here on the island of Vekianos.

Chapter 40

Callisto had been in Athens for nearly a week and she was feeling very sorry for herself. She had spent most of her time in her hotel room and when she had ventured out to meet up with friends it was a disaster. All they'd talked about were holidays and weekends away, something she used to love to join in with, but with no spare money she was on a tight budget and getaways were far down the list of essentials. To be honest, she didn't really know why she had come back. She had felt the need to get away from Keriaphos, but she could have gone anywhere. She shouldn't have assumed that she could fall back to her old habits when so much had changed since she left Athens.

It was a new day though, and she was determined to get out of her budget hotel room, get some fresh air, and hopefully clear her head and stop moping around feeling sorry for herself. That wasn't going to get her anywhere.

She quickly checked her work emails before heading out and was quietly surprised that she still hadn't received one from Tassos. Yes, they'd had a falling out, but she had expected him to be in touch for business reasons by now. That he hadn't meant it was reaching the point where she was starting to suspect he was avoiding her on purpose. If that was the case, fine. She knew she was the one in the right and he was the one who needed to apologise for trying to trick her into a partnership by being nice to her, suggesting days out, laughing and joking. She'd let her guard down and he'd gone in for the kill. The nerve of him!

She headed out for a walk around the centre of

Athens and was glad to be out of the hotel room. As she wandered into one of the quaint little squares she decided it was time to stop to have a coffee and watch the world go by.

I've gotten very good at watching everything happening around me, with little forward momentum of my own, she thought miserably.

As the waiter put the coffee down on her table and she placed her phone in her handbag, her eyes caught on someone she recognised coming towards her. Before she could hide she was spotted and she quickly schooled her features. It was time to put the act back on, the same one she'd used when she was out with her friends the other night. The look that said she was happy, her life was going well, and she was a successful businesswoman without a care in the world.

'Hello, Joanna.'

'Hi, Callisto, I thought it was you. Back in the big city for work?'

'Yes, I'm just taking a little break for a few hours.'

'Do you mind if I join you?'

'Take a seat.'

The last thing Callisto wanted was to make small talk with Joanna but at least it would give her a reprieve from her thoughts for a while.

'It's funny I ran into you as I was actually just thinking about Stelios,' Joanna said, surprising Callisto.

'You were?'

'Yes, I was thinking it's such a shame he didn't live long enough to start his next project on the piece of land he bought from me.'

'It is. I have to say though, I'm still baffled why he bought it in the first place, given how many issues we've had. Was it to help you out financially? I don't mean to pry, but, well … given you now have the rest of the land up for sale...'

'Honestly it's fine. Given it's been weighing on your mind, I don't think he'd mind me telling you that he bought it because he loved that bit of land. He spent time on that beach with Patricia and I think he was hoping that if he could build something magical on the land he might be able to win her back. He knew from mutual friends that she was retiring and that he wouldn't be in competition with her career anymore, so he decided to take the chance. I suspect his plan was to retire himself once the project was complete, and hand his company over to you to run at that point. You do know that that was always his plan, right? He knew it would be in safe hands with you and so he never considered any alternatives.'

'Safe hands,' Callisto scoffed. 'Thankfully he isn't here to see what a mess I've made of it so far.'

'I doubt he'd think so,' Joanna said kindly.

'He really did love Patricia, didn't he?'

'Oh yes. It's such a shame that Stelios was taken from us before they could reunite. I miss him so much. It was the simple things – a chat on the phone, a dinner or lunch out, and those moments when he gave me advice. It's his counsel that I think I miss most.'

'I'm surprised to hear you say that, Joanna. I wouldn't have thought you'd need advice; you always come across as so confident and in control.'

'Most of it's an act,' Joanna confided. 'It comes alive when I put the business suit on. The truth is that I doubt myself as much as the next person. For instance, am I doing the right thing selling all that's left of my family's land? I'm getting to the end of my career and I want to use the money to invest in the company I work for to create further retirement income. It's right out of my comfort zone but I've gone too far to turn back now. It reminds me of something your dad taught me. He said that when the doubts creep in and you feel like you should stop, you have to keep pushing onwards and hold your nerve. The easy way out is rarely the right choice.'

'He was very wise,' Callisto said, smiling to herself.

'He was. Now, I'd best get back to my office. It's been nice chatting to you, Callisto. I understand from Tassos that you aren't interested in being involved with buying the rest of my land but I hope you'll reconsider. From what Tassos has outlined it could be a very good investment and it's just the kind of ambitious project your dad always loved. He'd be proud to see you carrying on that legacy.'

As Joanna left Callisto thought over what she'd said. Was that where she had been going wrong? Instead of saying to herself 'what would Stelios do' she had instead been stumbling along and making mistakes that only made her feel sorry for herself.

Her phone beeped with a notification and she saw it was an email from Tassos asking if she had made a decision on the Athens apartment yet. She hadn't but she suddenly knew exactly what her dad would do: he would meet face to face with the people who wanted it and come to a solution that would suit everyone.

Looking through her phone for the contact details of the company that wanted the apartment, and then making sure the project manager was on site, she made a call to arrange a meeting for that evening. She then checked other listings for similar apartments as she headed back to the hotel to put on her business suit. Because as Joanna had pointed out, it gave you a much needed bit of confidence.

It was nearly six o'clock and Callisto was on her way to the apartment. The builders had finished for the day but the project manager had stayed behind to run through everything with her before the potential buyers arrived at seven o'clock. To say she was nervous was an understatement but she knew she had to stay focused. This was how her dad had done business, no messing around and straight to the point, but in a relaxed, informal, chatty way. She could do this; she just needed to keep her nerve.

The project manager had given her a full update on the various elements of the build before he left and Callisto used the short wait for the buyers to walk around the apartment. It still needed so much work but that was a good thing as it meant the people wanting to buy it could put their own spin on it, making it their taste.

She knew the figures inside out and braced herself when the knock came at the door, surprised to find a woman in place of the men in suits she'd been expecting.

'Eva Galanis. I'm here to see Miss Drakos,' the woman said.

'Please come in, are you on your own?'

'Yes, thankfully. I think it's nicer doing business with a woman, don't you? That way there's no messing around because we have a hundred and one other things going on in our lives that need to be sorted, like, yesterday.' Eva laughed and Callisto couldn't help joining in.

'Very true. Where would you like to begin? I'd suggest starting with the view.'

Eva smiled the minute she stepped into the living room and saw the massive window framing a truly incredible view.

'This is why I want to live in this apartment. It's all about this view of this wonderful city.'

'I agree. The inside can be turned into whichever look or design you want, but the view is already perfect and timeless.'

'Exactly. Now, down to business.'

'Did you not want to see the rest of the space?' Callisto asked, confused.

'I don't need to. I know that this apartment will work perfectly for me. It's going to be part of my divorce settlement and as my soon-to-be ex-husband will be paying for it, you can name your price. Oh, and given that he will no longer be my husband due to his little liaison with his twenty-year-old secretary, don't let him have it cheap.' Eva winked and Callisto couldn't help but laugh.

Callisto and Eva came to an agreement in no time at all and she wrapped up the paperwork back in her hotel a few hours later. There was just one more thing Callisto had to do before turning off the light: send an email to Tassos to tell him she had wrapped up the deal and sold the apartment for the same price they would have if they had finished the project. She couldn't help feeling a bit smug. She had done it, and she had done it all on her own. It was just the burst of confidence she needed.

As she went to turn the light off she paused. Maybe not entirely on her own. No, there was someone she definitely needed to give credit to.

'Thank you, Dad. I couldn't have done that if you hadn't been stood beside me. This is just the start. By the time I've finished I will make you very proud, I promise.'

Chapter 41

Lena's phone beeped when it was still very early and before she could look it beeped again.

As her eyes struggled to adjust she saw that it appeared to be texts from Callisto and Fotini. She read her sister's first:

Back on Vekianos by lunch time. Could we meet up to talk about the apartment? Shall we say around five p.m. at Fotini's villa?

Fotini's said:

Callisto's coming back today and wants us to meet her at the villa. Do you know what's happened?

Lena groaned. She hoped whatever it was would be easily addressed. She already had a lot on her mind as she'd agreed to go out for a meal with Jacob later on because he was scheduled to leave for America tomorrow.

And before all of that she needed to nip and see Pavlos who was getting the big food delivery today. She wanted to make sure he was ok sorting everything himself, and suspected he would tell her to leave him to it as he needed to get his head around everything and put things where he wanted them, and she would only be in the way.

'Hi, Pavlos, I'm just checking you still don't need me today.'

'No, you're fine. The lorry will be here in half an hour and then I have today and tomorrow to get organised before we open the following day. You should go out and enjoy your last couple of days off.'

'Ok, but only if you're sure, and if you promise you'll call me if you need anything.'

'I will, I promise.'

She made a quick stop at the supermarket before facing the hill. Thankfully she didn't need a lot, just a few bits for lunch. Continuing on her way, she saw Tassos coming towards her down the hill.

'Morning! Dare I ask how things are going? Is Jacob getting nervous about the move?'

'No, he seems to be fine. Of course he's still disappointed you aren't going with him, but like I keep telling him, the last thing he would want is for you to go and then be unhappy. By the way, why aren't you at the restaurant today? Doesn't it open in a couple of days?'

'Yes, the day after tomorrow, but Pavlos wants to be able to get things sorted without me being in the way, so he gave me the day off. I'm looking forward to some down time ahead of the business meeting with my aunt and sister later on.'

'Callisto is back? I knew she had finalised some business in Athens but I didn't realise she was back on the island already.'

'I don't think she is, not until lunchtime at least. Are you two still not talking?'

'Who knows with your sister. Good luck with the meeting.'

'Thanks. Have a nice day, Tassos.'

Once back in the apartment Lena put her shopping away and then sorted something nice to wear for her evening out with Jacob. While she was at it she went through all her t-shirts and shorts, setting aside ones that would work for down at the restaurant. She was glad that she and Pavlos had decided on a casual uniform as it would make life easier.

Lena was surprised when it was Callisto who answered the door of the villa, rather than Fotini.

'Thanks for being on time. Fotini should be here

very soon,' Callisto said as she ushered Lena inside. 'How are things coming along with the restaurant?'

'All ok, thank you. We open the day after tomorrow and to be honest I think Pavlos just needs to get that first day done and over with. He's a little stressed at the moment and just wants to be left alone but by this time next week I'm sure all the worry will be gone. How have you been? Have you had any thoughts on what you want to do with our rental apartment?'

'Yes, but shall we wait for Fotini to get here?'

'Did I hear my name?' Fotini asked as she came through the door.

'Yes, I was just saying to Lena we should wait until you get here before talking about the apartment. First, I thought we could look around the villa and see if you're happy with what's been done so far.'

'That sounds fine to me. I know I said I didn't want to come back in until it's finished but I really can't wait for that. I'm too excited!'

'It's going well so far. All the electrics are finished and the new pipe work for the plumping is all in place. And the walls are nearly finished being plastered in most of the rooms. I will warn you though, it does look like a building site.'

'That's not a problem. Lead the way, Callisto.'

They started in the bedrooms, which had been freshly painted and only needed decorating, then the bathrooms, which seemed very big to Lena, but that was probably because all that was in them were the pipes coming out the walls for the taps and the toilet. From there they moved on to the kitchen, which was also a work in progress with unfinished walls, and finally the living room, which was finished and had new sliding doors leading out onto the patio.

'Oh, Callisto, this is so lovely! So much light is

coming in,' Fotini gushed.

'Shall we sit outside and chat?'

'Yes, let's move on to the apartments,' Lena replied.

'Not quite yet. Are you happy with everything you've seen, Fotini?'

'Definitely. I'm going to need to rethink my living room furniture because the room looks so different from when there was just a window there.'

'Good. Now we need to talk money. As you know, the renovations Dad had designed for the villa were completely different and obviously would have cost so much more, but given that we've gone for a refresh instead of an overhaul there's still money in the budget to do other things to the property if you'd like.'

'That's very kind, Callisto, but could that money instead be used to help the business?'

'I'm pleased to say that we don't actually need it now. I've just completed a deal in Athens on an apartment, which went far better than I could ever have hoped, and with the money saved on this project things are looking a lot better. Whatever project the company invests in next will have to be given a lot of thought and consideration, but we're on the right track to get the company back to where it was when Dad was at the helm.'

Lena was impressed. This was a very different side to her sister and it felt as though she had come back from Athens a different person – more confident and more in control.

'Now, on to the rental apartments.'

'Well, girls,' Fotini began. 'I'm not sure about you two but I'm a bit concerned that if I make my apartment a holiday let I wouldn't know who was coming from one week to the next, and any unexpected noise and disruption could seriously impact the other residents. And then, of course, there is the cleaning and maintenance needed between each guest.'

'Yes, I was thinking the same. How about you, Lena?' Callisto asked.

'I'm happy to go along with whatever you both want to do. One thing I did think of was if we treated it as a yearly rental we could get somebody local in. Fotini, you would probably know people here on Vekianos who would be suitable, right?'

'Certainly. I can already think of a few people who would be very interested.'

'Which way is your head leaning towards, Callisto?' Lena asked.

'Do you know what, I asked myself what Dad would do if it was him that had to make the decision. And I think he would opt for yearly rentals as it would create homes for deserving people and would involve none of the hassle of holiday lets. And if it's good enough for Dad, it's good enough for me.'

Lena and Fotini shared a silent look.

'So, I think we have everything covered,' Callisto said, hurrying things along as though she didn't want to give anyone a chance to comment on what she'd revealed. 'Can you think of anything else, Fotini?'

'No, I don't think.'

'Lena?'

'Not really. But ... can I say something? Please don't think it's me being nasty or nosey or anything but you seem to have come back from Athens a little different, Callisto.'

'I suppose I have. I got to a point where I realised I needed to pick myself up and stop feeling sorry for myself. The company wasn't going to get back on its feet by itself. Striking such a good deal for the Athens property all by myself gave me a lot of confidence. I feel ... lighter, and more than ready to take on whatever challenge comes next.'

Before Lena or Fotini could say anything or congratulate her, Callisto was on her feet and picking up her paperwork. It was clear that both the conversation and the meeting were over.

Back in her apartment it was time for Lena to get ready for her evening out with Jacob. They were going to the restaurant they'd discovered the day they went for the long walk, but they wouldn't be walking there tonight as Jacob had booked a taxi for seven-thirty. She hoped it would be a fun evening and that Jacob wouldn't be too gloomy. Every time she'd tried to talk to him lately it had been like speaking with Eeyore.

She took one last look in the mirror and felt pleased. She had scrubbed up well.

As she got to the bottom of the main stairs she heard footsteps behind her. Turning around she saw it was Jacob and she was pleased to see that he had also gone to the effort of dressing up.

'Look at you, young man! So smart. Is this the new look for America?'

'No, this is just for you, Lena. Before we go I need to say that I'm not going to spoil our evening by being all miserable. The last thing I want to happen is for you to remember me in a bad way. I expect the taxi is here. Shall we?' he asked, ushering her out the door before she could respond.

Surprisingly it didn't take that long to get to the restaurant, and they joked about how perhaps they hadn't walked nearly as far as they'd thought they had when they'd been before. They chose a table inside and when the waiter came to offer them menus they waved them away, saying they both already knew they would be having the moussaka, with tzatziki to start.

'So, are you all packed and ready to go?' Lena asked once they were alone again.

'Yep. What have you been up to? How's the restaurant coming along? And Fotini's villa? Is she happy with how things are going?'

Lena was surprised by the rapid-fire questions and didn't know quite where she should start.

'The villa is coming along ok,' she began. 'I was there with Callisto and Fotini earlier today and my aunt is very happy with the work that's been completed so far. As for the restaurant, I'm feeling apprehensive. I just want it to open so we can get a few days under our belts and create a routine. The day after tomorrow is the big day and I'm sure it'll be fine. Once I've dropped a few things and spilled drinks over people everything will fall into place,' she joked.

'I don't think that's going to happen. I know it's going to be a huge success. You work so well together and make a great team.'

'Thanks. Are you looking forward to meeting your new team?'

'I am. The schedule sounds pretty intensive but they're entitled to get their money's worth out of me when they've made me such a great offer.'

'How about the creative side of the job? Are you excited about that part?'

'Definitely. There are a couple of projects in development that don't interest me that much, but when I get there I'll be able to see everything that they're doing and share my enthusiasm for the jobs that appeal to me more than others.'

Jacob topped up their wine glasses and Lena thought to herself that the evening was turning out much better than expected. There was a buzz in the air between them and it reminded her of what it had felt like when they'd first met and were getting to know each other. This was the perfect way to end their last night together.

'That was beautiful, Jacob,' she said as they

finally put down their cutlery and sat back. 'I'm so happy you found this gorgeous restaurant and that we had a chance to come back before you head off on your adventure. Are you ready to get a taxi back?'

'Yes, but do you think we could get the driver to drop us off down at the beach in Keriaphos so I can have one last look out to sea before I leave tomorrow?'

Lena knew a last goodbye under a starlit sky would be emotional but how could she say no?

'Of course!'

The minute they got in the taxi the atmosphere changed and Lena suspected things would only get more uncomfortable. She needed to remind Jacob that he was doing the right thing.

The driver stopped just at the end of the boardwalk leading down to the side of the beach café. Everything was in darkness apart from the lights behind them from the restaurants on the main street.

'I'll miss this,' Jacob said. It's such a shame I can't stay for the opening day of the restaurant, but by the time I come back to visit you and Pavlos will be in a real routine. Come on, let's go down to the water's edge. I want to dip my toes in the sea one last time and look back at the beach café with all the tables and chairs outside. It will help me to think of you working there.'

They walked down and stood in silence for a few moments, surrounded by the sound of the gentle waves.

'I'm going to miss you, Lena. And I want you to know that this isn't the end for us. I promise.'

With that he took her hands, pulled her towards him, and kissed her.

Chapter 42

Yesterday had been a successful day for Callisto. She was glad to see Fotini was happy with how the villa was coming along, and she felt she was growing closer to both her aunt and Lena. Given the way she had treated them in the past, it was more than she could have ever hoped for.

She hoped to ride the wave of yesterday's success into today, but given that first on her list was a call with Tassos, that seemed unlikely.

'Hi, Tassos, it's Callisto.'

'Welcome back to Vekianos. How can I help?'

'I wonder if it would be possible for you to meet me out at Thagistri later today. I've come up with an idea that could help us both. Would four o'clock down in the car park on the beach be ok?'

'Yes, that's fine. I can give you a lift if you'd like.'

'No, it's ok. I have other business to deal with before then.'

'Four o'clock it is then.'

Coming off the phone she felt good. Now to get ready and head off to Zagandros.

She had the driver drop her off at the end of the private road she and Tassos had walked down and arranged for him to pick her up in two hours' time from the same spot.

After double checking the time on her phone to make sure she would be back in time for the taxi, she started to walk and in a short time she came to the first of the villas. There was a car on the drive and she noticed the windows were open so she couldn't stand and stare. Hopefully one of the others was still closed up and she could risk taking a peek through the gate.

A few minutes later she came to the next house and she could see a woman putting bags in the back of the car out front.

'Can I help you? This is a private road... Oh! It's Callisto, isn't it? Stelios' daughter? I'm Maria. I work in the pizzeria in Keriaphos,' the woman called over.

'I'm sorry, I didn't see it was a private road,' Callisto said, sticking to the story she and Tassos had used. 'I was in my own little world. These villas are lovely. I can see why you'd want to keep the tourists out of your space.'

'Not me. I don't live here, I just clean a couple of them between guests coming and going.'

Callisto felt as though she had fallen on her feet bumping into Maria. If she had just finished cleaning the villa maybe Callisto could get a look inside.

'I don't remember these being here. Are they new? They're gorgeous and very private and best of all not too big. I presume they only have a couple of bedrooms each?'

'Yes, they were only built within the past few years. Most have three bedrooms and they're still quite expensive to rent but nothing like the big villas with the stunning views. Still, they're in the perfect location near the beach and they all have a little pool.'

'I expect they're rarely empty.'

'Yep, it's back to back bookings most of the time.'

'That's wonderful. I've kept you talking long enough, Maria, so I'll let you go. I'll have to go online at some point and look at the interiors. I expect they're stunning and very modern?'

'You're not holding me up. In fact, if you'd like, I could show you around this one. That is, if you have time?'

'I'd really like to have a quick tour. As long as

you're sure I wouldn't be putting you out?'

'Not at all. Come on,' Maria said.

Callisto followed Maria through the gate and into the grounds. The pool and the patio were quite small compared to other, bigger villas Callisto had seen on the island, but they were perfect for half a dozen people. The inside had a large, open plan living/dining/cooking area and off that were three double bedrooms, all with en suite bathrooms.

'It was so kind of you to show me around, Maria,' Callisto said as they made their way back outside. 'I really appreciate it.'

Callisto waved goodbye and headed towards the lovely beach café to grab a drink and make some notes. She also wanted to try and work out the square metres of the villa she had just seen. Kicking her sandals off and walking across the sand she felt happy, something she hadn't for such a long time.

Checking the time a while later, she saw she still had twenty minutes before the taxi was due to pick her up, which would give her enough time to walk back up past the villas and also to get her head in business mode before her meeting with Tassos.

Her first stop after arriving at Thagistri was Makis' restaurant as she had a few questions she wanted to ask him.

'Welcome back!' he greeted her warmly. 'People are going to start to think you're a local with all the time you've been spending in our little town. Not that I'm complaining, of course, you're bringing money to Thagistri and that's just what the town needs. Did you want your usual coffee and spinach pie?'

'Just a water today, please. You aren't very busy,' she observed as she glanced around the café.

'Sadly it's been quiet, with not too many holiday makers, but like I said before, there isn't a lot for visitors here apart from the beach.'

'It's a shame the island council doesn't get involved and help the town.'

'Oh they do. They would love it to be a tourist destination to take the pressure off of some of the other towns and to encourage more visitors to the island in general. They actually have quite a lot of incentives for developers and they even helped me with this place because I was willing to take a chance and set up here even though it's a bit off the beaten path. I couldn't have done it without the loans I was granted.'

Callisto was about to burst with excitement. Makis had answered her questions without her even having to ask them and now she had everything she needed. Quickly drinking her water she paid Makis and was on her way.

As she started to walk down the lane to the old property her first thought was that the lane needed a lot of work. It would be no good building gorgeous villas with no way to drive to them properly. But perhaps that's where the island council could help. With a little bit of creativity they could probably fit at least eight to twelve villas along the lane, all very private from one another.

After twenty minutes of walking around and taking photos she headed back onto the track towards the old polytunnels and tomato fields, seeing Tassos up ahead.

'Hi, Tassos,' she called and he whipped around to face her.

'Sorry, I didn't mean to make you jump.'

'That's ok. I was distracted.'

'Looking at what can be done with the land the polytunnels are on?'

'Yes, that's right.'

'To be honest, I've blocked them out of my mind

for now. They'll definitely factor into the big picture but they won't be part of phase one of the project as that side will need a lot more money thrown at it. For now, I've concentrated on the old house and the land behind it.'

'Sounds like you've given this a lot of thought. Does that mean you've come around to my suggestion of working together on the project?'

'Possibly. I think we need to rethink a few things first.'

'I'm sorry?'

'I agree we can work together on this, which I'm very happy about, but it has to be a joint project between my company and yours. My dad left me this company and I'm determined to keep the success he started going ... on my own. That's the deal on the table, Tassos, take it or leave it. Now, I'm off down the lane to sit on Dad's bench so you can give the deal some thought. That's where you'll find me for the next hour.'

As Callisto turned and walked away her heart was racing. Would he agree? She hoped so because she couldn't realistically do this project without him or the money he wanted to invest, and deep down she knew it wouldn't be a success if they didn't do it together. But she had to keep her nerve, even if he came back with other suggestions. This was the deal and she wasn't budging one little bit.

Sat on the bench staring out to sea she was daydreaming of what her dad would have thought. Had she done well? Would he be proud of her? She was so deep in thought that she physically jumped when her phone beeped. Her first thought was that it was probably a text from Tassos saying 'no deal', but looking at the screen she saw it was from Lena, inviting her to the new beach restaurant tomorrow at seven o'clock. Apparently Pavlos was having a little get-together for friends, family, and locals to celebrate the opening. Of course she would have to go, but more than that, she *wanted* to.

As she was replying she felt someone's presence behind her.

'Ok for me to sit down?' Tassos asked.

'Of course. I was just texting Lena.'

'About the opening of the restaurant? I just got a message as well. It will be a nice evening I hope.'

'I'm sure it will.'

'Back to business. Callisto, I accept your deal. I think you have come up with the perfect solution that will work for both of us. I'm excited and I know Stelios would be as well. He would be very proud of you.'

'That's very kind of you to say. Where should we start? I have lots of ideas and plans and projections to back it all up but that's all in my apartment. Would you like to go back to Keriaphos and take a look?'

'I'm sorry, I can't today. I've other business to finalise.'

She looked at him questioningly.

'I'm getting rid of my office and home in Athens. I'm going to be running my accountancy business from here on Vekianos from now on. Most things are done online these days and I could work from anywhere in the world, really, so I thought: why not here?'

Callisto didn't know what to say, surprised at how pleased she was to discover Tassos would be staying on the island.

'You look surprised,' Tassos laughed. 'So am I, to be honest. This was definitely not the plan, it's just ... I've fallen in love with this island, and I want to make it my forever home. I'm afraid I need to be going now. I would offer you a lift but I'm not heading back to Keriaphos just yet as I have a few details to tie up here. You'll find out soon enough so

I might as well share that I've bought the house behind us on the road, the one that we viewed together. I think it'll be a lovely home for me. I needed somewhere with an office and the apartment is far too small for that. I also love my private outside space, which the new house would give me. My life is taking a very unexpected turn but I'm really excited. See you tomorrow, Callisto.'

He waved as he headed off and Callisto was left alone on the bench, her mind whirling.

Chapter 43

'Are you sure you're ok going to the party down at the restaurant tonight?' Trisha asked Julie first thing. 'We really don't have to go if you don't want to. It is your final night before going back to England after all.'

'Of course I want to go! Anyway, I have to. I bought that lovely new dress over in the harbour especially for it.'

Trisha smiled. She was happy Julie was up for going to Pavlos' opening and as she stood waiting for the kettle to boil she looked back over the last two weeks and realised they'd been full of so much happiness. There had been a lot of laughter and a few tears and they'd grown closer than they'd ever been. She was so pleased her sister had agreed to come and stay, it was just what she'd needed and hopefully Julie felt the same.

'There you go,' she said as she served up the tea.

'Thank you, and more importantly, thank you for such a wonderful holiday. I've enjoyed myself so much.'

'Me too. You've really helped me to look at things in a new light, and you've shown me that my place is here. I'm going to sell my place in London. I'll miss certain things about my home there but life on the island is so much easier – slower, less stressful and so peaceful. I would be silly not to stay.'

'I'm so excited for you!'

'This is a new start for all of us as a family and that makes me so happy.'

The sisters shared a hug until the sound of a knock at the door rang through the apartment.

'I suspect that will be Fotini,' Trisha said as she went to answer.

'I hope I'm not disturbing you,' Fotini said as the door swung open. 'I just wanted to ask your opinion on something: which of these dresses do you think I should wear tonight down to the restaurant?'

'Come in and join us. Julie will want to weigh in.'

'Thank you. I've just passed Callisto going into Tassos' apartment with lots of paperwork. I wonder if they're friends again.'

'We'll soon find out because Lena told me they're both going to the party tonight. The big question is: will they be arriving together? We'll have to wait and see. Now, go on out to the roof terrace and I'll bring you out a coffee.'

'Thank you for letting me come over, Tassos. You can't move in my apartment for boxes but that's my own fault. As you know, I thought I was going to be moving into the top floor apartment.'

'It's fine. Now Jacob has gone, there's nothing here apart from me, a suitcase of clothes, and a laptop.'

'Perfect for our needs. I've brought all the information on Joanna's land along with a scaled map. I've also been looking into the little villas you took me to see over in Zagandros. I managed to talk my way into viewing one of them and it was gorgeous; very compact but perfect for smaller groups. They were constructed by a local builder and as he's worked with Dad before I've contacted him for quotes. I've also pulled together a rough plan of the different stages of the project, which unfold over several years, that is if we get planning permission of course—'

'Callisto, please stop and breathe,' Tassos

interrupted. 'You'll do yourself an injury if you carry on like this. I know you're excited and that you want to prove you can do this but please slow down. Before we talk about the project we need to talk about us.'

Tassos turned away to grab some cold drinks from the fridge and Callisto wandered outside onto the terrace. What had he meant by 'us'? Her heart was racing.

'There you go,' he said as he handed over an ice cold glass of some kind of fruit juice. 'I really can't get enough of this view. Of course it will be a different view once I move to the house in Thagistri, but thankfully it will still include the sea.'

'I'm still really shocked you're going to say goodbye to Athens. You have so much there: a fabulous home, a chic office, friends, important clients... Do you really think you can run your business from here?'

'I'm not sure, but I really hope so. I'll probably have to go to and fro a couple times a month, maybe once a fortnight or so, but I'm still going to rent out my office and get a smaller one for my secretary to work from that I can also use when I'm there. To be brutally honest, Callisto, I'm very nervous. If I'm not careful this could be the end of the business I've worked so hard to build up, but I'm at a stage in my life now where I need to change. Jacob's gone off to America, he doesn't need me anymore. And losing Stelios... When it first happened I kept myself so busy, working non-stop for weeks, and then I came to Vekianos and ... it hit me hard. My best friend had been taken away and it changed my life, my business, everything.'

They sat in silent reflection for a moment, the quiet so loud Callisto almost wanted to scream and shout to chase it away. She settled for changing the subject.

'Tell me about the new house. Did you know you wanted to move to the island before you went in to view it?'

'I knew I needed to make changes, and I was aware that as much as I love this apartment your father left me, it isn't big enough to work from. When we stepped into the villa I felt at peace, and it's perfectly placed for overseeing the new development, though I didn't know then that it would be going ahead. By the way, you're more than welcome to have one of the rooms as your office, if that would be helpful.'

'Thank you, that's very kind of you. It would be perfect to be on site on a daily basis, but that's still a ways off. We have to get planning permission first.'

'Somehow I don't think that will be an issue. The island authorities are very keen to help bring more tourists to Vekianos, and of course you have the Drakos name, which will be a huge advantage. There will be lots to keep you busy but are you sure you won't miss Athens? Surely you must miss your lifestyle and all your friends that you have there.'

'I have to admit I miss the city, but as for friends, they weren't real friends, just people I hung out and partied with. I've learned the hard way that I have to take responsibility for my life.'

'But you're already off to a great start there. The deal you made for the sale of the central Athens apartment was brilliant and you did that all by yourself, and I can see the fire in you for this new project. Since Stelios' death we've both been numb but it's time to start living again.'

'That's kind of you to say. And I think you're right. I'm looking forward to settling in here and putting everything into this new venture. My dad bringing me here really was the best thing that could have happened to me.'

'I know this new opportunity we've been given

will work out and I'm looking forward to working together, solving the problems, enjoying the successes, and making your dad proud.'

Callisto smiled. She had a feeling they'd already accomplished that last goal.

'This is it, Pavlos, time to welcome the world – well, perhaps not the world, just our friends and family – into your new venture! Are you ready?' Lena asked, throwing an arm around her friend.

'I'm ready but also so nervous. I just want to get tonight over with and then tomorrow will be the big day. Hopefully lots of holiday makers will flow through the door, spending money and enjoying what they get. How are you feeling? Any regrets about staying and not going to America with Jacob?'

'No, I'm where I'm meant to be. I miss him, of course, but from what he's told me he hasn't had a minute to himself since his plane touched down. He has long days that start with breakfast meetings and go straight through to dinner meetings. I would have been lonely if I'd gone with him, whereas here I have the restaurant to keep me busy and I have Fotini and Callisto close by. No, I'm doing what I've always done: getting on with life. On that note, I think I can hear our guests arriving. It's showtime! I think you should go and greet everyone at the door while I fetch the tray with the champagne glasses.'

As she walked to the bar for the tray Lena took a moment to think about what she'd said to Pavlos ... and what she hadn't.

Like the fact that there were times in the middle of the night when she was woken by the pain of missing Jacob. Like the fact that she thought she'd made a mistake she would always regret. Like the fact that she knew she should have said 'yes' and gone to LA with him when she had the chance.

Chapter 44

Three months later

Trisha was in a hurry to get over to the villa. It was a big day for Fotini – she was having a party to celebrate moving back in – and yesterday had been very busy between them cooking and cleaning. She walked by the hall mirror and stopped to ponder her reflection.

'Where have the last few months gone?' she asked the Trisha in the mirror. 'You haven't stopped! Your life has been busier than before you retired, but then, can you still say you're retired if you're working four days a week with Pavlos and Lena, helping to cover the busy lunchtime trade?' She decided that she could as it didn't feel like work. It was fun, entertaining relaxed holiday makers enjoying the beach. The work could be tiring but she found herself waking up raring to go every day, so she would continue until that feeling went away.

'Sorry I'm late!' she said as she rushed through Fotini's door a few minutes later. 'I've been busy having a conversation with myself in the mirror.' She laughed.

'I hope the conversation went well,' Fotini said, giggling along with Trisha. 'Take a seat on the patio. Drinks and snacks are on the way.'

'It was a lovely chat, thanks, none of the doom and gloom like it was when I first arrived here on Vekianos. My life is now so busy I haven't time to be miserable!'

Trish went out onto the patio and looked out into the garden. It was the one area that had largely avoided the refurbishment and for that she was glad. It still looked almost the same as when she was here all those years ago on holiday with Stelios and it brought back happy memories. That was another big change that had come over the past few months – the sadness had leached from the memories, leaving only the good. It had come naturally as she realised that couldn't change the past but she could forgive herself for the choices she had made, and – most importantly – she could move forward.

'There you go,' Fotini said as she set out a tray that was heaving with treats. 'We don't have that much to do as I was up early and finished the food preparation, the villa has been cleaned to within an inch of its life, and I've laid out all the drinks, so we can just have a pottering sort of day. Oh, I think that's my phone...' She broke off as she rooted around in her pocket for her mobile.

'Hi, Tassos.'

'Hello, Fotini, can you talk?'

'Yes, of course. I'm just sat here having a chat and a snack with Trisha.'

'I just wanted to let you know everything is on schedule for tonight. I'm looking forward to your party.'

'So am I and thank you for the update. Fingers crossed everything will go to plan.'

She hung up and took a bite of a pastry, pretending not to notice the look of confusion on Trisha's face.

'Did I tell you how much easier everything is with all the updates? I'm so lucky.'

Trisha realised Fotini wasn't going to share what the call was really about, so she decided not to press. Everyone was entitled to their secrets.

'No one is more deserving! I saw Callisto moving her boxes out the other day. Does that mean she's now working from Tassos' new home over in Thagistri, do you know?'

'Yes, she is. They're getting ready to start work on the villas any day now. She was showing me the plans and it's going to be gorgeous. I know Stelios would be so pleased with it.'

They were interrupted by the phone ringing again, but this time it was Trisha's.

'Hello?'

'Hi, Patricia, it's Karen from the estate agency here in the UK.'

'I hope you have good news for me.'

'Yes, very good news. The couple I was talking to you about last week have come back and have agreed to pay the full asking price on your property, so hopefully the sale should go through within six to eight weeks.'

'Thank you so much, Karen, I'm over the moon.'

They said their goodbyes and Trisha turned back to Fotini with a huge smile.

'I've sold my property in England!'

'Congratulations! I'm so pleased for you, and I just know all your friends here on Vekianos will be thrilled to hear that you're here to stay.'

'Thank you. Now, are you sure nothing else needs doing to prepare for the party?'

'All I have to do, really, is tidy up out here in the garden. All the cushions need putting out, and the tables need a wipe down, but that's it. I'm so looking forward to showing the place off. Lots of my friends from town haven't been here since Stelios died so the refurbishment will be a big surprise.'

'I know Stelios would be very happy with the final result.'

'Do you think so, Trisha?'

'Yes, because if there's one thing I've learned since arriving on the island it's that all he wanted to do was make his friends and family happy, and there is no one here on the island with a bigger smile on their face than you, Fotini.'

*

Callisto had finally got the furniture in her new office right where she wanted it. Her desk faced out the window into the garden and as she stood there, she couldn't help but laugh. This office couldn't be more different than the one she had left in Athens! There was nothing LA film set about this room, if anything it said 'junk yard' given it was a whole room full of things people had thrown away because they were old, broken, and very outdated. But saying that, she loved this room. She felt comfortable and relaxed here and she just knew this little office would serve her well for many years to come.

She was interrupted from her daydreaming by a knock at the door.

'I hope I haven't disturbed you with all the moving of the furniture,' she said as she waved Tassos inside.

'Not at all. It looks nice. It's strange but it reminds me of your dad's office in a lot of ways, it's very practical.'

'That's about the only nice word that can be used,' Callisto said with a laugh. 'I'll happily settle for that though, so thank you. How are you getting on? I have just the one room to sort whereas you have quite a few.'

'Yes, quite a few. To be honest I'm a bit concerned that perhaps the house is a little *too* big for me. Do I really need all these rooms?'

'I think you'll find uses for them all. For one thing, you'll have space for Jacob when he comes to visit.'

'Perhaps so, but something tells me he will be happier staying over in Keriaphos so he can be close to Lena. Right, I need to be getting on and of course we have Fotini's party to look forward to tonight.'

'But first the horrible job of unpacking all the boxes of paperwork and files. That's where this office will differ from my dad's, with all his piles of paperwork and things all over the floor and nothing put away. I don't know how he worked like that!'

'He did like his clutter, didn't he?' Tassos chuckled. 'I'll let you get on with your boxes and will see you at the party. I have a few things to do on my way there.'

'Nice things I hope.'

'Not just nice but special,' he said mysteriously.

As he left, Callisto was curious what he meant by 'special'. She supposed she would find out at the party.

'Aunt Fotini, where are you?' Lena called from the entryway.

'I'm here in the kitchen – my new, *sparkly* kitchen.'

'Pavlos let me finish early so I could come and give you a hand before the guests arrive. What do you want me to do?'

'Nothing, darling. Everything is ready as Trisha's been helping me the last couple of days. We just need everyone to arrive. While we're waiting we can have a drink out on the terrace. I think a gin and tonic first and we'll save the champagne until the celebrations begin.'

'Celebrations, plural? Do we have something else to celebrate as well as the villa?'

'There is always something to celebrate, Lena, the evening is still very young,' Fotini said with a wink and a giggle.

Fotini went off to get the drinks and Lena was left feeling a bit down. She wasn't really in the mood for a party but she knew she would have to put on a big smile. To be honest, she had no reason to be miserable. She had a gorgeous apartment, a fabulous job that she was enjoying so much, and lovely friends and family to spend time with when she wasn't working. But now the novelty of the new job had worn off and she was in a routine, she really missed Jacob. Though they often chatted on the phone when he had time in his busy schedule, it just wasn't the same as having him here on Vekianos.

'There you go, one gin and tonic. Now, tell me how are things at the beach café? Every time I see Pavlos he says he's really happy with how things are going, and I know how much Trisha is enjoying working there, but what about you?'

'It's all good, thank you,' Lena said vaguely.

'I sense a "but",' Fotini prompted.

'I miss my dad. He's the missing piece in my jigsaw.'

'I have to disagree with you there, Lena. Your dad will always be part of your jigsaw because he was part of its foundation. I suspect the missing piece you're actually looking for is Jacob. All I can tell you is that most jigsaw puzzles aren't put together in a day. Sometimes it can take weeks or months to build them; you just need to have a little patience... I think that sounds like people coming through the gate. It's party time!'

Fotini went off to greet her guests and Lena painted on a smile, swinging into action to serve drinks, and before she knew it the garden was full of people.

'Can we give you a hand?' Callisto asked as she and Trisha joined Lena. 'I bumped into Trisha as I was coming out of the apartments and I thought between the three of us we are more than capable of dealing with all the food and drinks so that Fotini can mingle with her guests,' Callisto suggested.

'Oh, thank you, yes, of course we can. Everyone that is in the garden or on the patio has a drink already so it should just be a question of topping everything up.'

'Should I go and sort the food out in the

kitchen? I know what's to do as I've been helping your aunt the last few days, preparing it all,' Trisha offered.

'That's perfect, thank you, Trisha. Lena and I will throw the booze at the locals out here.'

'Oh Callisto, what are you like? There will be no throwing of booze!' Lena laughed.

'Ok then, pouring down their necks. You forget that I know how these parties work. Whenever our dad had one here on Vekianos they would drink him dry, and do you know something, he never minded...' She trailed off, overcome by a wave of sadness.

'Are you ok, Callisto?' Lena asked gently.

'Yes. I just really miss him. In life, in business...'

'But now you have Tassos to help you and support you, that must help. And I know you don't believe me when I keep saying it, but I truly believe that the relationship you have with him is special, and so much more than just a working relationship.'

'Do you know what – and I've not said this to anyone else, not even to myself, come to that – since he's been here on the island there are times I completely forget he's a work colleague. But we can't stand here chatting about that now!' she said in a rush, looking embarrassed. 'We have guests to look after!'

The three of them spent the next two hours pouring drinks, serving food, clearing dirty plates, and generally keeping everyone in good spirits – literally and figuratively. Lena could see how happy and proud Fotini was to have everyone in her newly revitalised villa and that brought a genuine smile to her face.

All of a sudden a bell rang and everyone looked towards the patio where Fotini was standing.

'I just wanted to say I hope you are all having a

nice time and have had plenty to eat and drink. There is quite a bit of food left in the kitchen and the drinks are out on the side so please help yourself as waitress service has officially ended for the evening. It's time for my three fabulous helpers to sit down and enjoy the party. Thank you for all the hard work Trisha, Callisto, and Lena.'

The crowd cheered and Callisto moved to get herself a drink, spotting Tassos coming through the gate as she did so. He was late.

'I thought you had stood me up!' she joked as he joined her at the makeshift bar.

'Sorry, my little surprise took longer than I'd thought it would. I would never willingly stand you up because...' Tassos took a deep breath. 'Because I like you in my life, Callisto, and I don't want us to be apart. There. I've said it. And there's one other thing. I don't just want you to work from my house, I'd like you to consider living there as well. After all, it would be a shorter commute to work for you,' he said with a hopeful smile.

'It does make sense cutting those minutes off my journey, but that's not a good enough reason for me to say yes. If you were to ask me to move in with you for *another* reason, however, perhaps you might get a different answer...' she said leadingly.

'Callisto, after spending so much time with you these past few months I've fallen in love with you and I want to share my house and my life with you. I want it to become our home. Please say yes?'

Callisto was momentarily stunned by Tassos' declaration, but then a huge grin started to spread across her face.

'Now *that's* a good reason. And my answer is "yes" because I think I'm in love with you as well.' Tassos enveloped her in a hug and Callisto let out a giggle.

'Was that the surprise you were being so

mysterious about?' she asked once he'd let her go.

'No, that surprise is for Lena. Do you know where she is?'

'Over there, with her back to the path...' Callisto trailed off as her eyes caught on someone making his way towards her sister. She turned to Fotini and Trisha who were stood together and called them over, pointing towards Lena.

All three women held their breath as they watched.

'Excuse me, what does someone have to do to get a drink around here?' someone asked over Lena's shoulder, making her freeze in surprise.

She recognised that voice! But no, it couldn't be ... could it? Was she hearing things? Slowly she turned, delighted to find a smiling Jacob standing before her.

'Jacob! What are you doing here? You're meant to be in America! What has happened?'

'Too many questions, Lena. Let me kiss you first,' he said, pulling her into his arms.

Fotini squealed with delight and turned to share in the joy with Trisha and Callisto, only to be met by another surprise – Callisto and Tassos were kissing! She turned to Trisha to make sure she wasn't hallucinating and was greeted by the same shocked expression she was sure was on her own face. The two older women burst out in laughter. What a party this was turning out to be!

'I'm sorry to shock you, Lena, but long story short: the company has given me a couple of projects to work on and have agreed I can do it from here in Greece. I will have to go to the states three or four times a year, but my home will be here on Vekianos! Say something,' he added when she remained speechless.

'Sorry, Jacob, I'm just ... I'm shocked! But also so glad you're back. In fact, it gives me an idea,' she said, spotting Callisto and Tassos over Jacob's shoulder. 'I think your working situation would be better if you had an office, so you don't have to live and work in the same place. So, how about you work from your dad's apartment and live in mine?' She grinned.

'Lena Drakos, are you suggesting we move in together?' Jacob's grin was almost bigger than Lena's now.

'Yes, but only if you want to.'

'Want to? Of course I want to! You're the reason I've come back! Now come here and let me kiss you again and again. I never want to stop kissing you. If that's ok with you?'

'It's very ok with me. I've missed you, Jacob. Welcome home to Vekianos.'

THE END

Printed in Great Britain
by Amazon